I0817779

A Fugue of Small Spaces

A Novel

Reggie Hudson

A Fugue of Small Spaces is a work of fiction. The characters, locations and situations depicted within are fictional. Any resemblance to actual locations, events or people, alive or dead, is entirely coincidental.

Copyright © 2021 by Reginal Hudson

All rights reserved

Published in the United States by ALL CAPS

Hardcover ISBN: 978-1-7366160-0-0
Ebook ISBN: 978-1-7366160-1-7
Audiobook ISBN: 978-1-7366160-2-4

reggiedhudson.com

First Edition

Book design by Reggie Hudson

For Crissy, who is patience and generosity in human form.

CONTENTS

A Fugue of Small Spaces

first

1

He waits as the spitting rain weaves through the early morning haze. The gray face of the building before him only adds to the gloom, a stark steep cliff of concrete and fake stone. It's all texture and no real substance.

A tiny, imagined voice whispers convincing falsehoods about that facade into Lex's ear. It reminds him he's read less-than-reliable reports about the calamities that befall densely-packed city buildings. Ordinary citizens who are seen leaping from their heights, choosing demise by asphalt over being burned alive. He cranes his neck at the fake-stone and drab, weathered concrete, pierced by regular squares of shiny gray glass, and shivers.

He grips his backpack straps a little tighter.

As his imagination takes hold, sounds fill his ears: the hypothetical whoosh of the morning air whistling past as he falls the entire height of his new home; the sound his body would make splattering against the sidewalk; the screams of unsuspecting bystanders as his speeding body makes contact with the ground before them, covering them in his essence. He concludes that he would probably land spread-eagle like some weird cartoon.

"She's not much to look at," says the old guy at the building's front door with an obscenely large ring of keys. He's dressed like a lifelong bachelor. Everything he wears is probably the cheapest version of that thing he could find. "She's secure, though. Affordable for this part of town."

"Yeah, it's a great deal. For the location, I mean, and the way things around here are coming along," Lex says, rambling.

Despite this great deal, he's had to put nearly all of his savings toward the deposit. The cost of wanting to live in the heart of the city, close to the action, as they say. He's sure lots of people have needed to pay first month's, last two months', cleaning deposit and a key fee just for the privilege of living in a trending neighborhood. Lex harbors a healthy dose of embarrassment for having asked his parents for so much money. He'd been saving, but still needed help.

He's promised he would pay them back and, once he's truly started making money, buy them something nice. He honestly believes this, repeating it to himself every time he thinks about thanking them, telling them he'll be okay and that the apartment he's chosen is a perfect little place to start.

"Don't care," says the old guy. "C'mon, daylight's burning."

The metal-framed glass door creaks open as the superintendent tugs the handle with a wiry strength. He's probably not as brittle as he seems. Lex considers all the times he'd come to the city, all the times he'd visited people in beautiful, old high-rises with doormen and attended elevators. Every single one of these places had its own version of this old guy, the undersized super who could probably snap someone's neck in the time it would take a normal person to shake hands.

The super stands in the doorway, waiting for Lex to pass. He holds a posture he seems to have perfected after hundreds of rounds of practice. He waits with his back against the inside hall wall, holding the door open with his arm and a leg. He forms a crooked letter K with his body, a little wobbly as he's also trying to put out a cigarette he's never lit. The super shrugs, spitting onto the sidewalk just outside the doorway before tucking the crinkled stick of tobacco behind an ear.

"Need a key to get in the door," says the old guy. "There's a buzzer just there that goes to an intercom inside the apartment. You'll know what to do when it goes off unless you're simple. Are you? Simple?" The old man squints at Lex before sighing. "Never mind. I'll try to get around to putting your name on the panel before you move out."

Lex laughs a small, nervous laugh, looking into the super's face before realizing that the man wasn't making a joke. Lex coughs and mumbles something that even he can't understand. The super stays stoic, rigid, fingers working the ridiculously large key ring in circles. There's a faint clink as the keys bump each other. It reminds Lex of wind chimes.

"So, you coming in or am I just standing here for my health?" The super's voice sounds like he's steadily on the verge of coughing, an uncomfortable rasp that makes Lex really wish he would clear his throat.

Lex wipes his feet on the concrete just outside the door, thinking it's better to at least try and project the image that he's considerate, wishing to avoid tracking more water onto the glossy tiles of the entry hall. He guesses he's probably getting the soles of his feet wetter than they'd already been, standing in the street admiring the gray facade against the gray sky. He shrugs, wiping the soles of his Converse more earnestly.

"Don't bother," says the old man. "Polite bullshit! Come in, dammit."

Lex catches a faint whiff of stale tobacco mixed with some sort of deli meat from the super's breath as he takes the weight of the door from the man. A tightness grips his chest as Lex gets close to him. His ears are hot from the scolding. Something deep inside says he should be offended at the man's gruff chastisement, the assault on what's left of his manhood.

A burp rumbles up from the pits of the super's stomach, gurgling its way up his throat before gushing from between yellowing teeth. The air hits Lex squarely in the nose just as he passes into the building. Pastrami.

The keys chime again as they collide with each other, having been released from the super's grip and allowed to hang at his waist from a retractable cable. The old guy movements are sneaky-quick given his apparent lack of musculature. He zooms past the bank of mailboxes and points as he goes by.

"Mail's right there." He's taken the tone of an impatient substitute teacher. "Another key. You get all your keys after you sign. Name'll go right above the key slot. Maybe."

The super stops just at the bottom of the steep concrete and metal steps leading to the upper floors. There's a faint gurgling sound coming from down the hall just beyond the stairs. He leans out into the hall to catch the source of the sound. The super turns his head and Lex can see the man squinting severely, the deep crow's feet at his eyes branching in multiple directions down his cheek. The super finally clears his throat, blinks then turns to Lex.

"What did you say your name was?" the old man asks. The throat clearing didn't help one bit.

"Lex."

"Is that short for something?" The old man cranes his neck forward, looking directly into Lex's eyes.

"Yes," Lex stumbles. He doesn't know why he takes a half-step backward. He is, after all, nearly a full head-height taller than the super. "It's short for Lexington."

"Lexington?" The super chews this word for a while, glancing back once toward the gurgling sound before re-establishing his piercing stare. "Queer name."

The old man turns suddenly and Lex tries to ignore the soft sound of a dry fart as he ascends the first few steps.

They reach the fifth-floor landing quickly despite the steep pitch of the stairs. With each floor, Lex looks at the doors lining the halls, imagining the lives on the other sides. He smiles to himself thinking of the people he may run into, coming or going or loitering about the halls.

He also likes taking the moment to catch his breath at each landing, swallowing hard from all of the sudden labor he's subjected his legs to.

Each floor is identical, almost eerily so. Every wall and door is the same color gray, every floor is an identical pale tile. Each door has a small number/letter combo pasted just below a peephole. At each turn, each step, Lex appreciates how good the old super is at his job. All of the common spaces are spotless, especially in the far corners where all of the really dank stuff tends to gather. Impressive masterwork.

The stairway continues upward beyond the fifth floor, but Lex ignores it for the moment. He will have plenty of time later to explore the rest of the building, to get to know its quirks. Butterflies flutter in his gut as he thinks of all the possibilities before him.

The old man trudges to the gray door marked 5D while simultaneously shuffling through the ring of keys at his side. He sounds like he's singing softly to himself as his fingers fumble around the little sticks of metal for the one allowing access. He finds the one he's looking for just as he reaches the threshold and Lex is impressed at the efficiency of the old man's movements. He knows that, were it up to him, he would have fumbled through the keys starting at the second floor and wouldn't have found the correct one until a few minutes after they'd reached the apartment door.

The super stabs the deadbolt and twists the lock with a jerk. Soft click and he withdraws the key and repeats the stab at the doorknob. The knob sticks a little and he swears under his breath as he kicks the bottom of the door. Theres a small pop followed by the hiss of the sweeper brushing against the hardwood inside the apartment.

"Fuck you," the old man whispers as he withdraws the key and lets his key-ring zip back to his hip.

The smell of fresh paint mixed with cleaning products breeze across Lex's nose making his head swim. It is bright inside, gray light pouring unfiltered through the windows and bouncing around the freshly painted off-white walls. It makes Lex smile despite the slight stinging in his eyes.

The old man takes a deep breath as he walks through the door.

"Fresh paint," says the old man. "Can get high off fresh paint and floor wax."

"Yeah," says Lex, stepping into his first apartment for the first time. "Looks nice."

The super stands aside, staring at Lex as he passes into the apartment, throwing the type of impatient look that only hardened and grizzled city dwellers can pull off. It tells Lex that his time with the old man has expired.

The apartment is tiny by any standard. The door swings open to the right where it's immediately greeted by the apartment wall. A few feet in and one reaches the rearmost limit of the the space. The rest of the apartment stretches to the left after crossing the threshold. Stretching is such a generous word for the actual scale of the flat. The space peters out after about twenty-five feet or so. All of it, gleaming hardwoods and fresh off-white paint, trim included, is traversed in the space of a half-dozen paces, give or take.

Opposite the window wall, near the midway point of the space, is an alcove with a counter. A gas stove sits at one end, a single-bay sink at the other. The fridge sits against the side wall of the alcove closest to the door. Opposite that is the wall the kitchen shares with the bathroom.

Lex finds himself pirouetting about in the middle of the space, taking it all in as much as he can. He's excited, nervous, disappointed. He remembers it being larger somehow during his brief tour of the place with a broker, but that may have been nerves. He knows that it's the most space he can afford by himself, especially considering the building's location. He quickly comes to terms with the fact that he's arrived at his new home.

He's ready for the next stage of his life.

The old man by the door clears his throat. Lex stops spinning and looks. He's sure he knows what's coming next.

"Well," the old man says, "you want I should stand here like a moron while you practice your dance moves, princess?"

He didn't disappoint.

"Right," Lex says, remembering himself. "I'm so sorry, yes."

The walls are clean, fresh, There is a dent in the drywall here, a small off-color scrape there. The trim, upon closer look, has seen better days with some imperfections that even paint can't cover. The floors are in great shape, narrow, polished boards of deep tan maple in tight, straight lines running parallel to the window wall. The cloudy light glints off of their smooth surface. Lex walks into the impossibly white tiled bathroom and switches on the light and the fan. Everything jumps to life, no flicker in the fixture, no hiccup in the fan. He steps back and quickly looks over the kitchen space. Everything in the small apartment is clean, tidy, ready and waiting for him to move in.

The super is tapping his foot, arms crossed. His jaw hasn't stopped moving since he'd cleared his throat moments earlier. Whatever he's chewing is persistent.

"Everything okay?" asks the old man. His rattle of a voice is clipped, impatient. Lex nods.

The super pulls a folded piece of paper from the back pocket of his slightly oversized polyester slacks, unfolds it and shoves it into the air toward Lex. "Initial the top three parts, then sign and date the bottom."

It all feels very strange to Lex, the abruptness of signing something that he doesn't fully understand. He flashes back to signing that book of a lease agreement, his gut aching with each stroke of his pen. It's a new world compared to the carefree days of just drifting through his youth, letting things happen as they may with others taking care of the consequences.

Those days feel like they happened a lifetime ago, like his current state was the tortured reincarnation of the person he'd been.

His hesitation lasts less than a second, but he's apologetic nonetheless. The debate rages through his mind as he reaches for the page the old man presents. His inner child is screaming as he grabs for the pen. He feels downright faint as his hand forces the pen to form his initials in three places, draw his signature at the bottom.

The old man's face transforms, become instantly cordial. He almost looks downright friendly as he snatches the page from Lex's hand and replaces it with a cluster of three keys bound by a cheap, thin loop of metal. The shorter pair are jagged like the lower jaw of a predator, the third is big and blocky with round holes partially drilled at irregular intervals. The super jabs Lex's palm with a bony finger, landing at the big blocky key.

"Downstairs door," the old man croaks. He moves on to the jagged keys in one swift motion, "mailbox, apartment door. You need copies, call the office."

He's out the door before the imprint of his finger fades in Lex's palm.

2

LEX CLOSES THE DOOR BEHIND THE VANISHED SUPER. HE'S TEMPTED TO peek out the door and down the hall, see how quickly the old man's fled his company. He knows better. The last thing he needs in that moment of silence is to have the withering look-back of disapproval. He wants to enjoy this brief moment of emptiness.

The apartment is quiet. Uncomfortably quiet. The kind of quiet that makes his ears ring, where the blood rushing through the veins in his head is too loud. Lex is easing into the silence, finding it odd how serene his little piece of the city is.

He fears he may be living a cliché.

Lex rests his bag on the floor in the middle of the room, the thickening clouds outside shading his world further. There are a pair of ceiling fans overhead, each taking a half of the apartment as its jurisdiction. He finds a bank of switches mounted to the wall near the door and flicks one. The nearest fan begins to whir. The next and its light blinks on. The next pair work the other fan. He leaves both on as he takes another orbit around the apartment, planning his next move.

He imagines how the far end of the apartment will look once he's obtained a nice, wood-framed futon. He thinks about small, sensible Swedish side tables with nice lamps on top flanking it. He pictures the round dining table on the side nearest the door, the two areas separated by a simple, modern entertainment center, taller bookshelves on either side. His head nearly swims with the images of all the modern style his budget will allow him to stack into the place.

He feels moved to take his first, independent piss into his own toilet.

He pauses in the doorway, the bathroom fan whirring softly over his head, light flooding the bathroom and gleaming off of the tile, a small smile spreading across his face. He's feeling more like an adult than he has at nearly any other point in his life. He's free to be his own man.

It reminds him a little of his first day in his freshman dorm. That was a lifetime ago. Images flash of Oscar standing, arms crossed against his chest as Lexington hauled an oversized duffel along a short walkway leading to the mid-sixties era three-story dormitory. Lorraine had stayed home, arguing that she'd already been crying the entire morning and seeing her baby boy walking into his dorm would have been far too heartbreaking. So, there he'd been, hauling his stuff on his own as Oscar waited. At least his father didn't leave until after he'd passed through the front doors.

Lex was greeted by a very eager RA in a pale blue t-shirt emblazoned with the words "ASK HOW I CAN HELP."

He'd been pointed to a four-sleeper on the second floor somewhere near the middle of the building and found that he'd been the first of his roommates to arrive. For fifty-two glorious minutes, he'd had the entire place to himself, clean and pristine.

Fifty-two minutes of peace that he wouldn't experience again for six and a half years.

He flushes after using his new place's toilet and leaves the seat up and the light on as he saunters into the living space. He's going to grab the Ikea catalog out of his bag and really start game-planning his trip later that afternoon. He reaches the middle of the space and stops.

Blink.

". . .the fuck?" Lex asks aloud. He whirls around, scanning the small and empty space. He moves quickly to the door, opens and looks down the hall. It's empty as well, doors closed to the common space, light steady from the sconces positioned between the units. He closes the door and looks around the room once more.

He can't find his backpack.

The very backpack he'd sat in the center of the room. There had to be a reasonable explanation. He is, after all, in the middle of downtrodden downtown. In the time he was in the toilet, someone must have snuck into the apartment, quietly snatched his bag, and made off into the rainy morning. His good mood is fading and Lex is once again beginning to doubt his decision to move to the heart of the city. The old part of the city at that. The part of the city that was just beginning a resurgence, a new awakening. He should have listened to his father when he warned about getting mugged and robbed moving to such a haven of crime and amorality. Oscar's exact words.

Lex sighs and drags his feet to the kitchen. He stops again.

Blink.

"What the. . .?" Lex again speaks aloud to no one. His backpack sits on the kitchen counter. Placed neatly, leaning against the tile backsplash at the mid-point between the stainless steel stove and the sink. The straps are tucked neatly behind it. The contents have settled onto the counter, as if the pack had been there for hours. Days. The thing looks like a back-to-school retail display.

Lex stands for a few moments just beyond his kitchen, thinking. Maybe he'd moved the pack from the middle of the room to that spot on the counter. Perhaps he'd wanted to mentally measure the room for his imaginary furniture. He thinks it's likely he didn't sit the pack on the floor in the first place. The counter is, after all, the best place to sit a pack in such a small place.

He's done it to himself. It's early, he's not had a coffee yet, the paint fumes are still awfully strong. He begins calming himself, feeling a little less crazy.

His pulse slows as he opens the pack, retrieving his laptop computer and an edge-worn Ikea catalog. These two items are joined by a small, lined notepad. He turns a few pages past random scrawl and finds a blank sheet.

"This works," he says, leaning over the kitchen counter to map his morning.

He doesn't notice that the ceiling fans have stopped spinning.

3

"What's the place like?" asks Parker, his mouth full of fried rice.

"Small," says Lex, wiping partially chewed egg from his cheek. "It's a neat place, there's a lot I can do with it if I get creative."

The lights are bright inside the restaurant. The clouds outside have gotten more intense, amplifying the brightness of the interior. It feels like they're inside a lighthouse.

"Can't wait to see it," continues Parker. "When's the party? You know, the housewarming. Get some friendly friends up there, a little sunshine, a little liquid romance."

Lex shakes his head, focusing all of his efforts into trying to recall why he was friends with Parker. Sometimes Parker's odd little verbal flairs made his upper lip itch. He takes a deep breath, remembering that Parker has been his friend for six years and one of his final remaining for the past two. By default, this places him into the best-friend slot in Lex's hierarchy.

"So," Lex begins, getting to the point. "I'll need some help moving."

"No," says Parker. He's at least swallowed the mouthful of rice and was sipping from his teacup.

"It's not a lot," Lex persists. "Just a couple of boxes of random knick-knacks. A few suitcases."

"No."

"It's not going to take long. It's very easy, promise."

Parker pauses, thinking. It's the first time the during entire meal that he's completely stopped shoveling food into his mouth. There's an uneasy peace between Parker's fork and the surviving bits of his lunch that Lex knows will be short-lived. He needs to move fast.

"You know I wouldn't ask except, and that's the thing. . ." Lex spins his water glass a quarter turn. He hopes he looks adequately pathetic.

"What floor?" Parker asks, finally.

"Fifth, but. . ."

"Elevator?"

"Walk-up, but it's a really easy. . ."

"No."

Truce is over and Parker picks up his fork to shovel another mouthful of fried rice into his face. He's humming an annoying little happy song, something Lex typically only hears when Parker is particularly pleased with himself. Or when he's eating one of his favorite meals.

Parker has a lot of favorite meals.

"I'm not asking you to move a sofa," Lex continues. "I'll owe you."

He's telling the truth that he doesn't have any furniture. Part of his agreement with his parents, mostly between him and his father, is that he would take all of his junk with him. Junk is his father's term, not his. He likes to call the majority of his personal property collectible. At least forty-three percent. Twenty-four percent of it can be classified as electronic necessities. Eighteen percent is text-books he's yet to relinquish to the trash heap. The remaining fifteen percent are clothes.

He's agreed to leave his folks with the furniture they'd paid Oscar's hard-earned money for. If they were going to help him pay for the apartment, he would need to earn everything else he needed to place within it.

So, while the furniture statement is, for the time being, accurate, it failed to paint the full picture of what needed to be hauled up five flights of steps into his small studio. None of that could happen until he'd done a little more furniture shopping and had someone, preferably Parker, help him haul the sensible Swedish boxes up to the small apartment. He'd already arranged for a new futon to be delivered later that afternoon.

Then there was the matter of putting all of his new stuff together. Possibly over pizza. Or tacos. Cheap tacos. He was going to need his friend in the coming days and he needed to take the time to prime this friend for the dependency. The resistance was expected. He needed leverage.

"What do you say," Lex says, smiling. "You scratch my back now, I scratch your's later?"

"I'm not going anywhere near your back," Parker said. "Absolutely not. I don't help people move."

"Not even best friends?"

"Especially best friends. There's nothing I avoid more readily than helping anyone move. I can give you the number for a guy."

"I don't need a guy." Lex screws his mouth to one side. Something comes to him. "What's the name of that girl that you haven't quite found your way to hooking up with?" He deadens his face the same way he does when he's playing poker.

"Why have you deadened your face the way you do during poker?" Parker countered.

"This is my face. My face does what my face does."

"Angelica." Parker swallows, looking at Lex suspiciously. "What does she have to do with me not helping you move?"

"Just curious," Lex says. He takes a loud slurp of his hot and sour soup, the only item on the menu that fits into his current budget, especially after that morning's spending spree.

"And what the hell's with the damn poker face, Lex? You got me shaking, sweetheart."

"Don't call me sweetheart. I just couldn't remember the young lady's name, that's all."

"Don't call her a young lady, idiot. It makes you sound like somebody's dad. You're not someone's dad, are you? Seriously, are you?"

"You don't need to change the subject if you're embarrassed, Parker. I know how private you like to keep your private life. It just jumped into my head and I couldn't remember her name, that's all. Angelica. That's really pretty."

"Fuck you," Parker says right before chomping into his spring roll. Lex is able to dodge a minor splattering of oil spraying in his direction.

"Sorry I brought her up." Lex looks toward the other tables to hide that his poker face is cracking around the edges.

"I don't get why you did," Parker says. He's wiping his face, tossing his napkin onto his empty plate. "Bring her up. It's a dick move. Mentioning a guy's crush in the middle of a lunch in which you try desperately to recruit a fine human specimen like yours truly into manual labor, and failing. A mealtime tete-a-tete on how you're not getting your shit up to your fifth-floor walk-up. Stop me when I've missed the fucking mark."

The more Parker swears, the better Lex's chances. He's not entirely sure of what he's doing, but he likes the results so far.

"Nope, one-hundred percent dead on target," admits Lex. "You're right. It's a dick move to mention some hot chick that you have absolutely no chance with. Didn't you say she has a boyfriend? Some big ape-man from her gym."

"Had, motherfucker. Had!" Parker raises his voice a note. "Swinging dick fucked up and got caught cock-deep in a yoga instructor. Her eyes were red for a week. I helped her grab some of her shit, playing the consoling friend, listening to every acidic complaint she'd had about the neanderthal. Offering a tissue or a handkerchief or a shoulder. She was so open, she saw me as somebody who was so thoughtful. Fucking perfect."

Lex has heard this story before.

"How very friendly of you, Parker." Lex can feel the weight of the corners of his mouth. "Extremely friendly. What was your rule number whatever-the-fuck? Something about how you're never, ever so friendly as to make it impossible to get what you really want."

"Fuck you. I know the rules. I fucking wrote the rules. I'm getting things ready to get very close, not friendly. Plus, it doesn't matter, asshole." Parker is getting flustered, stuttering with flecks of spittle flying over the table. Lex puts down his spoon and pushes the final dregs of his soup away.

"My mistake. It sounded as though you were being helpful."

"Nah, I was just at her place," continues Parker. "Well, a place she shared with prince Meathead. She wanted to see if I could help her clear out a couple of things while she crashed at her sister's. She sees my potential."

"Uh-huh," says Lex.

"You're a fucking idiot."

"Uh-huh."

Parker stares at lex over his teacup. The rain clouds thicken outside, dimming the inside of the restaurant momentarily.

"Shit, man, she has a lot of stuff too," Parker says, laughing a little.

"She's the one with the massive sofa, right?"

Parker doesn't say anything for three whole seconds which is a Buddhist monk's lifetime of silence for him. He blinks. Check and mate.

After a few tense moments, Parker's ease returns. "She had this box of shit that was closed and sealed with about five layers of tape and shrink wrap. It had a weird weight to it, too. It was her box of marital aids. Her little jolly toys."

"Okay," Lex says.

"It was heavy, too. I shook it around a little bit when she was in another room slamming shit into garbage bags. Thing kinda clunked and I swear I heard a vibrator just buzzing away inside. I walked it out to her to ask where she wanted it."

"You're an animal, Parker." Lex is happy there's so little in his stomach. He didn't know how much more of Parker's personality he could take in this one dose.

"Fucking right, I am. So she looks at the box and she gets a little flustered and flushes red for a couple of seconds. Then, for whatever reason, she relaxes, kinda laughs, then tells me to just stack it at the door. It was the way she said that shit, too. Her head did that lean to one side thing and she smiled and she just said 'stack it at the door'. I bet you know where I kept that box the whole time I was carrying it."

Lex looks at his watch. Another of his morning's chores is almost done and right on schedule. He quickly runs through a couple of small stops he'll need to make before returning to his apartment to wait for his futon delivery.

Part of him feels a little guilty about the minor manipulation of his best friend. Parker's stuck around when he didn't need to, when most of that circle of acquaintances had abandoned him. Police investigations tend to have that effect on friendships, or so Lex has learned.

"Shit," Parker says, checking his own watch. "I gotta go, you fuck. I promised I'd bring back coffees for a call. Fucking prick Stuart always asks for the most complicated shit. I fuck it up on purpose. He gets so damn mad, but he still asks me to pick up a coffee for him. Some people, right?"

Parker reaches into his pocket and tosses a folded wad of bills onto the table as he stands, threading his arms through the sleeves of his overpriced hoodie. Parker has always had the uncanny ability to reach into his pocket and pull out the exact amount of cash needed to settle whatever bill he was paying, including the tip. Lex wonders if he's calculated how much his meal will cost beforehand and set up a dummy wad of cash to pay for it while trying to look cool. Someday he'll ask him about it.

Parker sighs as he checks the table for any forgotten glasses or electronics. Having unfolded himself from his seat, Parker practically towers over everything in the restaurant, his six-foot, six-inch lean frame stretching to its full height.

"So, when do you need me at your folks' place?" Parker asks with the same dismissive flair with which he'd thrown the cash onto the table.

"Sunday eleven A.M. work for you?" Lex allows his poker face to surrender a small smile. This is mostly for Parker's benefit, to show a little bit of his gratitude and to seal the deal.

"Fine," Parker returns the grin. "Fucker."

With that, Parker strides out the restaurant, his face in the screen of his cell phone. Lex sits back, adds a few bucks to his friend's cash, and sips from his water glass.

4

THE FUTON DELIVERY GUYS ARE VERY FRIENDLY, ESPECIALLY CONSIDERING Lex doesn't speak a lick of Russian. The team of three guys are fast, taking the wooden frame from the boxes, hauling the pieces and their hardware up five flights of stairs, and making the transport of the mattress look like they were simply carrying toss pillows. The one who speaks English smiles and offers compliments on the tidiness of the empty apartment. He bosses the other two around, a tall guy and a very tall guy who both seem to be in bad moods.

Lex can't really tell. He doesn't understand a word they say.

The afternoon has been a success for running errands, though he wonders if the Ikea delivery guys are going to be as helpful or as cheerful when they wind up delivering his fifteen rather large boxes up those same stairs. He's heard rumors about delivery guys just dropping boxes in the lobbies of walk-ups for the poor customers to haul up on their own. He's tempted to try and bribe the futon team to hang around for a couple of days and let them haul the rest of his new furniture up the stairs, but he understands how completely impractical that is.

The less tall of the tall guys stops in the middle of his task, bolting the bottom cross beam to the arms at the sides. He looks around as if he smells something foul and Lex checks to see if there's something off in the air. He only smells the fading off-gassing of the wall paint, the gradual decomposition of the powerful industrial cleaning products.

The worker stays still for an awkwardly long period of time. His counterparts don't really acknowledge what he's doing. One continues to put together the back frame, the other unwraps cushions and pillows from their plastic coverings.

Finally, the man stands and looks around the apartment, muttering something in Russian under his breath. It sounds almost like a song. His coworkers glimpse at him briefly before continuing their tasks. Finally, after a while, his cohort on frame assembly whispers something and the standing man resumes his task. He scans the room constantly, however, the rest of his time in the apartment.

After a half-hour or so, the team packs up their gear and, following a couple of test runs, leave Lex with his new piece of convertible furniture. The space starts to look larger, a sofa/bed taking up a space against the wall. He likes keeping the bathroom and closet doors closed. It makes him feel like the space is much larger, that the doors lead to other rooms.

Lex admires his new purchase before making his way to the kitchen and pours himself a red solo cup of water from a comically oversized bottle of spring water.

There's no real connection to the outside world apart from his phone because the cable and internet people wouldn't arrive for another week. Thursday next between the hours of 8:30AM and 1:45PM. He feels bad about needing to use another vacation day, but he's convinced his boss that it was vital to his getting his work done. The round-the-clock access an internet connection would provide meant he was technically never away from the office. It had been difficult to tell if the distracted manager believed him or truly didn't care.

Lex takes his cup of water and sits on the futon with his backpack. He fumbles around for a pen and a pad, ready to make another list. This one would include pending electronics purchases from the discount refurbished electronics retailer he'd passed while exploring the block. After writing down 'television' and 'surround sound', his mind wanders.

For no reason at all, he thinks of the amazing discovery of an online video he'd seen of a beagle playing the piano. While singing. In tune.

Lex laughs to himself as he thinks about the video and pulls out his phone to look it up. He gets distracted by his social media accounts, all of the jewel and candy-colored icons with playfully abstract images at their center, when he hears the tap turn on in the bathroom. The sudden sound of rushing water startles him and he nearly drops the phone as he whips his head around toward the closed door. The rushing water sounds violent, gallons of water tumbling over itself while fleeing the confines of the pipes.

He goes to the bathroom door and listens. Sure enough, through the door, he hears the water rushing into the sink. He also hears another strange sound. He swears there's someone splashing the water as it leaves the faucet. Someone is washing their face. There's also the sound of the water, having been splashed upward, hitting the floor. Someone is being a slob in Lex's new bathroom.

He reaches for the doorknob slowly, his other hand clinched in a fist. He's not sure what he plans to do. He's not much of a fighter in the traditional sense, though he suspects that some sort of homestead protection instinct has kicked in. More or less. He wants to call out to the person on the other side of the door who is clearly making themselves at home, but he's worried that the adrenaline coursing through his body will also cause his voice to crack, to pitch higher than he wants it to. Instead, he's decided that he's just going to open the door, try to catch the interloper in the act, perhaps punch them in the back of the head. Then he would call the authorities and his uninvited visitor would be hauled away having rued the day he crossed Lexington Theodore Delaware.

Lex twists the doorknob, and carefully pushes the door inward. That's when the sound of the splashing, of the running water, stops. The light is still switched off and the bathroom is still quite dark, the only light coming from the freshly cracked door.

Silence.

Lex reaches in carefully, flips the switch on the wall and the bathroom is filled with light, the fan whirrs softly. He throws open the door, prepared to defend himself.

The room is empty. The faucet is off. The tap doesn't even drip. Not once. The sink, the mirror, the floor surrounding the sink are all bone dry. There's no evidence that anyone's been there since he'd left that morning.

He reminds himself that he needs to get a shower curtain.

Lex stands in the door to the bathroom. He's trying to reconcile what he'd heard behind the door, the rush of water hitting the sink, the sound of splashing, with what he's seeing. Emptiness.

There's a weird, acrid taste in Lex's mouth and he feels a little like throwing up. He's not prone to wild fits of fantasy, so he has a very difficult time understanding what was happening. He blinks a few times to clear his head, switches off the light, and closes the door.

Deep breath with his eyes closed, Lex stretches his neck. He shakes his arms, ready to dismiss the incident a hallucination.

Perhaps the walls of the apartment are much thinner than he'd thought. He could have heard the neighbor, the person on the other side of the bathroom wall, washing their face. Perhaps the pipes are that noisy in the old building. Perhaps he was just imagining the whole damn thing.

"Lexington," he says to himself. When he was a kid, his mother would soothe him with his full name. Spoken softly, she would purr his name until he calmed down, stopped crying. "It's fine, there's nothing going on. Just adjusting to a new situation. It's fine."

She'd done that exact thing for days after he'd been released from jail. Oscar would sit for hours in their living room, staring at his son stony-faced and solemn. The fact that he would barely say three words to Lex for weeks was the extent to his outpouring of support. Lorraine, however, would sit as close as Lex would allow, a comforting hand on his wrist as she repeated his name over and over. He thinks it's the reason he didn't end it all in that dark period after.

He laughs, thinking how weird it is that this little trick still works, even when he's using it on himself.

He's forgotten what he was going to do, standing just outside the bathroom. He looks across the apartment toward the windows. It's getting darker and gloomier outside and he knows it'll be dusk soon. First night spent in his new place and he would spend it alone.

He takes a mental inventory of what he'd packed for that night with the plan to swing out to his parents' place after work the next day. He didn't bother with pajamas as they would probably take up too much space in his one pack. Instead, he'd opted for a change of clothes, a change of underwear, electronics chargers, and a few stolen snack bars swiped from his mother's kitchen that could pass as breakfast. Looking out the window at the deepening late-afternoon fog, a plan starts to coalesce.

He's decided to go out once more, take a nice long walk around the neighborhood. Perhaps he'll get to meet someone who looks wise, like they understand the goings-on of the block. Maybe he would find the most valued of all treasures, the hidden bodega. He already knows the fastest way to work, the bus that would take him just a half-block away from the office.

Lex turns toward his futon to grab his bag. He hadn't expected to see the futon fully folded out into sleeping position, his backpack resting neatly in the middle of it.

5

"SO, DID YOU GET MUGGED YET, COMING OUT OF THAT PLACE YOU'RE LIVING now?" asks Oscar, his hands hovering fork-less over his salad plate. He's gazing over his glasses across the table at Lex.

Lex hates the way he does that, peering in judgement without removing the glasses from his face. It's a trait he hopes to avoid picking up.

One of many.

"It's not so bad," Lex says. He's trying to keep the mood light even though he wants desperately to throw dishes about the room. "I think it gets a bad rap because of the way things used to be when you were young."

"I'm still young," says Oscar. He hasn't broken his stare, the pair of sharp, light brown laser-beam eyes are fixed on Lex. He isn't pleased at all. "Are you saying that I'm out of touch, Lexington?"

"Give the boy a break," says Lorraine. She's picking peas from her plate, eating them one by one and taking her sweet time with it. "He's just happy to be somewhere cool."

"I'm not a boy, mother," Lex interjects. He's losing patience quickly. He realizes he's not got very many of these opportunities left, a chance for a free meal. He reminds himself that he truly loves his parents. He has, however, reached his maximum level of tolerable exposure. It's no accident that he's chosen to live so far away from them.

At least he gets to take leftovers home.

He's not ungrateful for the shelter they'd provided, the twenty-seven months spent underneath their roof. He just feels constrained by their protection now that he's ready to move past it. He truly hopes he's ready to move past it.

"I'm not sure why you think I'm so old and out of it all of a sudden," says Oscar. "I can still run fifteen miles without stopping, did you know that, son?"

"Yes, dad, you've said as much." Lex is ready to leave. He has more clothes packed away, a few days-worth squeezed into a large rolling duffel. The same duffel he'd packed into his first dorm. All he has left to do is pack the food he wants to take. He'll work out how to make it to the train back to the city later. "You're not old. . . is that better?"

Silence settles awkwardly over the table. There's a ticking sound in the background from the large wall clock in the adjoining living room.

He wonders if he'd been as annoyed with all the little details of Oscar and Lorraine's house during the recent time he'd spent there. He can't remember. Perhaps it was the trauma of the Natalie ordeal, the steady accusations and endless scrutiny he'd endured. The nine weeks spent under observation by several different law enforcement agencies. That wasn't the worst of it. The worst had been the headlines, ones meant to grab attention and sell clicks. The way he was treated had been far from what he would call fair.

Then there were the amateur sleuths and zealots of justice who arose following those headlines and sensational local news stories. People who would implode his social media accounts and destroy his remaining friendships. Wannabe podcasters who thought they were on the trail of the next big true crime story. They hadn't left him alone, hounded him when he wasn't being questioned by the police, harassed his family and his friends.

Well, his friends didn't stick around very long for that.

It didn't stop right away after the police released a lukewarm statement saying that Lex was no longer a suspect in Nat's disappearance. It had taken several more weeks, weeks of menacing texts and rotten food thrown his way, of whispers and fingers pointed. Campus life became nearly impossible. So, he'd been left with his parents Oscar and Lorraine.

Lex withdrew after all of the hype finally died down. He's never considered himself much of a reader, but he would visit the depths of the university library, chasing every obscure reference to every random thought and idea he'd had. He isolated himself. He isolates himself still.

There are times he doesn't miss those friendships. He ignores the idea that he's never going to have the social advantages of his more pale-skinned counterparts, the assumptions of innocence. He'd once believed in himself, a belief that was shaken by the way they all looked at him. The way they detached themselves when the spotlight shone brightly on him. He'd become different. The other.

He's ready, recharged. His skin has thickened and resolve returned. He's also lonely. He doesn't admit the loneliness to anyone. It's something that can be worked through until he can get the wheels of fake extroversion rolling smoothly again. He's young, he can make anything happen.

His father doesn't seem to hold the same view and he continues to throw him the same looks he'd given him when he'd gone through the entire ordeal. Lex remains resolute, he would take his own damn sweet time.

"Are you taking all your stuff out today?" asks Oscar. He's managed to break off a chunk of yeast roll and was chewing rather earnestly. "You got quite a bit up there."

"No," says Lex, flashing a fake smile. "I'm coming back with help."

"When are you expecting to come back with this help?" presses Oscar.

"The weekend," Lex mumbles. "He's meeting me here this weekend, if that's okay."

Lex hates feeling like a five-year-old. It's a common feeling around his parents, especially around his father.

"Where did you say this apartment was?" asks Lorraine. "The Barnes Alley district, downtown?"

"Yeah," says Lex. "It's in Barnes' Alley, but I think it's a newly refurbished building. A walk-up. Nice."

"Bad part of town," says Oscar. Lex hates that Oscar is so damned stubborn. "Lorraine, you remember Lewis? Lewis Hanford?"

"Oscar," chides Lorraine.

"Lewis Hanford had his leg stolen down in Barnes Alley," Oscar continues. His face lights up for the first time all evening. He likes nothing more than delivering bad news. "War veteran. Sitting at the bus stop, minding his own business. He had his bus pass out, which I told him was his first mistake. You don't leave your money out, don't matter what kind of money it is. Bus pass, credit card. He said he wasn't even listening to music the way he liked to. He says he was humming to himself, under a streetlight, sitting at the bus stop."

"There's a point to this," mumbles Lex. Oscar doesn't hear him, but Lorraine does and throws her son a quick glance. Lex takes a sip from his water glass.

"Thugs come up to Lewis," continues Oscar. "About four of them. Clothes all torn up, bad look in the eyes. Lewis sees these kids coming. Knows he's probably about to lose his bus pass. Probably about to lose his wallet, too. Didn't matter to him, he didn't have but three dollars in his wallet. Never carried around credit cards. I told him he needed at least one credit card, just in case he got stuck somewhere. He always said that he never got stuck anywhere he couldn't walk. Fake leg and all. Lost the original one to a bomb on the side of a desert road. That's the way he always said it. 'A bomb on the side of a desert road.'"

"The Alley has changed a lot since your friend lost his leg a second time," says Lex, hoping to stop Oscar's story short. Oscar barely acknowledges that he's said anything. The man is lost in his story, the vision of it pulling at the corners of his mouth.

"What Lewis saw right there, coming toward him, were a group of rag-tag jokers about to try and rob him. He just sat there, humming. The boys surrounded him. Streets were empty, dark. Nobody else could see what was about to happen, but my buddy kept his calm. He just looked at the little hooligans around him. Each one, he looked right in the face. Didn't flinch, didn't blink. Just stared back at 'em while they closed in. The one right in front of him pulled out a bowie knife, long as his arm. That little boy says to Lewis 'give it up.' That's all the little idiot said, 'give it up.' Well, Lewis gives the one with the knife a look, says to the boy 'negro, please' then just threw his bus pass at him. Pop! The one on his left just punched him. Popped him in the jaw. One grabbed Lewis around the shoulders and pulled him up, somebody reached in his pocket and grabbed his wallet.

"In all the tussle, Lewis' leg comes off. It's not designed for wrestling matches. One of the thugs pulls on it and it comes right off. Well, those boys get freaked out by what they're seeing. Man's fighting with one leg, his other leg being in one of the thugs' hands. Bowie knife boy just stands there for a while, then he whistles and the other boys scatter. They take off. Lewis doesn't make a sound, just sighs. Pulls himself back up on the bench, a little bloody, a little bruised. That doesn't happen anywhere else except around Barnes Alley. Around where you've chosen to make your fresh, new start."

"It's not like that anymore," says Lex. The story has made him tired, eyelids moving slowly as he blinks. "It's much better, now. Not so much thuggery."

Oscar looks unconvinced. He folds his napkin slowly and places it over his plate, all while staring at Lex. Lex shifts in his chair, feeling a wave of mischief stretch across his chest.

"So, I don't suppose you'll want to help me carry some things up this week," says Lex. "Out of fear for your own leg?" Lorraine frowns.

second

6

The city's lights are persistent, drifting into the small apartment as Lex prepares for his first night's sleep in his new place with his only piece of furniture. His new sheets, a prominent grid pattern from the way they were folded in the packaging, are draped over the top. The two throw pillows that came with the futon are perched at the head of his bed.

During the entire train ride home, knapsack loaded with a week's worth of clothing and supplies, Lex kept thinking about his father's dinner story. Not that it has any influence on the way he sees his new neighborhood. He has a sudden, deep affection for the place. His father's story only illustrated just how much of a grudge the old man fostered against an idea of a piece of geography.

He wonders how much his father's negativity has stunted his own personal development.

There is a faint nagging somewhere in his mind reminding him that, while outside of his apartment was relatively safe, the inside held some peril. He's got an odd feeling in the pit of his stomach, something that he's quite willing to dismiss as first-night nerves. Similar to what he'd experienced that first night on campus, having spent his entire life to that point under his father's and mother's roof. He's in the middle of something new, reason enough to be nervous.

But that wasn't it. He grips his bag a little tighter and slouches in his rear-facing seat. The train is mostly empty, a few oddballs and misfits making late-night forays into downtown to face their own demons. Or create new ones. They hold more interest to each other and their varied upcoming conjurings than he does for them, so he feels adequately anonymous. Nonetheless, he withdraws as much comfort from the bag of his belongings as he can while he waits for the train to pull into the terminal.

What did that installation guy see? Or hear? Or smell? It was hard to come to terms with the odd vibes the encounter laid over the place. And the water. He shakes his head, reminding himself that he's a rational human being that isn't prone to flights of nonsense. He simply heard the neighbors. That's all. Case closed.

So, after dragging his week's worth of his old life, plastic containers filled with leftovers from his mother's meal included, he goes through his small apartment, switching on every light and checking the position of every possession. Everything, what little there is of it, is in its place. Once he's satisfied, he unpacks the sheets he'd gotten at the discount store down the street for less than five dollars. He then puts the food away, having almost forgotten it was in his duffel.

Bed made, clothes tucked into his surprisingly large closet, and everything else stowed, Lex washes up and brushes his teeth before steeling himself to lie down.

He sits there, all lights on in the apartment, both fans whirring softly overhead, staring at the light pollution streaming into the airshaft outside. It's beautiful. He stares at his own reflection, the reflection of the apartment behind him, in halftone against the background of the alley. Of the airshaft. The brick wall of the building across the way.

The sounds of the city trickle over the top of the buildings. Lex can see the ambers and the reds of the streetlights and vehicles and traffic lights as he sits on the edge of his bed. It's his space, his little personal corner of the universe and he lets the feeling of place wash over him. He closes his eyes, takes a deep breath and leans into the hand he feels brushing across his cheek.

His nose fills with roses and lavender, the hand on his cheek warm to the touch. Behind his eyelids he can see the rest of the figure the hand belongs to. Elongated slightly and thin, moving with a grace beyond what he'd thought was possible. It's in the shadows of the room, hidden. He sees the arm leading up to a shape. The fingers ease down his cheek toward his neck and he can't help but to lean into it further. He's losing himself, letting the moment melt the loneliness away.

It takes longer than it should have to realize the fingers dancing down his cheek didn't belong there. He should be alone in his apartment. The door is locked, he's made sure of that.

The room suddenly grows very cold. Lex chalks it up as fear wrapping its icy fingers around his heart. He opens his eyes, expecting to see. . .someone.

Anyone.

A woman with long, sinewy fingers stroking his face as she looks him in the eyes, head tilted, preparing to kiss him. All of these expectations despite knowing that he's alone.

So, it's no surprise to find, as he opens his eyes, that no one's there. The lights are still shining bright, the fans gently stirring the air around the studio. He's still facing the windows, still sees his own reflection staring back at him, the reflection of the room behind him in the clean glass. The aroma of roses and lavender is gone, replaced by the smell of paint and cleaning materials.

He's a little freaked out.

"Shit," Lex gasps. He's torn between laughing at himself for being so ridiculous and curling up into a ball to keep all the phantoms away. He decides to laugh, but only out of vanity.

While trying to calm himself, Lex makes an internal bargain. He would shut off most the lights save the one over the stove. He would close the bathroom and closet doors and would triple-check the locks on the entry. He would then make one final pass at the studio, placing things in unmistakably appropriate places, before crawling under his new sheets and resting his head on his new pillow, as firm as it may be. The entire apartment is visible from where he lay, so it's easy to reassure himself that everything is okay, that no one is mysteriously shuffling his things behind his back. There's no mystery woman surreptitiously trying to seduce him.

This is an easy bargain and he begins to execute the terms, pausing briefly to decide whether he's warm enough to leave the fans cycling while he sleeps. The weather has settled from a damp rain to a slightly damp chill and clouds were inconstant, drifting across the small sliver of sky he can still see. The flashing lights of the broadcast antennae atop a nearby building provide the steady though dim strobe of fake lightning, the perfect punctuation to a completely gray day.

Lex feels like a little kid as he pulls the covers over his head, hiding his face under the cheap sheer, synthetic fabrics. The pillow smells like chemicals and he hears the fibers of the stuffing compress under the weight of his head. He struggles to get comfortable. Not that the bed itself is inherently unrelenting, he's slept on much worse when he'd hopped from sofa to air mattress to beanbag chair over one restless summer. It was the summer he'd lost Natalie. It's a summer he doesn't like to dwell on anymore.

Lex pulls the sheets from over his head and lies with his eyes open, staring at the smooth ceiling as the shadows of the fan move in the faint light of the kitchen's vent hood. He steadies his breathing, listening to the faint sounds of the city fade toward sleep. He closes his eyes, hoping the sounds will coddle him like a lullaby.

He hears the taps in the bathroom sink squeak open and a torrent of water rush into the basin. His eyes snap open, but he makes no other move. He listens as, again, water splashes from the faucet into the sink. The sound of water being lifted from the basin, splashing against what must be someone's face, hitting the floor, drifts from the bathroom.

Lex sits up. There's a small gap between the threshold and the bottom of the bathroom door. He stares at this gap, expecting to see shadows moving. The bathroom is dark, but the sound of running water is definitely coming from within. There's no mistaking the source or fooling himself that it's an adjacent apartment heard through thin walls.

He takes a deep breath.

He's not taking any chances this time. He lifts himself from the futon, glancing once more over his entire space. No sneaking up on whatever is washing itself in his sink. Steeled and ready, he strides to the bathroom door, grasps the knob with authority and in one motion, twists and quickly yanks open the door.

Silence.

Lex switches on the lights. The sink is bone dry, just like he'd left it after brushing his teeth. The floor is dry as well, not a single sign of water anywhere. He steps closer to the bathroom sink, searching the small bathroom for the sign of anything other than himself. Apparently something with a dirty face.

Lex stands at his bathroom sink staring at his reflection in the small mirror. Confusion with a tinge of fear edged with complete fatigue stares back with bloodshot eyes. He is spent and is ready to collapse. He feels the cool tile floor with his toes and the pads of his feet. He wonders how comfortable the bathtub would be as a bed. Perhaps not so bad if he brings in the pillows from the futon. Maybe even with the sheets and some dirty clothes to act as added padding. He would be fine, he thinks, sleeping in the bathroom. That way, he would be able to solve the mystery of the running water.

It's a funny thought, curling up in the bathtub, watching the sink until he falls asleep. Lex chuckles weakly, eyelids growing heavy.

He snaps awake when he hears the kitchen faucet turn itself on at full blast, water drumming against the bottom of the steel sink. The splash is unmistakable. The water is clearly coming from the kitchen, drifting through the open bathroom door.

Lex is frozen. The confidence he'd demonstrated in getting out of bed and entering the bathroom was gone. He's shivering. The coolness of the floor, the same cool that seemed so comforting before, sends chills through his ankles and calves, up and down his spine.

Deep breath and Lex feels himself moving away from the vanity mirror. He sees the bathroom door approaching, feels the gentle drag of his feet against the tile floor.

The violence is more severe in the kitchen. Where, in the bathroom Lex heard a little splashing, he hears much more in the kitchen. It's as if whomever was bathing themselves in the kitchen sink was trying to start a flood, as if a waterfall were cascading over the front apron of the sink, hitting the kitchen floor. He hears water being splashed playfully, spraying onto the walls to either side and the cabinets above the counters. He can hear subtle, high-pitched tones as water drips from the bottoms of the cabinets.

Lex stands in the bathroom doorway. He switches the bathroom light off almost as if he's been hypnotized to do so. That part of the room darkened, allowing the vent light over the stove to be the only source of light in the apartment.

The sound of water showering every surface of the kitchen is loud, clear, close. There's a shadow that traces its way across the floor, the form of something reaching down into the sink, reaching up to a face. The water cascades down, rippling shadows linking the face and basin below. Lex turns the corner, the sound of water growing louder as he eases forward. He holds his breath and arches onto his tiptoes. He steels himself for whomever or whatever he's going to find around the corner, standing in his kitchen, washing itself.

The refrigerator comes into view, the oven and vent hood, the counter, all of the cabinets above. His eyes edge around to the sink and the sound suddenly stops. So does Lex. He gets the corner of the kitchen sink into his peripheral view and he freezes. There's nothing moving. No water crashing against the bottom of the stainless steel sink.

All is silent.

He finishes the trip around the corner and stands fully in the kitchen which is dry and quiet. There's no sign that the sink had been running, not a single drip from the faucet.

Lex isn't fond of the metallic taste that fills his mouth, the sting of each breath through his nostrils. He dares not move too quickly for fear of fainting. His eyes sweep across the counter, fearing what each moment reveals. What, he wonders, is hiding in the shadows?

He takes another deep breath. He repeats to himself that there's nothing in the room with him. That he's hearing things. That his imagination is running rampant. That he's being betrayed by fantasy.

Lex stares at the kitchen for a very long time. The entire moment is frozen like a photograph in a gallery. Man suspended by fear in his small kitchen, color. Photographer unknown.

He breaks the stalemate when he realizes that he's started to sway slightly. The fatigue is catching up with him, the adrenaline flowing from his body. He feels a crash coming.

"Shit," Lex mumbles. "Time for sleep." He doesn't know why he says this aloud. Perhaps he fears and answer. It's a test.

After a long blink and a spine-rattling yawn, Lex backs away from the kitchen, throwing one final long glance at the kitchen sink. He peers around the corner into his bathroom. There's not a single drip escaping from either faucet. After a momentary, exhaustion-addled debate, he decides to leave the bathroom door open. He doesn't want to take the chance at hearing another rush of water escaping from the taps.

Another wide yawn and Lex stretches before turning to dive back into bed. He stops himself, abruptly reawakened, adrenaline suddenly pumping through his nervous system once more.

The futon has been reconfigured to its upright, seated position, pillows resting against the arms, sheets neatly folded in the middle of the seat.

7

"YOU SHOULDN'T YAWN SO MUCH," SAYS CARMEN, SHAKING HER HEAD. "Especially so loud. And in the middle of the office. In such a small office. It's not polite."

Lex looks up from his computer, his head in a fog. He's not kept track of how much he's been yawning or how loudly, but apparently it's been beyond acceptable.

"Sorry," he mumbles. "Didn't realize how tired I was."

"Yeah, it's a little rude, to be honest," Carmen continues. She hasn't looked over from her screen at the adjacent workstation, focused as she is on a very colorful spreadsheet. It isn't a particularly sexy spreadsheet. The background is dark and the cells are very small, making the text and numbers within almost microscopic. It's been said in their office that the reason so many people wear glasses is because the numbers on their screens wreck their eyes. Human resources regularly rolls past the desks telling people to look away from their monitors to avoid fatigue and vision loss. This is how little eye contact she wishes to make with Lex. She's clearly annoyed.

"I haven't been sleeping a lot," says Lex.

"You've said that all week. Too busy being a party boy?"

Lex likes this back and forth. It passes the time. It helps him stay awake, keeps him engaged. Besides, he likes flirting with Carmen and he assumes that she likes flirting back. At least he guesses that it's flirting. It's hard for him to tell either way. He just wishes he could stop yawning.

"I'm not a party boy," Lex says, fighting back a yawn.

"I don't care," says Carmen. She has yet to look in his direction and is reaching for a pair of Bose noise-cancelling over-ear headphones.

"You asked," Lex mumbles. The computer screen before him is very blurry and he wipes his eyes with his palms to try and focus. He succeeds temporarily before another yawn racks his body causing tears to run down his cheeks.

There aren't a lot of people in the office which isn't unusual for a Thursday. Lots of weekend travel starts on Thursdays as clients like their long weekends and really don't pay much attention to what's being done with their money after Wednesday. Focus at the beginning of the week is rewarded by being allowed to work from home, which Lex takes as code for do anything else but work from home. The old-timers are spending the final handful of temperate afternoons wetting the bottoms of their boats.

Silence settles into the office once more as Lex simply gives in, leaning back in his chair and closing his eyes. He feels himself falling, drifting into the surf of sleep. He hears the blowers of the office's climate control system whine and the sound pushes him deeper into the trance of slumber. He relaxes, causing his spine to sink deeper into the chair.

He feels himself falling and doesn't care. The part of himself that wants to let it happen wins and he tumbles off of his seat, barely missing hitting the corner of his desk with his skull. He's somehow aware of how close he is to his desk and snaps awake just in time to see the hard edge of maple whisk past his face. Such a frightening sight quickens the heart.

"Glad to see you can catch up on a bit of sleep, Mister Delaware," calls a deep voice as he lands on the floor, inches from a pair of highly polished wingtips. The toe of one of the wingtips is tapping. The left one. Each tap spits small granules of dust into Lex's eye. "Get up at your leisure, if you'd like. Take your time. There's a fair amount of work to be done today and we are, of course, short-handed. Do not, however, let that influence your passion for the work."

Lex blinks the dust from his eyes the best he can. The tears help. He's not sure where they're coming from, if it's pain or embarrassment or the fact that there's dust rolling steadily into them. Once he clears the bulk of the crud in the corner of his left eye, he spots the cap to a water bottle. A blue one. From the way the threads roll up in neat ridges and the way the sides of the cap itself are ribbed, it's from a very fancy bottle of artisanal, hand-pressed water. The type of water one gets from the full body and mind organic grocers that line the blocks leading up to their fashionable studio office.

"Ease yourself back to your seat whenever you're ready, Mister Delaware," continues the voice above the wingtips. He hates the way the man says Mister Delaware. As if the façade of polite address can ease the jerkiness of the man's tone. It only makes Lex want to lie there for a few minutes, simply to dig under the skin of his manager.

"He's not that bright," says Carmen. Lex imagines her saying so with her headphones still glued to the sides of her face, staring intently at her screens. "Been yawning all day."

"Miss Nguyen," says wingtips. "I do believe you need to focus on your given assignment instead of concerning yourself with a minor issue of a lack of discipline."

Lex thinks wingtips has a great point. Carmen should mind her own business. Unless he can convince her that her business involves dinner at a reasonably priced restaurant followed by brown paper bag drinks at a great park with an overlook of the city. At that point, he'd be willing to make anything part of her business. Right there, though, in front of wingtips with Lex sprawled out on the ground in front of his desk staring at random trash and fugitive dust bunnies, he wants nothing more than for Carmen to keep her trap shut and to mind business that didn't involve him.

Lex hears a quick snort of disapproval from Carmen followed by some overly earnest tapping on a keyboard. He realizes that his time on the floor has expired. Much longer and he will pass from having had an amusing pratfall to being impertinently lazy. He pushes himself up, banging the back of his head on the bottom of the desk he'd avoided on the way down.

"That's the spirit," says wingtips. The toe has stopped tapping and the man now stands planted next to Lex's desk. His legs are spread slightly, as if he's getting ready to shoot a free-throw.

"I'm sorry," Lex manages to say as he unfolds himself, dusting off the front of his shirt and khakis as he does. The floor is filthy and he's certain that he's going to need to do a few loads of laundry before he'd initially intended. He thinks perhaps he can use the machine at his parents' while he picks up the rest of his stuff, but that's so far into the future he doesn't bother to take the thought any further.

The man in the expensive dress slacks, the man standing right in front of him in the stylish patterned shirt and contrasting tie, the man with the deep, authoritative voice stands planted with his arms crossed over his chest. He's a large guy, not fat. Definitely larger than Lex. His shoulders are broad. He looks like if he didn't work in personal finance he would be an MMA fighter. Heavyweight. His clean-shaven head reflects the overhead lights, spots of specularity gleaming off of his dome. His eyes smile behind his large, square glasses and seems like he's a very nice guy when he's allowed to be.

With Lex brushing himself off from his quasi face plant, he wasn't being allowed to be nice.

"Mister Delaware," says the large man, "I do hope that this isn't a harbinger for the quality of work we can expect from you during the remainder of your probationary period here. I would really hate to find a valid reason to terminate your stay with us at such an early juncture."

"No, of course not," Lex mumbles. He thinks of how little he likes the large man standing before him, layering threats onto an already humiliating situation. The fact that he's chosen to mock Lex does nothing to endear the man.

"Well, I'd hoped not," says the large man. The eyes are still smiling, still belying the sneer present in the man's upper lip. He hates Lex and enjoys doing so.

"I haven't been sleeping well," says Lex. He winces upon hearing himself. Carmen sighs. "It's been. . .I'll do better, I'm just so tired and. . ."

"We're all tired, Mister Delaware," says the man, sneer curling into a half-smile, "yet we persevere. Persevere, Mister Delaware. Don't make these types of displays a habit."

The man glides away from the desk, glancing toward Carmen with what Lex assumes was a mutual nod of disgust. Perhaps, he thinks, he's in the wrong place after all. Perhaps he would be better off resetting his life in a tax accountant's office.

"Good talk, Dean," Lex says under his breath. He stares, checking that Dean didn't hear him. Dean continues his route across the office, weaving past empty chairs at idle desks. He nods at someone who's doing some data entry near the wall before turning the corner into another section of the office.

Carmen begins to laugh without looking away from her terminal. She has her ears covered by her headphones, but there's clearly nothing playing through them. She wipes a tear from her eye then starts typing, hitting the delete button with every third keystroke.

8

"Fuck those people and fuck everything they represent," says Parker. He follows this with an impressive string of expletives that cause Lex to quickly cover the speaker of the phone and look around. The last thing he needs is someone admonishing him for inappropriate workplace language.

The coast is clear. Carmen has left for the day and Lex is pretty sure that the only other person on the entire floor is the intern sitting outside the VP's office. The VP having left hours previously with some thin excuse of needing to meet with a client at a nearby hotel.

"I talk to you to feel better, not so you can badmouth everyone," says Lex. He's grinning at the outburst and tries not to let his friend hear him laugh.

"Fuck cheering you up, dude," says Parker. "Listen, it's late, you've been there all day, you keep dozing off. Get your ass home, Lex. That's why we have homes. So we don't spend every hour of our existence in some soul-draining office."

"I know, but I can't do anything at home," says Lex, leaning back into his chair. He closes his eyes for a moment then catches himself, forcing them open again. He leans forward to fight the temptation to fall asleep on the phone. He'd never hear the end of it.

"You can take your ass to your swanky apartment, that's what you can do."

There's a burst of laughter in the background on Parker's end. It sounds predominantly female, mostly drunk. Perhaps naked. Lex can hear faint dance music pulsing in the background along with the snatches of random, bawdy conversations overlapping each other. Once again, predominantly female, mostly drunk.

"Should you get back to your party?" asks Lex. He's huddled closer to his desktop while speaking on his cell phone, hoping to muffle any stray sounds that may escape his conversation. He furtively glances about, confirming once again that he's alone in the darkened office.

"Fuck those people and fuck everything they represent," says Parker. "Look, nerd, you've got to get over this whole can't-sleep thing. I haven't slept but five hours in the past week and I'm great. That's not keeping me from my apartment."

The laughter on Parker's end of the phone is close and Lex can hear some faint moaning at a distance. He's not sure where Parker is, hasn't gotten the nerve to ask yet, and doesn't know why Parker called in the first place.

"Why did you call me, Parker?" asks Lex. "Where the hell are you?"

"Don't worry about it," says Parker. "Listen. You're being hard on yourself. Normal. New job, new place. You got a new girl, yet?"

If he lets on how deeply that girl comment cuts, it will dominate the rest of the conversation.

"No," Lex says. He thinks his inflection is flat, that there is no pain behind it.

"Right," answers Parker. There's a very long pause and Lex swears he can hear someone in the background being brought to orgasm. "Anyway, you need to get off of zero, kid. You're stuck. You've been stuck too long and inertia's taken over. You can't just sit around complaining about not getting sleep and zombie-walking through your day."

"Kid?" Lex asks softly.

"Take me, for example. I know you idolize me and my lifestyle, my swagger, how I hold myself. You can be like me, too. Just pick yourself up, live your best life. And, if you can, get laid."

"We're the same age, Parker. I actually may be a bit older than you." Lex tries to do the math quickly in his head. He ends up counting on his fingers. "I am older than you by three months, Parker. I'm no kid to you."

"Why haven't you been sleeping?" Parker asks. "Not that it matters. It doesn't matter. I withdraw the question. You need to not-sleep with purpose. I have the perfect plan. You should come here. Now. Ditch work and come over here right now and get yourself a drink. It'll settle you down and a friend, let's call her a friend, will give you a reason to stay up. Then you can see how to live life, kid."

Unsure if he should be grateful or insulted, Lex takes his time to answer. The delay gives Parker the chance to speak with people on his end. Lex gains a clearer picture of his friend's surroundings.

Parker, after the first few moments of phone silence, begins speaking to a young woman called Daphne who was nearby and, according to the bits of the conversation Lex hears, was being very stupid. Clearly not too stupid, or at least not a kind a of stupid that Parker wanted stopped because of the laughter in his voice. Daphne mumbles something which is followed by a brief eruption of laughter from several people near the phone, including Parker. Lex then hears Parker calling someone, or several someones, baby. Repeatedly. The word is said so many times in such a rapid succession it ceases to be a word at all. It's more of a sound that Parker makes trying to hold someone's attention. The sound of his voice trails away from the phone making Lex think that Parker has either set the phone down or given it to someone while he walks across whatever room he occupies.

"Who is this?" slurs a female voice. She had a faint southern accent that made her sound cute over the phone.

"Could you please put Parker back on?" sighs Lex.

"Who's Parker?" asks the voice before the entire aural background becomes muffled. "There a fucking Parker in here?" is what the southern accent shouts across the room. Lex truly hopes its a room. Another roil of laughter and what Lex could only interpret as multiple people moaning rhythmically drifts through the phone's speaker.

Everything he hears is run through the rough filter of flesh and cotton, as the southern accent is holding the phone pressed against herself while she searches the event. Wherever she has it, she's rubbing the microphone against something, creating a disorienting white noise. He's tempted to simply hang up but knows that once the phone reaches Parker, he's going to call back. Possibly angry that Lex hung up.

Lex thinks for the moment that he's alone with the muffled sound about how he'd gotten there. How he's sitting at his desk, night descending quickly outside the windows. How he's more tired than he's ever been in his life. That he's trying everything he can to not go home to his new apartment.

How it's been a week since he's truly slept and how he's not sure when he'll sleep again. He feels a little helpless. A little like the orphan cell phone being carted around a crowded room searching for its owner in the hands of a girl who occasionally lilts "are any of you fuckers Parker?" The word 'any' is drawn out into a three-note broken chord.

Lex begins to feel the time in his temples, how very late it is and how few excuses he has to stick around, as he hears the main door to the office swing open. He looks up as the short, dark-haired woman pulls a large rolling trash can through the door. She's followed by an equally small dark-haired man carrying a silver canister vacuum, the orange tubing coiled around his arms. Once through the door, they part ways with her wheeling the bin toward the offices to the right while he switches on the lights and plugs his vacuum in to his left.

"So, you coming out or not, big guy?" Parker's voice punches through the phone unmuffled. The noise in the background has changed. There aren't as many voices as there were before, the majority of the background is traffic. There are diesel engines and the squeals of tires on pavement, car horns and distant sirens. All of this blends with a steady breeze, creating a noise that causes Lex's shoulders to relax. Given the opportunity, he could easily curl under his desk with his phone at his ear and drift into a deep, deep sleep.

"Coming where, Parker?" Lex shoots back. "You haven't told me what you want. You haven't told me where you are. I'm at work, for the love of God. You call me and. . . not that I'm ungrateful for the invitation. I just don't know what you want."

"Forget all that, kid," says Parker. "Listen to me. Seriously, listen to me. Are you listening?"

"Yes, I'm listening."

"You're listening. Good. Lex, I gotta admit, brother, that I love you. You're a great fucking guy and if you put your mind to it, you're going to go far in this life. This has all just been a temporary setback, you know. A minor blip in the overall trajectory of where you're headed, my brother. I'm your number one fan."

"I hope you're right," Lex says. He looks at his watch before yawning wide. He hears the woman with the large rolling trash bin emptying the small trash cans scattered throughout the office with a single bang against the side of the bin. He hears the guy shuffling along the perimeter of the office wiping the glass on all the windows. The pair is working a well coordinated pattern, practiced and highly efficient.

"You hope I'm right. I'm right, motherfucker." Parker is yelling. He's gotten emotional. He's clearly very drunk. This means he should probably not be out on a balcony with a group of people who, according to all available evidence, don't all know who he is. "You're a fucking phoenix waiting for his fire. Your feathers are all falling out and your beak is drooping and you're low energy. Lady phoenixes don't like droopy beaks, my friend. They hate 'em. They like nice, strong, straight beaks, dude. Beaks that can get in there and really do shit, you know what I'm saying?"

"No."

"You're a phoenix, man. And there's so much shit that you need to do, but you haven't caught your fire yet. You're dragging, waiting for your fire. Your fire's coming, man. I know it. Your fire is fucking coming and you need to be ready for it. You need to be ready to catch your fire and get reborn and soar like the straight-beaked beast I know you are."

"Okay."

"But, okay listen to me. I don't feel like you're listening to me. Are you listening, Lex?"

"Yes, I'm listening. Fuck."

"Fuck you, man. You should listen when I'm laying down some love for you, man. I'm serious. It's really easy. You should just, you know, sleep or something. But if you don't sleep you should come down here and find out what I'm talking about. You know what I'm talking about, man?"

"No."

Lex has never been happier to hear the sound of a large, outdated canister vacuum as the man to the left begins his sweep across the office, starting at the far end and working his way back to the plug near the door. Perfect coordination with his partner, who is nearing his desk in her cycle of emptying the office's refuse cans.

"The fuck is that sound, kid?" says Parker, shouting through the telephone's speaker.

"Cleaning crew," answers Lex. "It's late and I should probably go get some food or something."

"Why are you still at work, Lex? You haven't been listening to a word I've said. I called you for a reason, goddammit. You've got to listen to me, man. I know some shit."

"I gotta go, Parker." Lex says. He switches the phone to his other ear as he yawns and begins packing his things. There aren't a lot of things to pack, but he scans his desk three times before zipping up his backpack. Notepad, check. Pen, check. Tablet, check. He wishes there was more to his life in the office, more things to pack to show that he's made a difference. He stands just as the woman with the rolling bin reaches his desk. The expression on her face is business-like and she's wearing white earbuds that Lex assumes plays music just loud enough so that she doesn't hear the vacuum running. Professional team and Lex respects it. He nods to her as he passes her. She doesn't react. Her moves are efficient, practiced.

"Yes!" says Parker. His shouting has reached a fever pitch and Lex can hear a faint cheer in the background. Apparently, Parker has recruited the people on the balcony with him as some sort of impromptu support squad. Lex hears random voices chanting 'come on up', their chant blending in with the sounds of the traffic below.

"I'll talk to you later, Parker," says Lex, pausing at the office door to gather himself for the journey home. He thinks he should perhaps eat something, but he's not sure what he wants. "I've got to get some food."

"We'll be waiting for you," says Parker. The background sounds abruptly change and Lex hears that he's back inside with the music and the other human noises. Lex shakes his head and walks to the stairwell. "We'll get started without you, though. As long as you don't mind."

"Good night, Parker. Please be careful," Lex sighs. He waits a beat before adding, "I worry about you sometimes, big guy." He ends the call and pushes the door into the stairwell to leave.

9

THE STUDIO APARTMENT LOOKS MUCH LARGER WITH FURNITURE HELPING to define the different living areas. Lex has tried to make the most of the space by choosing a small dining table, small bookcase, small side tables. Most of the items in the room, from what he's been told, are studio-sized. Tiny yet functional. It's a philosophy he's adopted with the prodding of the nice young stock clerk at Ikea, who was the encyclopedic example of 'solid dude'.

The delivery of his furniture, fifty-two boxes all told, had been unexpectedly uneventful. The delivery company called ahead like they said they would. The unmarked, yet generously scuffed, yellow delivery truck arrived with three guys squeezed into the cab. They popped out and the driver had Lex hold the manifest while all three guys efficiently transferred the boxes from the back of the truck, up the stairs, into Lex's mostly empty apartment. They checked the number of boxes to the numbers on the manifest, Lex signed it, and the men silently re-entered their truck, driving off into the grid of city streets.

Lex had almost been inspired to leave the guys a glowing review online, but was promptly distracted by the daunting task of sorting all of his newly acquired boxes into organized piles. He tried at first to sort by room. That failed quickly and he simply decided to begin assembling pieces as soon as he'd gathered all of the requisite boxes for the task.

Luckily for him, the first piece he completed was his retro-modern dining table. This came in handy as he needed a place to stack tools, instructions, small parts that might get lost in the cracks between floorboards. He made his way through the rest of the boxes over the course of a Saturday.

That's not to say he didn't suffer any setbacks.

On more than one occasion, boxes would simply vanish from their piles only to appear in a completely different stack. Once, while assembling one of his low bookcases, one of the boxes he'd accounted for, a box he'd sworn was on the bottom of that stack, was nowhere to be found. He searched the entire apartment, not a difficult task given the size of the unit. He even searched the closet, the kitchen cabinets, the trash pile that had been growing steadily as he stacked opened cardboard boxes. It wasn't there. He counted time and again to no avail. He'd decided that, instead of succumbing to mounting frustration, he would step outdoors and take a quick walk to get a coffee. A cheap coffee. The cheapest he could find. He'd thrown his jacket across his shoulders and opened the door to leave and there was the box, sitting just outside his door. He looked up and down the hall to see if there was someone watching the result of a rather cruel practical joke.

Nothing.

Just the box. Waiting for him as if it had always been there and he was just noticing it in that moment. Lex brought the box into the apartment and went for the walk anyway. He'd skipped the coffee.

So, there he sits at his dining room table in his fully furnished apartment wondering what will happen next. He's very tired but wide awake as he sits with a deli sandwich placed atop a sheet of unfolded deli paper, a small bag of potato chips lying unopened next to it. His senses are heightened, the world around him is saturated in color and sound and smell. He can't stop scanning the room, searching for the next weird misplacement. The next strange, unexplainable sound wafting across his face from someplace impossibly close.

The room has become less spartan in the week he's lived on his own. He's using low bookshelves as a room divider, separating his living space from the dining area. Most of the shelves are empty, walls undecorated. The furniture is nicely arranged and waiting to be stocked with personal belongings and a few electronics that Lex had his eyes on when he'd first signed the lease to the place.

That excitement has been replaced by a dread that will not ease.

He stops scanning the room long enough to consider eating the sandwich. He stares at the top bun and imagines the sesame seeds are stars, forming constellations from one end to the other. The patterns begin to sway, morphing in three dimensions from animal to abstract shape to faces of random people he'd seen in the street that day. The entire table top becomes blurry as Lex nods his head, jerking it back before he falls completely into his paper wrapper.

The apartment swims and he begins to smile. He's comfortable, relaxed, ready to finally sleep. He could sleep through anything at this point. He's not even certain he could make it to his futon as sleep has wrapped itself around him. The anxiety of having to live through another night of strange happenings, noises, unexplained relocations, all of it is being pushed into the background by an overwhelming urge to lie down.

He weakly folds the paper back over his sandwich, pushes it aside and hoists himself onto his feet. He uses the table as support being careful not to bring himself out of a blissful half-sleep. Not so much that he'd stumble over something and hurt himself, but not so little that he loses the sensation altogether. He shuffles his feet, leaning on the table, leaving his eyes closed as long as he can. After about a minute of shuffling, stopping to find something else to support himself, letting the waves of sleep crash through him, he makes it to his futon. It's up, sofa-style. He doesn't care.

Lex throws himself onto the futon, fully clothed, arm draped over his eyes as he releases his last holds on consciousness. The darkness deepens as he loses himself fully to sleep. The world drifts away.

There's a pounding on the front door to the apartment and he is instantly pulled from nocturnal bliss. Eyes wide open, a little confused, he looks to the front door.

"Fuck," he whispers as the floating fades, as sleep retreats once more. He sits up and looks again to the front door, waiting. He wonders if he'd imagined the knock. If he'd willed it, wishing for something to happen as he drifted off to sleep. The idea bounces around off the walls of his mind. What if there were nothing, no knock, no interruption? What if he was sabotaging himself, just when he was beginning to allow himself a little rest from the week's ordeal.

These were not normal times. Sure, things disappeared only to reappear in completely unexpected places. He could chalk most of that to mindlessness. A lack of focus. Most of those things didn't bother him.

The strangest things happened at night as he tried to sleep. There were noises, bumps. The sounds of water pouring from taps. The sounds of feet dragging, heavy breathing, constant tapping. There were voices saying nothing he could understand, laughter too close to be from different apartments. He would begin to doze off, drift before hearing the clod of heavy feet, the scraping of large and metallic objects, the grunt of someone laboring. Always in the dark, always in a place out of view. This was so odd for such a small space.

Sounds just out of view but always present in his tiny studio.

He suspects that it's happened again, that whatever oddities abide in his place have stirred to taunt him for another night. Tears begin to trickle down his face. He's very, very tired and feels on edge. Lex thinks to yell, but he hasn't the energy. His voice would be too feeble. There's nothing he wants more than to simply lie there on his sofa, waiting out the noise, hoping that his fatigue can outmuscle the disturbance.

He waits.

He doesn't wait long as the knocking resumes. It's more earnest than before. Lex rises weakly, stumbles for a moment as he finds his feet. He drags himself to the door. It's still pounding. The door vibrates a little.

Still not certain if the pounding, the shaking, the rattling is in his head, Lex freezes. He stares at the doorknob, watching to see if it turns or moves. He tries to look under the door, but the sweeper blocks his efforts. There's a peephole, a tiny disk of light in the middle of the door. The pounding, the slight bowing in the middle where whatever's on the other side hits, keeps him from using it. He thinks the door might give way at any moment, smacking him squarely in the nose.

Something compels him forward. An inner voice whispers nothing would be there when he opens the door. Perhaps this causes him, languor and all, to stride the remaining distance, grasp the knob firmly, and pull the door open.

Lex lets out a yelp, causing the round man with the wispy blonde hair to let out a scream. It's high pitched, like a child on the playground being chased by another child armed with a stick.

"Oh, my goodness," says the round man, breathless, pressing his hand against his chest. "What is wrong with you?"

"Me?" asks Lex. Fatigue has transformed to anger and confusion. "What are you doing?"

"I was knocking to introduce myself," says the stranger at the door. "I'd seen you come in, I knew you were home. I wanted to give you time to get settled and situated. Realized you've been here a couple weeks and I had yet to introduce myself. You seemed nice enough, so I thought I'd let you get yourself moved in before I came over to bother you. Welcome you to the building. Didn't think I'd get hollered at."

Lex stands at the door, dumbfounded. His tongue lolls around his mouth, working to form a coherent words. All of his previous exhaustion is forgotten.

"What?" stumbles Lex, hand still on the doorknob.

"You could invite me in," says the round man, fanning himself. "Not that I'm expecting anything, I've only been pounding on your door for the last five minutes. Almost called the police, thought you may have passed out or come to some kind of harm. I knew you were home, saw you come in. Didn't see you come back out. Knew you had to still be in. So, I said to myself, I said 'Merle, get your butt over there and say hello' and so here I am. Didn't expect to get screamed at when you opened the door."

"Why were you pounding?"

"Was I pounding? I couldn't tell. These doors are so thick, you know. So solid. If I didn't give a little effort into letting you know I was out here you wouldn't notice. I could just scratch at the thing all day long and you'd never even hear me. I don't think I was pounding on the door, as you say. I just needed to make sure you heard me. Plus, who knows if you were in the bathroom or fixing yourself some dinner on the stove and couldn't hear anything over the vent fans or whatever. I knew that if I just got in there and let you know that it was somebody outside knocking, you'd come and let me in. So, you gonna invite me in?"

The round man has calmed himself and caught his breath. He looks at Lex wide-eyed and extends a hand at the end of a delicately angled wrist.

"The name is Merle," says the round man at the door. "Merle Ogden. Was in the first group that moved in. Been living here three years."

"Lex," says Lex. He feels defeated, though he can't pinpoint specifically what has him more deflated. He takes Merle Ogden's hand and gives it a weak shake while Merle tries to peek around him to look into the apartment.

"Did I catch you at a bad time?" asks Merle. He does so while never making eye contact with Lex, holding his hand captive in what seems to be an old wrestling move, pulling Lex off balance in order to get a better view into the small apartment. Lex, tired as he is, stands his ground.

"Yes, actually, you kinda did," Lex answers. "Thank you for coming by, but perhaps we can sit and talk another time."

"Oh, well of course," says Merle, visibly disappointed. "How rude of me. I can never tell, everyone keeps their own hours, you know. Nobody has that old-fashioned set schedule anymore. It's always leave early, stay late, bunch of ships passing in the night. No one gets to know each other even though they're just a few doors away. Not that I'm complaining to you. You know what it's like to work odd hours. Clearly. Anyway, I'll let you get back to whatever it was you were doing. You don't have company over, do you? I hate to interrupt you and your company."

"Thank you, Merle," Lex says as warmly as he can manage. "I'm just trying to catch a little sleep. Long day and another early one tomorrow."

"Yes, certainly. Well, I'm just down the hall. I'm sure I'll run into you at some point. If you ever need anything, just come knock on my door. I'm just down there at 5B. Oh, and be sure you put your shoulder into knocking. These doors are solid. Otherwise, I might not hear you over the vent fans or I might be in the bathroom. But, keep knocking, you know. I'll answer. I work from home mostly, anyway. Online marketing and correspondence, you know. It's a pretty good living. Can't complain."

"Yes, I'll be sure to stop by."

"Good! Please do. I'll be around. Well, don't let me keep you. I know you've got to get to it, I suppose. Don't let me hold you up."

"Thank you."

Lex begins closing the door. He doesn't want to appear rude and he's not sure why. Merle backs away from the door, still trying to look into Lex's apartment. He's not being subtle about it, standing on his tiptoes, craning his neck to try to see around Lex's body. Lex merely smiles and waves as he closes the door. He hears the click and slowly engages the deadbolt.

"Sleep well," says Merle, muffled through the closed door. "Talk to you later, then. Welcome to the neighborhood."

Lex sighs and shakes his head as he pulls himself back into his apartment. His shoulders and back ache from holding himself upright during his Merle encounter. He drags himself to the bathroom and closes the door.

On his small dining room table, an unopened bag of potato chips balances neatly atop a perfectly rewrapped sandwich.

10

"OSCAR IS ONE CRAZY SON OF A BITCH," SAYS PARKER. HE'S SITTING ON Lex's childhood bed, flipping through an old copy of Popular Mechanics. He approaches the task as if he's expecting to find an adult magazine centerfold buried among pages of engine diagrams and computer-drawn isometrics. He looks disappointed with every turn. "You grew up with that guy all up in your shit trying to guide you to be a better man? No wonder you're so fucked up."

"Thanks for the support, asshole," answers Lex. He's forcing as many clothes as he can into a large rolling suitcase, the kind that street salesmen use to display their counterfeit goods.

"You have a lot of clothes for a dude who doesn't go out," continues Parker, tossing aside the magazine and lying on the bed. He looks bored.

"I'm getting rid of some of them. All this stuff won't fit in the apartment. I'll get most of this over there and sort it all later. Give me something to do."

Lex doesn't want to let on to Parker that he's been hallucinating the entire time they've been at his parents. Tracers and phantom images of things he's picked up, put down, picked up again. He's been very indecisive, sometimes lingering on a piece of kitch or an item of clothing for much longer than should have been necessary. He's taking longer and longer to blink, eyes stinging every time. He's rubbed them so much that the corners of his eyelids are sore, raw.

"I'm telling you," Parker says. "You claim to not have a lot of room and you just went out and bought a bunch of new furniture."

"Small, cheap furniture," Lex interrupted.

"Ain't it all, man? Our whole fucking lives are small and cheap. You said the apartment is small."

"Tiny."

Parker laughs, looking around at Lex's smallish bedroom.

"From small to small?" Parker asks. "Representative of anything, stud?"

Lex holds up a middle finger.

"Hell, man. Your whole life is a fugue of small spaces. You repeat the same movements endlessly with just the tiniest of variations."

"My apartment is a little larger than this. . ."

"I wouldn't know because you haven't had me up yet, not that I'm bitter about that shit or anything."

"I just got settled. It's only been a week and a half. Besides, where do you think we're going after we leave here?"

"I invite you to my place all the time, kid. Just wanted to remind you of that fact. Not that you ever take me up on the offer."

"You run a brothel up in your place. I would get lost."

"Too much space for you? Beats where you could have been. Small room to small cell."

Lex shrugs. "At least I'd get some sleep."

The past couple of nights have started a little easier, but only because he's been able to ignore most of the happenings in his apartment, nap through the minor disturbances. The water still runs violently in the bathroom and the kitchen every night and he's been able to plan for those, thinking of them as his own bizarre noise machine. He's remained unstirred by the sounds of footfalls on the floor next to his bed and has even been able to fall asleep despite voices. It's the knocking that wakes him these days.

Sometimes it sounds like Merle is pounding on the door again, trying desperately to get his attention. Two nights ago, there was pounding on both the closet and bathroom doors. Simultaneously. As if there was one room there with two doors and an army of trapped animals trying feverishly to escape. He's even seen the doors move, rattle with each strike as if the doors were about to be jettisoned from the frame, hinges and all. There are times where the pounding would stop and the scratching would begin. He's never been able to get back to sleep after that.

So, there in his old bedroom in his parents' house deep in the darkest corners of Bayport, Lex looks longingly at his bed. He's not sure if he should be glad or disappointed that Parker has sprawled himself across its queen-sized confines. Were he not so eager to leave the house, if he were completely alone for an hour, he would have taken advantage of the quiet and slept. A greedy sleep filled with nothing but darkness and silence. A sleep that would have held on, wrapping itself around him like a constrictor.

Parker, in what would be a rare moment of empathy, seems to notice that his friend is struggling and tries to help in his own way.

"Let's get fucked up." A crooked smile pushes Parker's lips to one side. "Let's ditch, go get a bite and some adult consumables, lose track of time and see where the night takes us."

"How is that going to help me, Parker?"

"How can it not, my friend. You've got too much of the world on your shoulders. I can see you, all hunched over like some goddamned Quasimoto, trying to carry all the shit of creation on your back."

"Unbelievable," whispers Lex.

"You're goddamn right, unbelievable. You've got to look at this a different way, Lex. You've got a place of your own, you've got somebody who'll pay you to do god-knows what while sitting at a desk six hours a day."

"Risk scoring," says Lex. He's stopped packing and is standing, rapt, listening to Parker work himself up. "And I work way more than six hours a day."

"Seven, then. Point is, you've got too much going on between those big, floppy ears to worry as much as you do. So what if you don't have the perfect job? Who cares? What matters is that you're young, you got a lot of life ahead of you, plenty of time to worry about what or who you could be doing or how much sleep you're getting."

Lex blinks.

"Look at me, for example. I'm crushing it. I'm blowing my own mind, that's how much I'm crushing it. People see me and think, 'damn, that dude right there is winning life.' And they should. I don't worry about how little sleep I get. I don't worry about going from point A to point B. I just let things happen. If I'm out doing something, that's the thing I'm supposed to be doing at that time. Like, right now, I'm supposed to be here, preaching to you about how you need to pull yourself together and act like the dominant motherfucker I know you can be."

"What does any of this have to do with helping me move my shit out of my father's house, Parker?" He can feel the tears perched on the edges of his lower eyelids. His fingers slowly curl into a fist.

"I'm helping you in other ways, kid," says Parker. He sits up on Lex's bed and crosses his legs. He's fixed an expression onto his face, his fingers tented beneath his chin. The counselor is in whether you've asked for him or not. He's about to share some of his vast, infallible wisdom and all present should recognize the magnitude of the moment in which they're living.

"Not helping in the way that counts," Lex mumbles as he resumes packing the last of the items from his bedroom closet.

"I just want you to soak in the history that you're witnessing," says Parker. His tone is all motivational speaker, clipped and aggressive. "Just take a moment to soak in the fact that you're among all your earthly possessions. All of this stuff, packed into bags just waiting to be hauled off to some other place, become a part of some other life. Just recognize that you're joined with your past life in an unusually poignant period of your life."

"I'm almost ready," says Lex, moving more quickly than he had all afternoon. He's feeling more awake than he has in a few days. Parker is stirring things he wants no part of. He wants to get everything ready to go into the rental van he'd nabbed and get back to his tiny, uncomfortable apartment.

"No, you're not almost ready," says Parker, moving to the edge of the bed. Lex tosses shoes into a garbage bag almost frantically. "You are ready, Lex. That's why you've got your own place. That's why you're moving away from the shadow of your parents and that college bullshit. You're ready to take on this next period of your life. But, you can only fully embrace it if you open yourself up to the possibility that, at any given time, you'll be doing exactly the thing you're supposed to. Don't worry about consequences. There are none. You're simply fulfilling your destiny."

"Great," says Lex, tossing aside the garbage bag-full of shoes and moving toward a tower of boxes near the wide wood dresser. "All of that sounds great."

"You know it does," says Parker. He rises to his feet and places a hand on Lex's shoulder. "Follow me and you'll go far."

"Let's start now," Lex smiles, planting a moving box squarely into Parker's chest, his outstretched arms grasping it at the last moment. "I'll follow you all the way down to the van for a start. Then we can take it from there."

"You fucking animal." Parker begins to laugh as he shifts the weight of the box around in his arms. "You're not as dumb as you pretend to be sometimes."

"Thanks for that." Lex grabs another box from the pile and looks out of the bedroom door both ways down the hall. "So, let's finish with all of this stuff so that we can go meet our destiny elsewhere. That way, I can avoid another sad-sack story from Oscar."

11

LEX FEELS A LOT BETTER ABOUT HIS LIFE'S CHOICES AFTER GETTING SOME SLEEP. The night after he's moved the remainder of his belongings to his own apartment, nothing happens. Not a single bump, not a single scratch. He remains uneasy most of the night, expecting to be roused from his sleep by the usual sounds and disturbances. He's almost disappointed by the lack of activity.

After the second night, having actually slept the entire way through, he begins to see a dappling of hope. He comes up with a few plausible excuses to explain the week of sleeplessness, the odd rearrangements and everything else. He concludes that the empty apartment acted as a speaker, magnifying all of the sounds he'd heard in the building around him, making them sound like they were much closer. He thinks that, with boxes full of things and a closet full of clothes, the sound has been dampened, the vibrations lessened. He even thinks that the weight of all of his belongings have helped to settle the floors, making them sound less like someone is dragging a chain-wrapped dead body across their surface.

He doesn't have an explanation for the pounding on the doors. He ignores this and continues to sleep blissfully through the night. Having been deprived of it the first few days in his apartment, he's greedy for the peace, the silence, the rest.

So, he's settled into a routine that's become comfortable, one that he hopes to continue for a good, long while.

He's never been very good at cooking, so breakfast is usually something that he can toss from the freezer to the small microwave oven he's purchased for a shockingly low price at the refurbished electronics shop. The number seven doesn't always respond immediately, but he works around it. He heats things up in two-minute increments, anyway.

He then takes the no-longer-frozen pastry-based breakfast item into the bathroom. It's not the most sanitary order of things, but it works in his mind as the most efficient way of getting his morning going. He brushes his teeth just after he's swallowed the last bite of breakfast, runs himself through the shower, then towels himself quickly before throwing on some clean underwear.

He knows it's clean, he has a system.

He dresses himself with little effort, mainly because all of his work clothes are essentially copies of the same shirt/khaki combo in slightly varying shades. Ties are not required, so he doesn't bother with either of the two he owns.

Lex is usually out of the door in about thirty minutes after the microwave beeps. That usually means he's going to be ten minutes early to work depending on how quickly he's able to wipe the sleep from his eyes and roll himself off of his bed. Sometimes he bothers to "make" his bed, folding his sheets and reposition the futon as a sofa. Mostly, as he becomes accustomed to having his own space, to being accountable to no one but himself, he's started to let some of his old habits go. He doesn't always put the seat down on the toilet after using it. He'd paid for this lax practice dearly one night when he decided not to turn on the bathroom light while he stumbled to relieve himself. He can almost feel himself maturing into a bona fide adult.

He strolls to his desk, unpacks a pad and a pen from his pack, and gets to work sorting exotically calculated numbers in a multi-colored terminal window. At lunch, he'll stroll around the neighborhood, taking in as much of the late autumn sun as he can. It doesn't always peek through the perpetual cloud cover and on such days, Lex ducks in to the Japanese beef and noodle place with the cheap veggies and extra sesame. On the nicer days, he'll stop at a street vendor, grab a sandwich or a hot dog and sit in the small park near the office, watching the people stroll by. He tells himself their stories based on their gait or who they're talking to or what they're carrying. It's these times when he misses his Natalie the most.

He's frequently the penultimate person to exit the floor, the windows reflecting the indoor hanging fixtures against a dark autumn sky. He takes the stairs, feeling that it's something adults should do. On the way to his apartment, he stops at a grocery store if he feels up to cooking in two-minute increments. If not, he'll stop at a place for a sandwich or some soup, something easy. He lets himself into the building, checks the mailbox to make sure it's still empty, then takes his time walking up the stairs to his apartment. At this point, Lex is usually singing some alternate-universe version of whatever song he'd heard on his way past the sketchy electronics shops lining the sidewalks of his route.

It was on one of those walks past the refurbished consumer electronics boutiques that Lex spotted an impossible deal for a decently large television. At least it's decently large compared to the overall size of the apartment. He hauled it home and up the five flights of stairs one day after work and set it in a designated spot atop the low bookcases that separate his living and dining rooms. He occasionally sits and stares at it, turned off, wondering how he got such a bargain. The only defect he sees is a slight discoloration in a very small part of the plastic housing on the back of the set. Otherwise, it's a modern-looking flat-screen television.

So, when he sometimes sits on his futon to watch television, he does so without actually switching it on. He has yet to hook up cable, deciding that he would wait for a few more paychecks to clear before making the plunge into that specific pool of adulthood, the part that makes one consume media in exchange for a monthly fee. He is perfectly happy, for the moment, watching streaming videos on his parents' accounts from his phone.

Lex enjoys those quiet evenings a great deal, having satisfied himself that the days of strange occurrences had passed. He is no longer dreading the lonely hours between dinner and bed time. Slouched on his sofa in front of his big-screen television watching shows and movies on his small-screen phone, one earbud in so as not to disturb the quiet of the apartment.

He has yet to hang curtains and thinks they might be his next purchase, but he's content looking into the space between buildings outside his windows. The city lights cast a glow all around, creating a perpetual twilight he finds comforting. Most evenings he leaves the lights inside the apartment off, letting the city's glow color his immediate surroundings. He's certain no one can see inside his apartment, but he gets undressed inside his bathroom nonetheless. It's ingrained in him, not wanting to be seen.

Then he settles into bed and sleeps. After the third day of this routine, Lex begins to miss the bizarre encounters. Just a little. He wouldn't mind just a little extra noise, a small bump to let him know that he wasn't the only traveller on his life's road. After the fifth, he's pretty sure that it was pure madness to want some mysterious happening to keep himself company and laughs at himself for such a foolish thought. By the twelfth day, he's dragging his own feet across the floor, slamming the bathroom and closet doors, even randomly tossing objects across the apartment to see if they would somehow reappear elsewhere. He laughs, almost maniacally, when they never do. By the twenty-first day, he fights the powerful urge to walk down the hall to 5B and invite Merle over for a cheap beer and conversation. After some quick math, he calculates that his loneliness hasn't reached that level, yet.

He channels this new freedom into potentially meeting new people. He reluctantly fills in the online form for a matchmaking website with nice pastel colors.

It's the one with the picture of an old guy telling him it's his own fault should he fail to find a match among their options. Two of the people that contact him are clearly catfishing, four of them are the same woman trying different approaches, and a half-dozen don't respond to his initial queries. He does manage to strike up a correspondence with someone called Felicia who is out of his league, so he thinks she must be stringing him along for her own amusement.

He doesn't mind.

So, Lex celebrates the day of the clearing of his first regular rent check, a Friday, by changing from his work uniform into something he imagines will look good in a dark bar, refreshes his deodorant, brushes his teeth, and prepares to take himself out on the town. He's so happy about his patterns, settled enough that he wants desperately to change it up, to do something a little different. He's found a bar online, one that has only two dollar-signs next to its three-and-a-half star review average, not too far from his apartment. He can walk there, see what happens, and, if need be, stumble home.

Lex isn't practiced at impromptu social interactions. The alcohol makes it easier, but building himself up to that point always makes him nervous. He's going through the night's potential in his head as he throws on a jacket and performs one final pocket and under-arm check. Everything is in order, but he's tossing scenarios around in his head, making certain that he's prepared for everything. He doesn't remember when he'd folded the work clothes that he'd stripped so quickly and tossed aside onto the apartment floor. Surely, during his preparations he'd placed them neatly atop the pile of neatly folded sheets on his futon. He shrugs.

He backs out of the apartment and eases the door closed just as his television switches on and something dark moves across the screen.

third

12

"YOU'RE DRUNK," SAYS FELICIA, GIRL WITH THE GOLDEN-BROWN HAIR, girl with the model's face. The girl who smiles at Lex's stupid jokes and joins in on his hyper-critical put-down of the masses. "That's okay, I'm a little drunk."

He's trying not to grin at the circumstances around her sitting on his futon. He thinks about how he'd arrived at the decent hipster bar near the apartment, about how he'd ordered a drink that was much stronger than he'd planned. With a half-finger of brown liquid left in the glass, his unexpectedly buzzed brain guided his hands to send a message to Felicia informing her of his intentions to imbibe and inviting her to join him.

She'd responded.

She'd shown up.

They drank. A lot.

"I'm not drunk," says Lex, filling two new drinking glasses with ice from his freezer. He is drunk. "I'm relaxed for the first time in weeks. It's a very nice feeling. Glad you can share it with me."

He pours water from a filter pitcher into the glasses before turning to the young woman perched on the edge of his futon, right next to his neatly folded clothes.

"Water? Really?" Felicia asks. She looks up at Lex sideways, somewhat suspiciously. "Don't you have something even a little bit stronger?" She smiles briefly in a way that almost makes Lex think that she's joking. The smile fades as she stares at the glasses in his hands indicating that she's not.

"Well, yes. Of course," Lex lies. He sits the glasses on the side table next to the futon before turning back to the fridge. He knows exactly what he'll find inside, but he looks anyway. There's a half-empty water filter pitcher, a small bottle of ketchup, a large bottle of soy sauce, an uneaten deli sandwich and a paper container of rice. Not a drop of alcohol. Not even juice.

"Are you sure," says Felicia, gathering her purse and jacket. She looks disappointed, which also makes her look sleepy. Could be a side effect of the all the alcohol, but he reads it as disappointment nonetheless. "I can just go, it's no big deal. I had fun."

His heart drops and he's not sure if the sudden wave of vertigo is because of his blood-alcohol level or because he's afraid his evening is about to come to an unsatisfying end. His mind races, grasping for clues during the evening that might salvage things.

He'd never felt as smooth as he had talking to Felicia. She is, he's found, very easy to talk to. There was genuine conversation about the quirks of life and the varied merits of binge-watching vs the measuring of one's episodic television consumption. After a few hours and a few more drinks, they began pointing out the flaws in their bar companions' wardrobe choices. With one group, they played a game of "count the teeth," the rules of which changed when a member of a particularly rag-tag group strolled to the bar to order a round of soda-waters with lime.

Lex wasn't sure what came over him when he invited Felicia back to his apartment to continue their conversation. They'd discussed the apparent pitfalls involved with an adult attempting to revive their show-biz career after an interrupted turn as a child star. Perhaps it was the silliness of the conversation or the fact that she laughed at most of his jokes. He tried repeating the ones that worked to diminishing returns. Felicia isn't stupid.

He was taken aback when she'd agreed. The bar was in last call and they both seemed to genuinely enjoy each other's company. Besides, Lex didn't want to waste such a hard-earned buzz by simply going home and sleeping. He'd grown accustomed to the promise of sleep and felt he could delay it this one night for a little female company.

"I had fun, too," says Lex. He fights what he calls the pathetic tense, a tone in his voice that sounds desperate. "Tell you what, and you should really hear me out here before you go."

"Okay," Felicia says. She hasn't released her belongings, but hasn't made any further moves to leave. "What do you propose?"

"I actually wouldn't mind continuing our debate and perhaps starting a few more," begins Lex. He's trying to assume a non-threatening posture. Shoulders slouched slightly, hands clasped before him, head bowed slightly. Pure beta-male.

He's sure he looks ridiculous, but he continues. "So, why don't I run down to the store on the corner, grab a bottle of wine, and we can close out the debate over a few glasses of vino?"

He hates that he called it vino. He wants a do-over for that last sentence.

"You do know we're only talking, right?" asks Felicia. She apparently wasn't overly fond of the use of the word vino, either.

"Yes, that's perfectly clear. Yes, we're just talking. No. . .we're just having a conversation. I like talking to you. Yes, we're talking. Two adults talking. To each other."

"You're ridiculous," says Felicia as she puts down her coat and purse. "Red wine. No merlot."

"Great," says Lex. He hopes he doesn't sound desperate. He plays his voice back in his head and knows he sounds desperate. Over-excited. Like a puppy whose owner just got home from work. "I'll be right back. Make yourself comfortable. Or not. Not too comfortable. Two seconds."

"Down boy," Felicia laughs. "Is your bathroom okay for visitors or will I need to visit the bodega to pee?"

"Yes, of course," Lex answers while trying to remember if he'd cleaned before he left. He didn't shower before going out for the night and he doesn't remember if he'd flushed the toilet. Yet another thing he sometimes forgets to do as a newly-minted adult out on his own. "Just give me one second."

He slips into the bathroom, closing the door behind himself before turning on the light. Much to his relief, the room is fairly clean. He hadn't left things lying around, there are no stains on any of the fixtures, and he'd not only remembered to flush, he'd left the seat down. He slips back out of the bathroom, almost too pleased with himself.

"All clear," he smiles.

"Thank goodness," says Felicia. "Now, run along. I'll try not to rummage through too much of your stuff while you're gone. Or at least try to make it so you don't notice."

Lex grabs his jacket and heads for the door. He turns back to the kitchen counter, grabs the keys lying there, checks his pockets for other essentials, then walks out of the door. He tries to make a show of being casual about it, that he's not in a hurry to run down and run back to spend time with her, but he feels ridiculous doing so. He feels his body too keenly and the room is still pitching and rolling a bit from the effects of all those drinks. He thinks briefly about laughing it off but decides instead to finish the cool-casual charade, closing his door gently behind him as he leaves.

He looks around to make sure no one is watching and listens to hear if someone else is coming up the stairs. He bounds down five flights of stairs and out of the building like it was an olympic sport and he was the reigning gold-medal champion. He lands awkwardly on the third floor landing, nearly twisting his ankle and spoiling the rest of his night, but he recovers, takes a beat, then continues quickly.

The twenty-four-hour convenience store, while well lit, always makes Lex uneasy. He immediately feels the weight of the man inside the booth staring at him from the moment he pushes through the door. The booth is very much like a fortress that occupies one-fifth of the storefront's total volume, all metal grating and scratched-up glass. The rest of the store is somewhat spartan, low metal shelves ending at shoulder height so that one could work the aisles and still keep an eye on the rest of the store. There are large convex mirrors in both back corners providing full fish-eyed coverage of the entire shop floor.

If the store had a voice, it would growl at customers to come in, get what they needed, pay for it quickly, and leave without lingering. It would also ask that customers do so without engaging in superfluous conversation.

Lex grins as he thinks of this, making his way to the very back of the store where the wine and beer are kept. He makes note of the video cameras everywhere, fighting the urge to wave at each one while smiling.

The store's wine selection, while not vast, is cheap. Lex understands that, were he in a proper grocery store, the prices would read two- to three-dollars less than they do in the shop, but he shrugs. He figures it's the price for convenience, good conversation and some soft company. Very soft company. With a nice smile.

He shakes off the thought of perhaps returning to a partially dressed Felicia waiting in his apartment, reminding himself that she's made it very clear. Conversation and company only. No bathing-suit-area-type stuff. He stops his train of thought from derailing again, grabbing two bottles of something that describes itself an American red table wine. They weren't the least expensive bottles there, but he was certain that bringing back wine in plastic bottles would be a strike against him. He's completely ignored the ones in boxes and cans.

As he pays for his wine, he does a little quick math in his head and concludes that, if he's very careful over the next couple of weeks, eating only when absolutely necessary, the evening's spending spree would not put him into too much financial jeopardy. Besides, he thinks, it's not like he does this every week.

The clerk frowns as he shoves Lex's change atop a brown paper bag underneath the small gap between the heavily-scratched glass and the metal counter, both littered with various tobacco and alcohol advertising stickers.

"Put in bag before you leave," says the man inside the booth, almost as an admonishment. His squint makes Lex think the man suspects Lex of being up to no good. Lex merely smiles, shoves his change into his pocket and eases the two bottles into the paper bag, clinking them softly as he does so.

Lex doesn't want to arouse any of the man's suspicions further, so he cooly, casually strolls through the bodega's door, trying not to seem like he's in a fevered rush to get back to the pretty woman waiting in his apartment. He eases the first few steps out of the store, again resisting the urge to smile and wave at a camera mounted just beneath the awning, then power speed-walks the rest of the way back to his building.

With each step closer to home, Lex tries on different conversational angles. He wants to seem casual, smart, unrehearsed. All of these, he feels, takes work. He tries at first to remember their last thread, remembering it was something silly like the merits of crossover characters in non-related television shows. Or it could have been serious like how to get past paying college athletes by providing them with free gym memberships. Either way, he works through several different clever talking points until he reaches the building's door.

He only fumbles with his keys once, nearly dropping the paper bag of wine, but opens the door rather easily, breezes past the mailboxes and heads up the stairs. He ignores the earnest gurgling sound coming from the basement and by the first-floor landing, he starts to feel anxious.

He hears footsteps descending quickly from an upper floor and what sounds like someone crying. Lex's heart sinks as he presses upward, not breaking his stride.

At the second-floor landing, the sounds of crying are clearer and the footsteps are closer. They're the footsteps of someone moving as quickly as they can in a pair of nice-yet-comfortable wedge-heeled boots. Lex bounds up the next set of stairs and almost drops his wine again as he nearly runs head-first into Felicia who is looking over her shoulder, purse and jacket clutched in her arms.

She sees him, throws a teary-eyed look of terror his way, then proceeds past him down the next set of steps.

"Felicia," Lex calls after her. He turns and follows her down the stairs, forgetting about the two bottles he has clutched in a brown paper bag. The bottom of the sack is starting to give way, but he's preoccupied. Every time she looks back over her shoulder as if something is following, he sees a mania in her eyes that's almost contagious. He even looks back a couple of times himself, just to ensure that he's not being chased by whatever she's running from.

She turns sharply around the handrail on the second floor, fumbling in her bag for something while trying to keep her balance. She seems more unstable now, like she's forgotten how to walk in boots she'd had no problem with before. Her movements are frantic. She seems out of sorts, different from the woman he'd left alone not ten minutes before. He's never seen anyone act this way, in the throes of an adrenaline-fueled panic.

"What's happened?" Lex asks as he reaches the bottom of the steps behind her, turning the corner to follow. He sees her just ahead, looking up toward the higher floors as if she's expecting something to leap down the stairwell and pounce on her as she makes her escape. This thought seems to wash over her and she speeds up. She rounds the corner to descend the final flight of stairs between her and freedom.

The entire time, she doesn't answer. She doesn't acknowledge that Lex is there, that he's following her down the stairs. She doesn't try to calm herself by taking a breath. She's focused on leaving as quickly as she can. To escape some unknown horror. Lex wants to get in front of her, to stop her. He needs to know what happened. It's important that he knows what she's seen, what came to her while she was alone.

There's a loud ripping sound and his paper bag gets suddenly lighter. A clang and the tinkling of shattering glass followed by the rush of liquid echoes through the stairwell as wine and shards of bottle spray across the first floor landing. That accounts for one bottle.

The other hits the the edge of the second floor, bounces off of the handrail, and flips toward the middle of the stairs. Felicia is unfazed by the crashing sound, the ping of the glass wine bottle as it knocks its way to the ground. She continues on her escape, possibly sensing that she's very close to getting away from— whatever. She doesn't see the wine bottle bounding toward her.

Lex rounds the corner, remnants of brown paper bag in his grasp, just in time to see the rogue bottle strike Felicia squarely over her left eye. She loses her balance and begins to tumble down the stairs, her feet briefly leaving the concrete. The wine bottle, after striking her, flies down the rest of the stairs ahead of her, shattering as it hits the tile floor in front of the mailboxes. Felicia hits the side wall face-first as her body turns and begins to tumble backward toward the ground floor. There's a loud metal clang as she hits the handrail first with her leg, then with the opposite foot.

A soft crunch as she lands with her neck at an odd angle against the bottom step. The rest of her body folds over itself thanks to gravity. She goes limp as she concludes her tumble over broken glass and spilled red wine just in front of the bank of mailboxes in the entrance.

She doesn't make a sound the entire time her body tumbles through the space. Lex stops a few steps down from the top of the landing. He opens his fist and the tattered paper bag floats to the floor like an oversized autumn leaf. It lands near a slowly spreading puddle as her blood and the spilled wine mixes around the broken glass.

She twitches once, eyes unblinking, staring upward, neck at a cartoonishly strange angle. She lies still.

13

"Hell of an accident," says detective Flake, scribbling small circles with a pen in her notebook. She's not looked away from Lex for about a half-hour. "I tell ya, the wine was an odd touch. Never seen wine as part of that scenario before."

"Neither have I," says detective Newhouse. She hasn't stopped pacing laps around Lex's small apartment since they arrived. She shakes her head as she peeks briefly out of the window toward the brightening airshaft.

Lex is sitting at his dining room table, staring at his cuticles. All this feels far too familiar.

He'd called the police almost immediately once he realized that Felicia wasn't breathing, wasn't moving. That the angle of her head relative to her shoulders more severe implications. The paramedics arrived quickly and silently. He was thankful for the silence, that there weren't sirens blaring through the city's streets on their way to his building. He'd decided to stand outside and wait for the ambulance and police which meant that he'd needed to step gingerly over the woman crumpled at the bottom of the stairs.

Lex thought about the repetitive procedural television shows as he tried to contort himself over body and broken glass, red wine and pooling blood. He tried not to stare, but the image of her lying below him as he released the remnants of the paper bag, the crumpled brown craft paper fluttering to the ground was burned into his memory. Just like a crime scene photo. His imagination had even thrown a sepia filter over the memory. An oddball trick for his mind to play.

He'd held the door for the paramedics as they hauled their kit on a stretcher into the building, lights flashing against the windows of the office building across the street. The strobes transformed the entry hall into a macabre disco, blinding warm and cool lights throwing dancing shadows against the walls, the stairs, the mailbox fronts.

Two cars with blue flashing lights arrived shortly after, their drivers nodding to Lex as they entered the hall. They took in the grizzly scene, looked at the stairwell, then nodded to the paramedics. One of the officers moved Lex away from the entry door, guiding him to the rear quarter panel of his cruiser.

That had been the first time he'd detailed his clumsy evening of courtship, pointing in the directions of the bar, the bodega, and finally back to his building, gesturing to the fifth floor. He would tell the story to different people as he stood on the sidewalk among flashing lights at least six more times. Each time, the story would be the same. Bar, flirtation, water, wine, panic, fall. Sometimes, the person he was recounting the story to would laugh, as if his story was being added to their own personal encyclopedia, a place to store story ideas for when they needed to impress someone. Most of the times, he would get a suspicious squint, a frown, a head shake. The person would write his story in their notebook, underlining whatever details they thought was important to their theory, then call someone else over to listen to him tell the story all over again.

An old muscle kicked in, telling the same story time and again to people who, by the nature of their jobs, were suspicious. No, Lex didn't touch her. No, she wasn't being held against her will. No, she hadn't been drugged. As far as he knew, she was only drunk and not high. He blacked out a couple of times, body running on autopilot. Panic was held in check as Lex waited for the time to pass.

No crowd gathered around the building in the two-hours it took for paramedics to leave and for the first-response officers to be replaced by detectives. He wasn't even sure if anyone from inside his building had been curious enough to leave their apartments, to investigate the goings-on in the ground-floor hallway. His pocket of the universe felt abandoned. No one else was around.

"How did you know her?" asks detective Flake, snapping Lex out of the memory. "I think I've got it all down, but just tell me one more time. Just so that the record is clear."

Lex rolls his eyes. This will be the eighth time he's answered this question this morning. He's told the exact same version of it every time. Perhaps it's too perfect. Perhaps he should change it up, make it a little more interesting. Maybe the detectives are looking for a little variation in the story. Natural variation is good, right? He ultimately decides against it and tells the story of the evening again, flat, clinical. The exact same way he's told it.

Just like with Nat.

"Great," says Detective Newhouse. "That's what we thought. So you didn't do it intentionally, then?"

"What?" asks Lex. A small change-up. It feels like a blind-side assault. Like something meant to trip him into admitting something that he didn't do. "Do what intentionally?"

"You said you threw the bottle of wine down after miss. . ." Flake flips through her notebook, as if she's trying to remember Felicia Carmichael's name. As if she hadn't repeated it time and again. As if she hasn't just heard Lex say his date's name repeatedly while recounting the events of the evening, down to the embarrassing details of shopping for impromptu wine in a bodega. "Miss Carmichael. She was running in fear from you and you threw the bottle after her, but unintentionally."

"That's not what I said," says Lex. He's tired of this questioning and wants to sleep.

Flake flips more pages in her notebook, reading, looking to her partner, then looking back into her notebook. She looks genuinely puzzled and Newhouse ceases her orbit long enough to go and look over her partner's shoulder. They look to each other then to Lex who is tapping his foot under the table. He fights back a yawn.

"Are you sure you didn't say that you accidentally threw a bottle after Miss Carmichael as she ran down the stairs?" asks Newhouse. She looks like she just swallowed a lemon whole, peel and all.

"Of course I didn't," says Lex. He's straining to keep his cool.

"Then why are you laughing?" asks Flake.

"I'm not laughing," Lex throws back. He hears it, too.

The detectives both stare at Lex for a long time. They appear to be simultaneously disappointed and confused. Lex laughing at them would be just the excuse they would need to mete some instant justice. The laughter is clearly coming from somewhere in the room, but not from anyone in the room.

"Are you sure?" asks Newhouse. She's still having trouble syncing her visual with the audio surrounding her. She seems to be the kind of cop who needs to keep things simple, the kind who feels the only answer to a problem is the obvious one, no matter how that may skew other facts involved.

Lex shrugs then shakes his head. Detective Flake rises from her seat at the dining room table and begins to walk around the apartment trying to trace the sound. It's close. She stands next to Lex and pauses, trying to make as little noise as she can. The sound is distant again. Newhouse hasn't looked away from Lex, her eyes are all focus.

"I promise you," says Lex, "I'm not laughing. You can see I'm not laughing. There's nothing funny here to laugh at."

The laughter in the room intensifies. It's more than one voice coming from two different places. She leans in to Lex who has also become unsettled by the constant, borderline maniacal laughter. Lex can barely maintain eye contact. He can no longer think about how tired he is.

Flake goes over to the television and stares at it for a few seconds. She then kneels and holds her ear to the speaker. She keeps this position for a while, her body tensed. The addition of more voices, whispering something just beyond comprehension causes her to jump suddenly. She nearly falls onto her side, but catches herself and noisily regains her balance.

More laughter and voices surround them. Newhouse finally breaks eye contact with Lex. Flake reaches for her gun as the knob to the bathroom door begins to rattle. Newhouse has also taken a defensive stance, clearing the table and keeping her back to the far wall next to the front door. Both detectives are silent, in tense coordination. Newhouse nods to Flake even though Flake isn't looking in her direction, her focus locked on the bathroom door.

The laughter subsides, replaced by rapid, unintelligible whispering. The number of voices have multiplied and seem to be coming from the walls themselves. The doorknob continues to shake and starts to turn. The detectives hunker themselves, preparing. Flake keeps one hand on her hip while extending the other forward toward the bathroom door. Newhouse draws her weapon, keeping it trained on the doorframe. Flake edges forward, the doorknob twisting back and forth. Newhouse presses her back foot against the bottom of the wall, bracing herself to fire.

Lex has quietly tucked himself into a fetal position underneath the table.

Flake reaches the doorknob, grasping it with her forward hand. She glances quickly to her partner and nods before refocusing on the door. She takes a deep breath and, in one motion, twists the doorknob and yanks open the bathroom door.

The apartment falls silent. The only sound comes from the breathing of the three occupants. Well, the breathing of the two detectives and a subtle whimpering coming from under the dining table.

Flake walks into the bathroom, hand still on the weapon at her hip and Newhouse moves toward her to get a look inside the room. Flake flips on the lights and looks around the small chamber, pressing the open shower curtain to reassure herself that no one is hiding there. Newhouse appears, gun still ready but posture more relaxed, just behind Flake as she turns back toward the door, puzzled.

"The hell was that?" asks Newhouse, hesitantly re-holstering her gun. Her chest is rising and falling in a way that shows she's working really hard at calming herself through meditation. In through the nose, out through the nose, nostrils flaring with each breath. The corners of her mouth turning down to show how much focus she's committing to calming herself. The middle finger on her right hand starts to twitch, so she forms a fist with that hand as if he's ready to punch a wall. Hard.

"You heard that, right?" asks Flake. She's standing in the bathroom door, her back to the mirror. She's ashen, eyes darting around the room. They both seem to have forgotten Lex.

"That was the weirdest thing," continues Newhouse. "You ever hear anything like that before?"

"No."

Flake sniffs the air in a deep inhale. She still hasn't taken her hand from her holstered pistol. Newhouse eases into the kitchen, looking around the entire apartment as she does. She seems to be clearing the room over and over, reassuring herself that there's no longer a threat. If there truly was one in the first place. Flake joins her in the kitchen, absently grabs a glass from the dish rack, and pours herself some water from the tap. She leans against the counter as she drinks.

"You can come out now," Newhouse commands as her eyes land on Lex, still curled under the dining table.

"I'm comfortable where I am, thanks," says Lex, voice muffled by his knees.

"Suit yourself," Flake says. She finishes his water, rinses the glass and places it back in the dish rack. She looks to her partner and finally removes her hand from the holster. Both detectives move toward the exit, occasionally panning the walls for anything they may have missed. Flake removes a card from her shirt pocket and slaps it onto the dining table.

"If you think of anything else, call me," says Flake. Her voice is shaky, a little quieter than it was when they were asking Lex the same question over and over again. "We may need you to come in and answer some questions."

"We'll let you know," adds Newhouse. She has the posture and movements of a brave woman who's trying not to appear to be in a hurry. She's overly casual as she opens the apartment door. She tries to mask that she hasn't turned her back on the apartment but is steadily, carefully backing from the room.

Flake is making similarly cautious movements, side-shuffling from the table while her head sweeps back and forth across the room.

The door slams shut, and Lex unfolds himself from hugging his knees and rolls himself onto his back, staring up at the pressboard bottom of his table.

14

"MOTHERFUCKING COPS," SAYS PARKER AFTER SWALLOWING A MOUTHFUL of hot and sour soup. He'd waited a full twenty minutes, even dumping most of their shared dish of fried wontons into the bowl, trying to let the thick brown broth cool. It's out of character to start with soup, mainly because it takes him so long to eat the large bowls of it the restaurant serves, but he claims to have a great reason.

"They were a weird pair," says Lex, crunching on one of the fried wontons he'd snagged before Parker upended the bowl into his own soup. "Different from the ones with Natalie —" He can't bring himself to finish that sentence. "They were trying to get me to trip up on something. I'd told the truth from the beginning, I told them. Repeatedly."

"They're just a pair of power-tripping pigs who couldn't get out of their own way. Assholes."

"They had a point."

"You didn't kill the girl. At least not on purpose." Parker slurps the last of his soup loudly and pushes the bowl away. He's been all smiles since he'd met Lex for lunch. His morbid side shines through. Parker breezes past how Lex made the acquaintance of the unfortunate young woman who'd met her demise on his building's staircase. Instead, he'd wanted details of how she'd looked lying there in the hall beneath the mailboxes, her head twisted ever so slightly in the wrong direction.

"I feel you're somehow missing the point," Lex says. He flicks the wrapping from his straw across the table before leaning back from the table. He hasn't had much of an appetite since his adventure-filled weekend. The soaring high of having actual physical contact with another human being, though brief as it was, was brought to a crashing low when that human being tumbled to her death. Partially because of a faulty paper bag which had been overloaded with cheap wine. It had been expensive cheap wine to be sure and a very small, nagging part of him is still bitter about having paid for something he didn't get to have at least a sip of.

"I haven't missed a single point, kid," says Parker, looking around the restaurant, flirtatiously smiling at a group of teenagers piled into a nearby booth, hovering over a dish of soup dumplings. "You had yourself an interesting weekend. That's the gist of it, right? Your weekend was so action packed, you're still hungover from it on a Tuesday afternoon. It's perfectly understandable. I, for one, would have been partying the rest of the weekend."

"Parker," says Lex, his hands curling into claws against the formica table top. "I don't get why she was running down the stairs. That's mystery number one."

"Mystery number one is how she made it up to your place," says Parker, not really paying attention to the man across the table from him. "From what I've gathered, you brought your JV game to a pro scouting combine. I'm guessing that she was crazy. Or desperate. Both points in your favor, by the way."

Lex pauses for a moment, seriously considering his life's choices. He needs Parker to get it, truly get it. There are some things that his buddy is excellent in providing emotional support for, things that Parker's perpetually skewed sunny disposition helps with. He realizes in this moment that Parker is not the deep and nurturing shoulder he needs for his current mood.

Lex slept cautiously and fitfully the rest of the weekend, tossing in his bed and getting up frequently to check his phone for messages or news updates. He'd set a search alert for his name and for Felicia's name and only one thing came up the entire weekend. The obituary notice was painfully short and Lex felt a twinge in his chest when he read the very short list of people surviving her. Other than that, the incident remained largely unregarded. He was surprised, considering how much coverage a person stubbing their toe while crossing the street gets in the nightly news.

Or how an entire town converged on his parents' home with the mere mention of a girl's disappearance.

So, Lex's troubles in connecting with Parker stem from not being able to come to grips with the silence of the entire situation. No one seems to care and that includes his best friend, who at that very moment is eyeing other people's food.

"She wasn't crazy," answers Lex. "At least, she wasn't crazy when she came up to the apartment. There was a ton of crazy to answer for later, but we were having fun. It was a nice time."

"You don't need nice times right now, Lexy," says Parker. He refocused his attention on his own conversation. "Listen to me. . ."

"I'd rather you called me 'kid'."

"You shouldn't dwell too much on this. The cops are gonna do what the cops are gonna do, they're gonna go away and then all you're left with is a bad taste in your mouth because the motherfucking cops have been poking their filthy-assed fingers in it."

"I hate when you call me Lexy."

"You need to get back up on your horse, man. I mean it. You can't strike out every time, it defies the laws of averages."

"Wait, their ass-fingers in my mouth? What the. . ."

"It's easy, now that you've already done some of the heavy lifting. Most of the, well, some of the hard work. You need to turn this into an advantage. Make it so that you let it inform your next move. Know to have wine in the house already, know to get some music ready. I'll send you a playlist."

"I don't understand," Lex rubs his eyes with the palms of his hands. He lets the colors spill across his vision as he presses in. Hard.

"Did you clean your apartment yet?" continues Parker. "Probably why you didn't get laid. She saw all the dust and dirt and shit in your apartment, probably didn't want to touch anything, you slob."

"What are we even talking about right now?" Lex shakes his head.

Just then, the main course arrives carried on a tray by a chubby-cheeked woman. She balances the tray, setting down each dish while smiling bashfully to her customers. Parker takes this as a cue to flirt and he assumes the appropriate posture. Relaxed, casual, moving and swaying like a drunken night club owner. He then smiles, a broad opening into his immaculate dental hygiene, and fires imaginary bullets from his finger as she slides his plate of Kung Pao in before him. She gently places a plate of fried rice in front of Lex while trying to politely return Parker's smile. He fires another imaginary bullet, tilts his head in a way he clearly thinks makes him look movie-star handsome, then nods to the poor waitress.

Lex wonders if Parker can help himself. He wonders if he even knows he's doing it or if it's some twisted instinct formed from endless repetition. Asshole behavior muscle memory.

After the server leaves, Parker turns back to Lex, staring at him over the steaming plates of food.

"We're talking about you, you hick," says Parker. "Focus. Pay attention. I've been telling you this whole time that you need to hone your focus, get better at really concentrating on the important things. Take the food in front of you, for example. Do you know exactly what's in it?"

Lex looks down at the brown clumps of rice clinging to bits of egg and random vegetables, chunks of chicken winding throughout.

"I can see what's in my fried rice, Parker," Lex says. His stomach turns a little and he's unsure if he's going to be able to eat his lunch. "I also see that you're refusing to take any of this seriously."

"I take it all seriously," Parker says before shoveling a forkful of chicken into his mouth. He nearly spits it back out again and holds his jaw open as he fans the food in his mouth with his hand.

"Great," Lex says as he pushes his own plate of food away. "Now listen while you deal with a scalded palate."

"Na-haya-na-yur-ya-aah," is the sound coming from Parker's mouth.

"As I was saying, I don't know why she was running down the steps. I know but, I don't know. What did she see? Or hear? It's probably hear, but the noises in the apartment have been more of the whisper-slash-strange sound type, not the sheer-terror-get-the-fuck-out type. She kept looking over her shoulder. Why?"

"Dude," Parker says, having finally swallowed his scalding-hot food. "That's going to leave a mark."

"Parker, c'mon."

"Okay. No, I'm with you. I hear you. Something weird happened to her up at your place while you were gone. Was anything missing? She could've been trying to rob you."

"Nothing's missing, Parker. She didn't have a lot on her to begin with, so there was nowhere to hide something if she was trying to rob me."

"Just covering all the bases. Damn, why do they make that stuff so hot?"

"But she looked at me like she would never be safe again. Absolute terror."

"You'd think they'd let it cool off at least a little before bringing it to the table."

"Then there was the shit that happened while the detectives were talking to me. The whole place felt like it was about to go haywire. They were freaking out, I thought I was going to get shot."

"Motherfucking cops," Parker says. He shovels a lump of rice into his mouth to try and ease the scalding.

"That's not helpful."

Lex's stomach is doing flips and he feels the faint strains of a headache tugging on the base of his skull. He's considering just standing and leaving, letting the crisp autumn air clear his head. He stares at the steaming plate of fried rice he'd ordered, seeing patterns that he imagines are animals, castles, corpses.

"It wasn't your fault," Parker says. Lex looks up and is surprised to see his friend looking directly at him, full focus.

"But, what about. . ." Lex's voice trails off. He's not sure which option he should use to finish the question. What about the voices? What about the laughter?

What about the running water? The footsteps? The shadows? The sheer look of terror on Felicia's face as she hurried down the steep steps of his building?

"Look at me," says Parker. "None of the stuff you're thinking. None of it is your fault. There's no way you could have known that any of this would happen. It's beyond your control. You're not responsible for what happened to her."

A heavy silence follows where neither man moves. The group of teenagers in the booth just across the restaurant get up noisily to leave. Parker doesn't acknowledge them at all.

"Here's what I know," says Parker, breaking the still between the men. "You've been feeling really bad for a long time. You've been in your head. A lot. When I met you, we had a lot in common."

"Big Thought," mumbles Lex. He smiles a little at the memory.

"Big Fucking Thought, man. Follow the mind-trail until it ends, then go a little bit further. It was great. We went to some dark, dark places, but it was all a part of it. In some ways, though, I think you never left. You just stayed in the darkest places we'd found. Set up residence there. Fucking homesteaded in the most uninhabitable places ever."

"What does that have to do with the mad shit that's happening now?" asks Lex. There's a small voice in the back of his mind that whispers the connection over and over, but he pushes it back. He ignores it.

"You're taking this all on yourself as punishment. You've never forgiven yourself. You haven't for then and you won't for now."

"Parker, she was in my apartment. Nothing was going to happen. We were going to talk and watch the sun rise over the tops of the buildings and then we were going to say good morning to each other and promise to talk later. It was a nice time. We were having fun, connecting."

"I know you were. So hold on to that, man. Hold on to the good. The rest isn't up to you."

Parker, who'd been leaning into what he was saying, eased back into his seat and pulled his plate toward him. There was less steam coming off of it and he tested how much it had cooled by scooping a forkful into his mouth and waiting a second or two. Having approved of the temperature, Parker resumes his regular technique of hunkering down and tossing the food into his open mouth.

This lets Lex off the hook. He relaxes, blinks for a very long time before making an effort on his own lunch. In some strange way, the talk with Parker has made him feel better and, before he knows it, Lex has cleaned his plate.

15

Lex runs along the sidewalk, being careful not to slip in the cold, hard rain that's dominated the streets for two days. He's wondered why, if it's so cold, none of it has frozen beneath his feet, causing no end to calamity and chaos all around him.

The other city dwellers seem to be similarly uncomfortable, collars turned up against chilled necks and ears, hats pulled down over eyebrows. There's the occasional umbrella, but most of the natives see them as signs of weakness. Members of the herd that don't quite have what it takes to survive on their own despite what the streets, or in this case the skies, throw at them. They catch sidelong glances from the every-day person making their way from storefront to bus stop to building lobby. It's an entertaining thing to see and Lex almost forgets how cold he is as he watches one of these scenarios play out.

He reaches the door to his own building, shaking water droplets from his bag, from his coat. It's not a very heavy coat. Something in a waterproof material with just enough lining to prevent death by hypothermia, at least in your standard sub-arctic city setting. He's seen the ridicule suffered by the tourists who felt it necessary to pack their heaviest winter parka to roam through the streets. He doesn't want to be lumped in with those that don't seem to belong, those that don't know what's up. He shivers, even through the layers he's had the wisdom to apply underneath, but he feels accepted among the commuters who've been hardened by their experience in the city.

His numb fingers fumble with his key, but he manages to open his door within the first minute of trying. He considers it a small triumph and smirks. Lex stomps his feet on the lobby's industrial-grade floor mat, a large, dark-gray piece that extends nearly halfway to the mailboxes. He looks down, making sure all of the little droplets of gray-brown water are shed from his soles. There's no hope for the hems of his slacks and he knows the same is true for the shoulders on his coat. After a while, the waterproofing had failed to bead the steady stream of water pouring from the sky and had begun absorbing some of the icy-cold rain.

"Shitty weather so close to Halloween," rasps a voice directly before Lex. He's startled and nearly jumps back into the door. He opts, instead, to yelp just under his breath, sounding as if he'd just swallowed a newborn rat.

He looks up and sees the old superintendent standing at the mailboxes with his arms crossed. He'd been mopping the floor at the bottom of the stairs, the mops handle leaning against the stair railing with the bucket resting askew just beneath it. Lex assumes that, somewhere hidden in the dark murky waters is the mop's head itself.

"Yeah," Lex says. He's stopped stomping his feet on the mat and regards it once more, making certain he hasn't spilled any water onto the floor outside of the mat's boundaries. "It'll hopefully clear up soon."

Lex is horrible at small-talk.

"The fuck do I care?" spits the old man. He squints at Lex in a way that makes him uncomfortable. This doesn't take a lot as there are many things that have made Lex uncomfortable over the course of the week.

"Sorry," says Lex. He says it out of instinct and almost immediately regrets doing so.

"Whatever," replies the old super. "You're that Delaware kid, right?"

"Yes, sir."

"Good. Been waiting here half the night. Does no fucking good mopping this hallway. Just gonna get wet again. I don't do this shit for my health, you know. I coulda just left you a note under your door or some shit, but I didn't feel like sprinting up five goddamn flights of stairs."

There's a knot in the pit of Lex's stomach. He wonders if he's being thrown out of the building, if he's made too much trouble for his landlords and now they've sent their enforcer to toss him on his ass. He imagines being locked in the grip of an old mob guy, one hand on his arm while another tightens around his throat. He could hardly breath as the anxiety took hold. His face apparently shows that he's playing out a doomsday scenario in his mind because he hears the old man laugh a raspy, dry chuckle that shakes his entire frame.

"You're a goddamn psycho, kid," says the old super. "I just came by to offer an unofficial apology from management. They wanted to make sure you wasn't thinking about suing them for your girlfriend's unfortunate fall down the stairs."

Lex stands at the door dumbfounded. He doesn't know what to make of what the old super is telling him. The knot in his stomach has tightened. He doesn't know what to do next, so he simply stands there with his jaw slightly ajar, making "ah" sounds with his throat.

"Yeah, didn't think so," grumbles the old man. "Told them it was a waste of time to even worry about it."

The super turns and grabs the mop's handle, using it to push the bucket down the hall past the stairwell. He gets to the supply coset door, opens it, then turns back to Lex.

"Go on back to whatever it is you're calling a fuckin' life, kid," shouts the old man from down the hall. "World'll probably spit out what's left of you soon enough."

The old man turns back to the supply closet, pushes the mop and bucket in, then follows it closing the door behind him. Lex could swear he heard one last "fucking idiot" grumbling from the old man and the deep vibration of a sigh from inside before the door closed with a click.

His head buzzes with what he thinks the old man is telling him. The landlords were worried that the fall was their fault and they didn't want any trouble from Lex. This is at odds with how he felt, where he thought the blame should lie. He thought it strange that management would assume responsibility for something he thought was clearly his fault. He floats up the stairs lost in the thought, not bothering to stop at the mailboxes to collect the random pieces of junk mail he knows will be there. Before he realizes it, he's standing at the top of the stairs on the fifth-floor landing.

He couldn't continue any further because of the round man standing before him, toes tapping on the hallway tile.

"Oh, hey," says Merle. He looks like someone who's trying to look casual. Like someone who doesn't want the person they were waiting for to know they were waiting for them. Lex finds it very awkward.

"Sorry, Merle," says Lex after almost running directly into the man's belly. He's flustered and, after his experience with the super on the first floor, not really present.

"Don't you worry about it," says Merle. He doesn't move, making Lex wallow in his discomfort. He's keenly aware of the small amount of space he and Merle are sharing just at the top of the steps. One false step and he would go tumbling. He's not sure it wouldn't be better for everyone in the end.

"Thinking of other things, you know," says Lex. He tries looking past Merle as an indication that he wants to continue home.

"Right, of course, how can you not," says Merle. "Just one thing, though, while I have you here. Won't take a second."

"I just," Lex starts, trying a subtle side-step. "If I could —"

His voice trails off. He shifts his weight, looks back, then looks to Merle who still doesn't move.

"Good, I just want to say, if I could, one little thing. I'll be out of your hair in just a moment. Just let me —" Merle takes a deep breath as if he's trying to wrangle his emotions. Lex thinks, for a moment, that it makes a very good show. "Let me say how so sorry I am about your loss. It must be so devastating for you to have lost someone so close to you. And to have the police here questioning you for hours on end. What you must have gone through."

"Thank you, but —"

"It's must be so hard, moving to a new place, adjusting to a new routine. And here, you have a nice, young lady-friend over and she winds up taking a header down the stairs. Sometimes I almost fall down 'em myself. They're kinda rickety. Don't you think they're kinda rickety? Like they could take someone's life any moment if they're not careful? Like they did with your girlfriend, what was her name?"

"We weren't," Lex is considering simply turning around, retreating back down to the first floor and out into the frigid downpour. "Her name is Felicia. Was Felicia. She was not my — Thank you, but she was just here that once and she was —"

"Oh, poor Felicia," says Merle, placing a hand over his heart. A small part of Lex is hoping that Merle is having a heart attack there on the spot. It would provide him some cover to escape to his apartment. To close the door and lock it tight behind him. No luck. "I bet she was a sweet one. Anyway, I wanted to let you know, first, how sorry I am. You must be devastated. Second, I wanted to ask you if there was going to be any further authoritative action, you know, because of the accident. If so, I just need to let you know that I support you one-hundred percent. Anything you need from me, I'm here for you."

The rain was looking better and better with every passing moment.

"Okay, Merle," says Lex. "Thank you and all, but nothing is going to happen. There's probably not going to be a big investigation or anything. Cops are probably going to narrow their focus quickly. It was an accident and I just want to leave it at that."

Merle hears him and drops the concern. His face falls and his hands drop to his sides. He tilts his head to one side and regards Lex with something akin to suspicion. Lex never realized that someone's demeanor could shift from concern to contempt so quickly.

"Well," says Merle. "That's just too bad, that's what that is. Too bad."

He makes a clicking sound with his tongue and sighs heavily. Merle regards Lex once more before turning and shuffling toward his apartment. Relieved to be released from his interrogation, Lex edges around the stair rail and sidesteps toward his own door. He's not sure if the conversation has ended or if Merle merely needs a break due to a shock of disappointment, but Lex doesn't stick around to find out.

"It's just," Merle says just before reaching his door, "an investigation may uncover some serious neglect around here. So might a lawsuit, if you were to feel aggrieved by the ordeal. Shine a much needed light on the plight of the residents here."

Lex looks over and Merle appears to be holding a conversation with the wall next to his door. He doesn't look over in Lex's direction but is clearly speaking loud enough so that Lex can understand every word.

"You have a chance to make things better for everyone," continues Merle. "I'm not just talking about money, although that would be nice to have a little something to spread around and help everyone that's helped you along, you know, to get adjusted and all that. I'm talking about making a real difference."

Merle pauses. By his profile, he looks stern, almost angry. A shadow has fallen over his eyes and his complexion has gone an odd shade of gray, as if the life had suddenly drained from his face. As if he were dying in place. His is also different. There is no light, playful lilting drawl, no musicality. He speaks again and he sounds like a man trapped in a well.

"There are things here that people should know about," Merle says. He still has not looked back to Lex, who is planted in his spot outside his own door. "Things that people shouldn't be allowed to get away with. You could go a long way in helping shed light on it. You could make a difference, one that no one else here could. You're new, people will believe you if you just told them."

Merle bows his head and closes his eyes for a moment. Then, just as quickly as his mood darkened, color returns to his cheeks. He smiles instantly and turns his head. His eyes are sparkling and he regards Lex with the same, familiar lightness that has been his signature.

"Of course, it's your call," Merle says to Lex, reaching out to his doorknob and twisting. "Whatever you think is best. I'm just glad you're okay."

Lex is numb and his limbs weigh a ton. He should probably say something.

"Thank you," Lex mumbles. "Yeah, thanks."

"Uh-huh," Merle fires back. He's halfway into his apartment and he finishes with, "I'm very sorry for your loss. Perhaps it'll be the only one."

Merle disappears into his own apartment closing his door behind him.

16

"I REMEMBER THE TIME WE TOOK YOU TRICK-OR-TREATING AND YOU WANTED so badly to dress up in a Spider-Man costume," says Lorraine, rocking in a chair on her front porch. "Only we couldn't quite afford to get you the official costume. We'd given you a choice, you could be a vampire or you could be a ghost. 'No,' you said, 'I don't want to wear an old sheet with the eyes cut out and I don't want to wear your old makeup on my head!' It took all I had to keep from splitting my side laughing."

Lex smiles even though his heart isn't completely in it. He hears the same story every year, sitting on the front porch waiting for costumed kids to approach. Lorraine would reminisce with the same seven stories, sometimes to kids who simply wanted their two pieces of fruit candy and to leave.

"I wound up making my own Spidey costume out of holiday ribbon and masking tape," says Lex, hoping to speed the progress of his mother's tale. "I got two pillowcases full of candy and it took two whole days to get all the tape off."

Lorraine laughs, rocking to the limits of the sleds on her chair. She absently picks through the pieces of candy in the bowl on her lap then continues.

"Two whole days to get all of that tape off. I scrubbed you so hard in the tub you cried."

"Great memory, mother," says Lex.

"My point is, smarty-pants, that you were very resourceful as a child. You wouldn't let anything stand in the way of what you wanted to do. If we said you couldn't do something for some reason or another, you would find your way around us and get it done anyway."

"That was a long time ago."

Lex stares out over the porch and across the front lawn at the clusters of children in bright costumes roaming from house to house across the street. They look like little gangs of mismatched mutants, a superhero little girl and a zombified boy with braces across his overbite. A shambling mummy comparing treats with a princess. He remembers a time when he was as fearless, as ready to parade himself through the world as those kids collecting candy from his parents' neighbors. He imagines what it would be like to return to that place, to soar again unencumbered by self-awareness and it scares him. He pauses his rocking to let the feeling pass.

"It wasn't so long ago, I don't think," says Lorraine, looking out over the same scene. "Not as long ago as you would have people believe, Lexington. You're not as old and wizened as you pretend to be, sometimes."

"Things aren't as carefree anymore," Lex replies. He feels distant, disconnected for a moment. "Can we change the subject?"

"You don't want to talk about Halloween on Halloween? You must have something really juicy and heavy to talk about if we're going to diverge from being topical."

"It's not that I don't want to talk about Halloween, I just don't want to. . ."

"Talk about yourself."

"No."

"Well, I like talking about you, even if you don't."

Lorraine turns her attention to a small cluster of children bounding across her lawn toward the porch. They're clearly dressed as something, likely from a television show that neither of them watch. The kids look like a family of four, father, mother, and two sons, but there's something askew about their demeanor. The kid dressed as the father is wearing clothes and makeup that make him look like Hunter S. Thompson, a little girl is dressed like a sixties housewife complete with a large red bob. The other two kids, who are clearly the children of the play group, are dressed in burlap sacks with bonnets on their heads. It's a strange sight and Lex finds himself staring intensely.

"What are you guys supposed to be?" Lex asks as the cluster reaches the porch.

The oldest kid, the one playing the father, looks at Lex while the other kids grab candy from Lorraine's bowl. He wears a look that borders on open contempt as he leans forward. The makeup is creepy, making a pre-teen kid look like a pot-bellied, balding, lanky, middle-aged gentlemen likely to do anything. His eyebrows are emphasized with extra-black makeup and he wears a sneer. Clearly, this is in character for whomever the kid was pretending to be.

"You're too old to know," whispers the kid in an accented faux rasp. "The cool kids are hip."

Lex isn't sure if he should laugh at the kid's off-base response, laugh at the kid's attempt at intimidation, or laugh at the surreal aspect of the entire encounter. He decides, instead, to laugh at how, when the kid snarls, there's a large piece of pink taffy stuck between his incisor and canine. The kid doesn't take it to well, sticking out a purple-coated tongue.

"Thanks," says Lex, turning his attention to the rest of the quartet receiving candy from his mother. "I'm sure you look very convincing, being whatever it is I'm not cool enough to know about."

The kid looks at Lex more closely, sniffing as if he's a bloodhound trying to catch the scent of something. He stops and leans back, looking briefly over his shoulder at the rest of his party as they leave the porch heading toward the street. He then turns to Lex.

"You got issues," the kid says. "I feel sorry for you."

He then turns and rejoins his party without retrieving his share of candy from Lorraine. He maintains character, ambling with this shoulders back and his hips thrust forward. Lex shakes his head at the peculiar sight.

"What did that young man mean by that, Lexington?" asks Lorraine, resuming her happy rocking.

"He was just being a brat," says Lex staring at the back of the kid's head as he rejoins his horde at the street. "I hate kids."

Lorraine wrinkles her nose and shakes her head at his response. She absently fiddles with a few of the candies in her bowl, fingers working as if she were knitting.

"You just don't have the patience for them right now," she says. "You have patience for a lot of things, just not kids that age."

"I'm not sure I have the patience for very much right now. Things don't seem to be coming together the way I'd hoped they would."

"You mean that young woman? Terrible, terrible stuff."

Lorraine stops rocking and seems to take a moment of silence in the memory of the young woman who died in Lex's lobby. Lex rolls his eyes. He sometimes regrets updating his parents on the events of that evening, but he felt he should be at least somewhat open with them considering how it was covered in the news. At least that's what he'd told himself. In reality, he knows that they probably hadn't paid very much attention to the fifteen-second segment she'd received on one of the channels, a brief blurb squeezed in between a massive warehouse fire and the police shooting of a raccoon that the officer had sworn was "leaping for his jugular."

"No," Lex stutters. He's always had a difficult time correcting his mother, contradicting anything she says. "It's not that. Well, it's not just that. I'm not even really thinking about that."

"How can you not," says Lorraine.

Lex frowns, feeing like the little kid who was told that his favorite costume wouldn't be waiting for him when he got home from school. That it was too expensive and he wouldn't be wearing it for Halloween this year. He's trying to hide his frustration while thinking of ways he could get his mother to change to subject. He knows it's an uphill fight that he's likely to lose, but he needs to try.

"Not too cold out, tonight," Lex says. He immediately cringes.

"You're not going to get away with that, Lexington," says Lorraine. She has that tone in her voice that immediately lets Lex know that he's still her child. "You need to deal with how this whole thing is making you feel. You need to look at how much it brings back the past."

There it is, the reference that he'd been running from the entire week. It was what he'd been trying to dance around as he spoke to his mother about life, the past, his childhood. He'd hoped it would be a nice escape from his everyday, time spent out of his own head. He doesn't want to revisit the past. He seems to have no choice.

"It was a long time ago," says Lex quietly.

"It wasn't as long ago as you try to believe," his mother says. "It's only been two years. You hadn't had enough time to truly process what happened before this young lady came into your life."

Lex closes his eyes, hoping that he will simply vanish in a puff of darkness and shadow. He's afraid of what picking at that wound would do to him, being on the verge of losing his sanity in his current circumstances. He'd spent so much time, some would call it time wasted, trying to regain his footing. He's not as delicate as he may seem, but he's not a Greek god, either. He can only carry so much of that burden on his shoulders.

He is ready to respond. Ready to open his eyes and look at his mother, tell her that he is fine. Tell her that he just needs a little more time to adjust to being on his own. That he is invested in being on his own for the long haul. He's forming the words, gathering the courage to lay everything bare before his mother, trying to make her understand that he's on track.

Lex's eyes open and is stunned to see a small boy standing at the edge of the porch, staring at him silently. The kid looks like a throw-back, dressed as a toy cowboy from a cartoon. He's bedecked in checkered shirt, red bandanna, deep blue jeans and an oversized cowboy hat with boots and belt to match. He has a shiny tin star on his chest matching the shiny, chromed plastic toy six-shooter at his hip. He has all the intensity of someone ten times his size, a stare that shoots cannonballs.

It catches Lex completely off-guard. Everything he'd been planning to say is replaced by a deep befuddlement. The young cowboy standing stock still before him appears to be reading his soul as if it's written across his face. Lorraine also seems to be taken aback by the child's demeanor.

"Oh, hey there," says Lorraine. She stops fumbling with the candy in her bowl and leans forward in her rocking chair, causing the porch boards to creak ever so slightly. "Let's have a look at you, then."

She smiles as she extends the bowl toward the boy in an attempt to entice him closer. He doesn't budge. He doesn't even flinch. Lex is equally entranced by the boy's stare, feeling locked in by the intensity.

"What kind of candy do you like?" asks Lorraine. She sounds unsure. She seems aware of how oddly tense the atmosphere has grown and is trying to diffuse it. The boy doesn't move.

For Lex, the stalemate lasts hours. He feels the beads of sweat trickling down the side of his face. He's so tense he starts to shake. He wants to shout at the kid. He imagines himself telling the kid to scram and the kid complying. His face twitches and he curls his fingers into a fist.

The boy is a statue, unflinching and constant.

The rest of the world drops away and it's just Lex and the cowboy, two spots of light in a dark, foggy world.

"Lex? Lex Delaware?" the woman's voice cuts through the atmosphere landing awkwardly in Lex's ears. There's a familiar tinge to the voice and he manages to pull his gaze away from the little boy just enough to see a very thin woman with large eyes making her way up the lawn. He almost recognizes her.

"Oh my goodness," says the woman, smiling broadly. "I thought that was you. I'd heard you were hanging out around here, but I wasn't sure if I was gonna get to see you. I'm only here for a couple of weeks."

Lex is almost to the point where he nearly recognizes her.

"Anyway, how have you been?" the woman continues. "Wait 'till I tell momma that I ran into you, sitting here on your front porch giving out candy at Halloween."

The woman makes her way to behind the small cowboy who is still standing statue-like, barely appearing to breathe. She rests her hands on his shoulders and beams.

"So, this is my boy," says the woman. She seems undaunted by the fact that she hasn't gotten a single response from Lex or Lorraine. She's clearly not possessed of an abundance of self-awareness. "Trig, this is Lex Delaware. He and your momma knew each other in grade school all the way to high school. Well, before your momma had to take the early exit."

Patricia Holloway! The name comes tumbling into Lex's mind. The woman standing before him now was a girl cloaked in scandal during their high school years. A girl who was, as the understanding went, very popular with the young athletes. Two years older than Lex but only one grade further ahead, she'd never met a boy she wouldn't flirt with. Warmth rose to Lex's cheeks as he faintly remembered how well he'd once known her.

The boy before her must be the very reason she'd taken that early exit.

"Lex," says Patricia, still seemingly unaware that she's been the only one speaking, "this is my little boy, Trigger. We call him Trig for short. He's a royal handful, let me tell you. He was so upset when I told him we needed to come and see his granny over Halloween. Said that we were ruining it all for him. That we were taking back our promise to let him go dressed as a TV cowboy this year. That's exactly what you said, isn't it. That we weren't letting you dress up like the TV cowboy. Well, I made it up to you didn't I. You didn't get to go trick-or-treating at home, but here you are. And I bet it's better here than way out in the country, anyway. Isn't it?"

The boy still hasn't moved. Lex wonders if he's on the spectrum.

"Well hello, Patricia," says Lorraine. Her greeting is seasoned with the spice of disapproval. "It's so good to see you again. When did you get in."

It's a question that doesn't require a long answer.

"Hey, Miss Lorraine," Patricia says, face beaming in Lorraine's direction. A long answer is coming. "It's so good to see you. We got in late last week, but there was so much drama, you know. Trying to get my things here, making sure everything else gets put into storage, getting all of Trig's stuff here in one piece so he doesn't have a meltdown. Then there's the clothes. I had to make sure he had enough warm clothes that he wouldn't freeze playing outside, but not so warm that he comes back in soaking wet from sweat. You know how that is, right? Get the right thing, this not that. Otherwise he never gets adjusted and you spend three hours every night trying to get him to sleep."

"That's very nice, dear," says Lorraine, hand plunging deeply into her candy bowl.

Patricia nods. Trig has yet to budge.

"Well, we should go," says Patricia, glancing down at her little cowboy. "Lots more houses to hit. But, Lex, we should get together. Are you still here?" Patricia nods up to the house behind him, hands firmly gripping Trig's shoulders. She looks a little desperate and Lex understands why. He once again breaks his stare with Trig and smirks to Patricia.

"No, I'm actually in a place downtown, now," Lex says with a small hint of pride.

"You should go before its too late," says Trig. The sound of his voice startles everyone. Lex looks across the yard, making sure that the tiny voice didn't come from some other kid making his way across their drive to collect more candy. Lorraine stops fiddling through tightly-wrapped Jolly Ranchers candies and focuses her attention on the little boy in the cowboy costume. Even Patricia looks down at the top of her little boy's head. He still hasn't moved and betrays no sign of having spoken.

"You heard that, right?" says Lex to no one specifically. They're all staring at Trig which is how they know that he's the one that speaks next.

"You can't stay," Trig says, eyes unblinking. "You'll be empty soon."

The boy's voice has a distant quality. Lex could see his lips moving, but the sound comes from somewhere else. It makes his ears hurt.

Patricia looks down at her son and Lex could see the flash of a deep frown. She addresses Lex and Lorraine sheepishly, pulling her son toward her as she tries to move past the oddity of what's occurred.

"I'm so sorry," says Patricia. Her voice wavers but the smile does not. "His blood sugar must be low. Lex, we need to catch up. I'll get your number from Miss Lorraine and we can have coffee or something."

It clearly takes a good deal of effort to pry Trig away from his spot at the edge of the porch and Patricia grumbles something under her breath as her claws dig into the cowboy's shoulder, finally causing him to stumble backward in stiff little steps. He doesn't break eye contact with Lex, but backpedals as Patricia all but lifts him across the lawn toward the street.

"What do you think he meant by that?" Lorraine whispers as she watches Trig being dragged down the street by Patricia. "Boy's probably not all there, I would guess."

"I don't know," answers Lex. He leans back in his chair as he begins to breathe again.

17

THE TECHNIQUE IS THE SAME EVERY TIME. IT'S BEEN PRACTICED FOR YEARS, perfected over hours and hours. There's not a hitch in the movements, not a single flaw in the results. Every time, consistency, which has been the goal since the technique was adopted many, many years ago.

No words are needed to walk Lex through each step. He knows what he must do. The movements are deeply ingrained, part of his muscle memory. He associates it with walking. Breathing, even. Once he gets going, there's no stopping him. He is tidy, efficient, and to any who takes a moment to observe him, stunningly adept.

He credits the perfection of his technique to the summers he spent with a maternal great-uncle watching the old men, each with his own method. He was a smart enough child that he could combine the things the men got right, discarding the mistakes he'd noticed. Eventually, he felt he could do it much better than any of the old guys he'd supposedly learned from. The student has become the master.

Not that any of the old guys could really care at all. They couldn't be bothered. They had boats to unload.

It always started simply. He would select his target carefully. Sometimes it would be the one next to the piece he'd just been working on, sometimes it would be a random piece that caught his attention. Either way, he would decisively pick it up and examine it closely. Much like an engineer inspecting a steel beam before it's bolted into place on the structure of a bridge. He checks for flaws, irregularities. This may make it seem like it takes a very long time to get to each one, but he's so adept at this part of the process that it only takes him a couple of seconds to determine the best approach after inspecting the piece.

After that, he picks up the shell cracking utensils.

With a couple of quick, certain moves, he separates the knuckles at each joint of the crab leg, pulling with precision as the tendons pull cleanly from the meat still in the shells. He grasps the handles of the shell cracker and pops the edges, exposing the meat within each segment and extracting it with his fingers in long, red and white unbroken strips.

It was a sight to behold, how quickly he could move, how many crab legs he could shell and devour in a short space of time. It was one of Lex's few notable skills.

He sits in the bar, finishing his third beer, enjoying all-you-can-eat crab legs while a hockey game plays on the televisions overhead. There's no shame in his crabmeat dotted smile, it's the most relaxed he's been in a very long time. It certainly, for him, beats sitting in his apartment alone waiting for something to happen.

Lex's crab dinner is a result of pure serendipity. He'd been walking through the maze of streets, odd angles and loops, in an effort to get himself lost. It was a game he played with himself in the almost three months since moving into his downtown apartment. He thought there would be no better way of getting to know the city than to try and lose himself in it. He'd succeeded more than once, suddenly finding the need to backtrack for blocks in order to find something familiar. It was a less-than-subtle way of avoiding going straight home.

That evening, he'd decided to do the same again with the weather being unseasonably mild for early November. He'd packed his things at his desk, shouldered his backpack, and set off in the direction opposite his normal route home. The Thursday night crowd was robust, people enjoying the end of the frigid rains that had been falling for what seemed like weeks. There had been a slight warming for Halloween, but it proved to be a short-lived tease for four straight days of shockingly cold rain and tear-inducing wind.

After a stroll through some very, very nice residential streets and more than a couple of scary, empty ones, he happened across a new-looking place toward the edges of one of the more recently rehabilitated neighborhoods. He was halted by the a-frame sign out front that promised a constant supply of beer and crab legs for a suspiciously low price. After taking note of the nearest transit stop, a mere half-block away, he ventured inside and made his "party of one" at home on a stool at the freshly-oiled bar.

So, he finishes the last bits of crab and sips down his beer, increasingly aware of the older couple staring at him from across the restaurant. Not in disgust, not in disapproval, merely out of curiosity. At first, he ignores it, focusing instead on achieving nirvana through plates of steaming shellfish. As his belly signaled that he should probably stop with the popping, cracking, and peeling, he'd become increasingly aware of them. He doesn't like an audience to his somewhat messy bliss.

Lex finishes the last knuckle of his last crab leg and waves for the check. The almost-friendly waiter peels off his check before wandering over to a petite blond who's having trouble with a beverage dispenser. Lex finishes the dregs of his beer and gathers enough cash to cover the bill and a modest tip, then gathers his things to make his exit. He glances at the couple, keenly aware of how long he's had their attention, as he dons his coat and shoulders his pack.

They whisper something to each other, both keeping their attentions pasted on Lex. If he were the type of person who confronted people, he would go right up to their table and demand to know why he's being observed without his permission. Instead, he timidly lowers his head, zips his coat, and rushes into the night.

The air has grown more brisk in the time he's spent in the restaurant reducing the crustacean population. Lex pulls his collar around his ears and heads to the bus stop. Glancing at the schedule then to his watch, he does some quick math and calculates that he should be back at his apartment in less than twenty-seven minutes, if the bus sticks to its posted schedule. He's proud of himself that he's burned off enough of his evening to allow the minimum amount of time in his apartment. He can get home and go straight to sleep, missing the countless minutes spent alone waiting for something to happen.

He leans against the post of the bus shelter blinking slowly, holding himself in the space between fatigue and sleep. He doesn't want to fall asleep on the bus and risk missing his stop, but he doesn't want to lose the floaty bliss feeling he's worked himself into by shaking himself awake. He looks around at the buildings and streetscape, a small trickle of foot traffic making its way up and down the streets. It's not a bad neighborhood, he thinks to himself. It's going to get very expensive very quickly, a thought that causes him to chuckle to himself.

If he were further along in his career, he imagines himself buying up a place as an investment, primed to cash in while still being brash and young.

The bus rounds a corner and approaches his stop just as he's imagining how cool people would think he was if he'd just jumped right into life right after school. All the hip, tastemaker-style possessions he would have surrounded himself with in order to impress everyone he came across. He shakes off the vain daydream and climbs aboard the bus, taking a seat near the middle exit doors. He's ready to continue his journey along his alternate timeline when he's jolted back to the present. The older couple from the restaurant climb onto the bus just before it's set to pull away from the curb.

The man steps onto the bus and looks down the aisle before spotting Lex.

He then turns to the woman, whispers something, then steps fully onto the bus while the woman pays the fare. They stare directly at Lex as they make their way along the aisle, grabbing hold of a handle as the bus pulls into traffic. Lex squirms, bracing himself for some sort of confrontation. They get closer without looking away. Their focus, though not menacing, is clearly on Lex. They're simply staring, clinically. As if they're observing a cockroach making its way across a high wall.

Lex shrinks against the window as the couple passes, turning their heads, craning to get a better look. They say nothing, do nothing as both walk slowly past where Lex is seated.

He watches them in return, trying to anticipate any move they may make, any word they may say. They pass silently, taking a seat two rows behind him. They say nothing to each other, moving in unison onto the bench, staring at Lex the entire time.

Lex looks away, thinking perhaps that he's being paranoid. That perhaps he has something on his face that's drawing attention. There are eight other passengers on the bus and no one else is even acknowledging his existence. Perhaps out of politeness. He runs a hand over his face, feeling around for perhaps a stray bit of crab, a smudge of butter. He feels nothing out of the ordinary, merely his face as he's always known it. He checks his nose and finds nothing.

Lex closes his eyes and counts to three as the bus rocks having hit a pothole before bearing right at an intersection. He's not fond of the paranoid feeling, the nagging thought that someone's ill will is bent toward him. He wants to believe the couple is no longer staring, but are engaged in a lively conversation with each other, laughing at an old punchline to an old story. He tries to release some tension in his shoulders. He's trying to convince himself that he has been imagining the whole experience with the couple. He thinks to himself how ridiculous he's being, especially after enjoying such a magical feast. He feels a little embarrassment at not being able to let himself enjoy even the simplest of things.

All of this and another count of three and he's certain that, when he opens his eyes, he will resume his life unobserved. Lex's eyes open and looks back to the couple.

Still staring. Still clinical and cold, as if they were taking mental notes on everything he does. They're both observing, ready to compare notes later. Still focused, for unknown reasons, on Lex.

Questions perch at the edge of his tongue. He almost asks what they want. He nearly jumps up and demands to know what they're looking at. Instead, Lex hunches down and stares at his ankles, trying to will the bus to move faster through the streets. It isn't working.

The bus makes several stops on the way across town before it finally lurches to a halt where he should get off. The older couple seems to know this and they rise from their seat a full block in advance. Lex toys with staying on the bus, getting off at the following stop. If they were anticipating his departure, perhaps he could throw them off by letting them disembark and leaving them behind.

This wouldn't work, he concluded. They could simply wait at his building if they know where he lives. He would need to pass them anyway. Besides, he could feel the cold blast of chilling evening air every time the side exit opens, making it an uncomfortable proposition to walk an extra three blocks to avoid confrontation with the unknown duo. He would risk it, counting on the lobby doors of his apartment to provide the final buffer between them.

So, just as he's anticipated, they follow him off of the bus and onto the sidewalk. They never get close enough for him simply to ask aloud why they're following him. He looks back and there they are, walking a few yards behind him. They're huddled together. All the while, they're staring holes into his back. Lex can feel it. It makes him increasingly uneasy and he's fighting the urge to do something.

Lex pauses, waiting to see if he's overrun. He glances back once more. The couple has stopped beneath a streetlight, maintaining the same distance they've held the entire stroll. Twin clouds drift from their mouths as their breath hangs in the air.

Lex can see the door to his building a few short yards away. He's desperate. His adrenaline is pumping. He's wide awake, his heart racing and his head buzzing.

He must get there.

If he can get to the door without seeming panicked, he can close it behind himself, race upstairs, and leave the couple far, far behind.

He wonders what would happen if he ran for the door. Would his shadows pick up their pace, a final move to intercept him and execute whatever twisted plot caused them to follow him so far in the first place.

He pushes those thoughts aside and focuses on the door. So close. His stomach lurches, anticipating something evil and foul. He breathes deeply and steps toward the door. Stops. Looks back. The couple is still standing huddled together underneath the streetlight, eyes locked on him. They don't look like their ready to move from that spot. They've followed him so far, why should they stop once he's just outside his door.

Lex throws caution aside and speed-walks to the door. He looks back and the couple are still huddled under the streetlight. Still staring. He turns back and swears at himself, fumbling with the door key in his pocket. He'd forgotten to get the key out while he was stopped. His breathing becomes heavy as he nearly drops the keys before finally recovering, slotting the correct key into the lock. He scurries through the door into the lobby and closes the door firmly behind himself. Looking outward once he's satisfied the door is secure.

He's feeling a little light-headed, partially from the excitement and partially from the three beers he'd had at the bar. Everything's pitching and reeling. He grips the door handle firmly to recover. It takes a moment for him to screw up the courage to look through the glass door.

His eyes go directly to the the square of concrete just outside the door. Nothing. His view pans up toward the streetlight. There's no one in the sidewalk between the building's door and the streetlamp. His eyes stop at the streetlight where he'd last left the couple, watching. They aren't there.

The street is empty.

They've vanished.

Lex takes a moment, scanning up and down the street from the relative safety of his position behind the locked entry door. No one passes on the street, no one on the sidewalk. The couple is gone.

The hair stands on the back of Lex's neck. He's no longer nursing the prospect of sleep. Wide awake, he rests his hand on the door handle. Just a little pressure and he would be able to open the door, look unobstructed onto the street. Just a little applied force and he could be sure that they were no longer following.

He glances back into the entry hall, past the mailboxes and toward the stairwell. He's alone. He thinks of how ridiculous he probably looks, guarding the building against an invader that doesn't exist.

Lex thinks.

He presses on the handle.

The door opens again to the cool night air.

He checks the corners, both sides of the doorway against the building and down the block.

No one's there. The street is deserted.

Closing the door once more, Lex shakes his head. He backs a few steps toward the stairwell, ensuring that he's no longer being followed. With his heart racing, he dares to turn and takes the stairs two steps at a time all the way to the fifth floor.

fourth

18

Every small noise is magnified, every small creak or bump or knock. The appliances alone make enough noise to keep Lex awake. The fridge is the the most egregious culprit. It hums then pops. He swears that theres water running down the back, collecting into some unseen pan that recirculates it back into the body of the appliance. He doesn't remember hearing so much racket from the fridge before, but it's keeping him from sleeping.

He's tempted to unplug it. He's certain that it would make things a lot more peaceful in his small flat. He resolves to simply lie there, to try and let the sound of the compressor wash over him. He tries to use it to lull himself to sleep.

The second week of November had worn him down to bare nerve. He almost wishes the strange noises, the unexplained water and the unbodied whispers would return. He'd seen the older couple everywhere. They were walking across the street from him as he made his way to work. They were standing at the corner near where he would hail a cab. They were two rows behind him when he would go see a movie.

They would never engage him, keeping their distance. They wore the same expression every time. Clinical observation. Never betraying a motivation, any emotion.

He could never get close enough to speak to them, not that he would. He can never bring himself to say anything to them each time he sees them. It's right there, on the edge. All he has to do is draw the breath and it would come out, pouring from him like a cascade of salt from a busted box of Mortons.

"Who are you and why are you following me?"

He practices the words in the shower. He says them to himself time and again as he lies on his bed, waiting for sleep to take him. He rehearses it while at work, unable to concentrate on the flow of the numbers dribbling down his spreadsheets. He has the words imprinted onto his vocal cords to the point that he wonders how he gets through a day without randomly spraying them onto any random passer-by.

"Who are you and why are you following me?"

Nine simple words that he should have no problem delivering with aplomb and expertise. There's nothing complicated about them and he should be able to extract the exact information he desires. If only he can get into range. If only, and he thinks every time he pictures the old couple, he weren't such a chicken-shit.

Lex tosses these thoughts around lying on his back staring at his ceiling. It was approaching two o'clock in the morning the last time he checked his phone. The shadows are deep and creeping, pushing their way across the ceiling. They remind him of fingers making their way across a dusty chalkboard, leaving dark voids across a flat pale surface. He reaches up and traces the pattern with his own fingers, the traces of utility lights reflected from glass across the alley.

He tries to relax, to settle himself into something resembling sleep. The drips catch his attention again and he's tempted to get up and explore. If anything, he could turn off the water to the sink and unplug the refrigerator, allowing himself a night of rest. He doesn't know, however, how the cranky old super will react once he finds out. Lex should, after all, leave these kinds of maintenance matters to the professionals.

Lex closes his eyes and tries to coax his racing mind to settle. He knows that he's his own worst enemy. He knows that he should be able to simply drift off in peace. The nagging rolling in his gut that prevents rest. Curling into the fetal position, grasping his stomach like a child, doesn't help. Plugging his ears with his fingers doesn't keep the noises out.

"Just go to sleep," Lex says out loud. He closes his eyes and repeats, "Dammit, just go to sleep."

The idea of talking himself to sleep was ridiculous and it sends Lex's mind on a different tangent.

"Why is it so cold?" he asks. As soon as he says it, he realizes how uncomfortable he is. How the chill has settled onto his nose and across his cheeks and ears. He opens his eyes and looks around the room as if other objects would demonstrate the same signs of chill he's feeling. As if the screen on his television would have frost tendrils creeping in from the corners.

Lex sits up, finding himself suddenly stiff from the cold.

"It wasn't cold in here before," says Lex. He ignores the fact that he says so out loud and continues with his reasoning. "At least not this cold. Fuck!"

He realizes it's getting colder by the moment. The corners of the windows show signs of frost. He can see his breath hover in front of him before finally dissipating.

Lex begins to shiver. He feels a chill that starts at the top of his head and cascades quickly across his shoulders, following the path down his spine. His jaw spasms, teeth chatter, bringing a headache with it. He pulls his blanket up around his neck to fight off the violent tremors which are rattling his futon frame.

Nothing is helping and the temperature continues to plummet.

Lex does a quick scan around the apartment, looking toward the windows, the kitchen, the closed doors of the closet and the bathroom. He notices the light changing, getting darker, cooler. He wants to get up and move. Get some circulation going in his limbs. Run around his tiny apartment trying to build up heat. Run until the sweat sublimates off of his body and joins his breath in a rising mist that fills the room.

He gets up and the cold stiffens his limbs as he tries to stretch his legs, swinging them over the edge of the futon. The floor feels like a sheet of ice beneath his bare feet. Lex winces as he plants them firmly before standing, draping his blankets and sheets over his shoulders.

The room has gotten impossibly dark, the only sources of light being a crack beneath the front door and the clocks on the kitchen appliances. The air is slightly foggy so the little light is diffused. He shuffles to the thermostat on the wall, trying to remember where he'd set it before going to bed. He didn't hear anything about a sudden cold front moving through, a drastic dip in the exterior temperature, so he's certain the thermostat isn't set to fight the onset of the deep freeze.

The steps become painful. His ears and the skin over his jaw hurts. His nose wants to fall from his face and shatter onto the floor. Tears form in the corners of his eyes and feel as if they've frozen to the spot. The darkness deepens.

His feet feel like they're sticking to the floor, like each step peels a layer of skin away from the soles. He's shivering violently, teeth chattering so hard that they feel on the verge of pulverizing, filling his mouth with frost-filled blood and shards of ragged enamel. It grows darker, the glow from under the door fading into a gray halo. He can no longer read the time on the clocks in the kitchen, their readouts blurred into obscurity.

He pushes forward toward the thermostat mounted to the far wall near the front door.

The glass in the windows begin to crackle, the high pitch sound of ice grabbing hold and pulling inward. The hardwood floors pop and creak with each step. Lex feels like he's on the deck of a ship in the arctic, the frozen and weathered boards complaining loudly about the extreme cold. He feels a pop beneath the pinky-toe on his right foot and dares not look down fearing that it's just fallen off. He doesn't feel his feet anymore, so he couldn't tell. Unless he looks. He presses on.

Lex reaches the wall, the darkness hovering like pitch. He blinks, trying to get a better view of the thermostat readout. He's shaking to the point that every other move he makes hurts. The small metal dome feels rough under his fingers, feels like there are small ice formations across its surface. He can't see the numbers, obscured as they are by a layer of frost.

He licks his fingers and they feel like lumps of ice on his tongue. The finger sticks briefly to his tooth as he moves it to the thermostat. He tries to wipe off the small piece of plastic guarding the temperature readout. Leaning forward, Lex almost touches the wall with his forehead but stops himself. He can feel the waves of cold cascading down the wall. He knows his forehead will stick instantly.

Even after trying to clear the readout, he can't make out the numbers. It doesn't matter, he thinks. He realizes that he needs to get out before his toe isn't the only thing lost to the sudden deep freeze. He wonders for a moment if the entire building is frozen solid and, if so, how much time he has to get out before he succumbs to it.

Lex nearly screams out in pain as he moves his feet. He's stayed in one spot too long and his feet bonded to the frozen hardwoods. He manages to pry them from where he's standing and suddenly feels a burning sensation at the soles of his feet. He thinks this must be the result of losing all the skin on the bottoms of his feet.

His lungs are screaming and he tries to catch his breath as he struggles toward the front door. He can barely see the weak, gray light pushing from the threshold. He gasps in short bursts, forcing himself to stay upright as he drags himself to the exit. He can't tell how much further he has to go, only that he needs to, in morbid terms, move toward the light.

His shivering stops and he suddenly feels a euphoric wave of warmth wash down his spine. Lex's muscles begin to relax and the feeling of bliss is difficult to fight. He knows that if he surrenders, stops struggling toward the door and stays there, he'll be asleep in no time. Wonderful, elusive sleep just right there. Within his reach.

He shakes it, understanding that it's his body temperature dropping dangerously low. He struggles, the promise of comfort and rest are so present. So real.

He reaches out, hoping that he's made it close to the door. His head rolls around on his shoulders and he slumps forward. His knees are failing and he doesn't have a single step left. His outstretched hand still reaches forward. One final, desperate move.

His numb fingers wrap around the doorknob. He twitches, twists the knob, and pulls the door open as he loses the rest of the feeling in his legs. He collapses through the open door into the bright hallway. He feels the light against his eyelids and wonders if he's reached the end.

Lex feels warm air pressing against his face and wonders if it's part of the process of freezing to death. He'd heard about climbers dying at the top of Mt. Everest and how they'd supposedly felt warmth and comfort. Some even removed articles of clothing as they froze. Lex thinks this is what he's experiencing as he freezes in the comfort of his own apartment building.

It doesn't feel like freezing.

He opens his eyes to the well-lit hallway just outside his apartment. His door is open and he can see clearly all the way across to the windows.

They're clear to the building directly across the alley. No frost, no ice. He looks down at his hands and there's no sign of freezing or frostbite. Down at his feet, he counts ten toes. The soles are intact. He wiggles his toes. They seem to work just fine.

The fifth-floor hall is quiet. Lights pour from the overhead fixtures as they always have. The floor is gleaming with bits of dirt sticking stubbornly to the edges by the baseboards and inside the grout lines. The temperature feels normal, warm enough to knock off any chill someone may carry with them from outdoors. The walls show no signs of frost or ice or any form of damp for that matter. All the doors stand closed, silent, unmarred by extreme temperature fluctuations.

Lex scrambles to his feet, his blanket and sheets still wrapped around him. His apartment looks normal. There are no cascading billows of mist pouring from the ceiling down the walls and across the floor. He touches a toe to the floor just inside the door. It feels more like hardwood and less like a skating rink. Looking around the hallway one last time, he eases his way back into his apartment, closing the door behind him. The air is comfortable. Warm. He looks at the thermostat. Seventy-four degrees.

Comfortable.

Warm.

19

"THAT GIRL'S NOT RIGHT IN THE HEAD," SAYS OSCAR AS HE GATHERS DEAD rose bush leaves from around the shrubs. "Neither is her boy, but that doesn't stop her from parading him around everywhere." He glances past Lex and toward the street

"I'm sure she's had a tough time of it lately," says Lex, holding the lawn bag open, helping. "I know what it's like to move back home."

Oscar visibly bristles at this, yanking very hard on a root, nearly ripping it from the shrub bed. The root fights back, nicking him on the thumb. A small bead of blood trickles from under his thumbnail which he promptly ignores. Lex can't help but notice.

"Shouldn't you be wearing gloves?" Lex asks. The sight of blood now makes him queasy, so he asks partially out of concern for Oscar, mostly out of the desire to not lose his lunch.

"Fuck it," Oscar grumbles. He gets his revenge on the root by grasping it with both hands and yanking it out of the ground causing the entire rosebush to list forward. Oscar smiles and it makes Lex lean back just a little.

Lex can't be certain that Oscar actually smiled after destroying the roots to one of his rose bushes. He's not even certain that Oscar had really pulled the roots. He's been wandering through the day in a daze, barely aware of anything. He's having trouble remembering things, top of which is how he got out to his parent's house from the city. He's pretty sure it's Saturday, fairly sure that his mother is in the kitchen preparing lunch while his father does some last-minute gardening before the truly cold weather settles in for the season. He's not sure how he got roped into helping his father in the yard as opposed to helping his mother in the kitchen.

He's more handy in the yard, he supposes, than in the kitchen. He hasn't real aptitude for either, but at least in the yard he can't really set things on fire. That's what he tells himself as he sways while holding open the lawn bag.

"Too much partying dulls the mind," Oscar says, finishing his hack-job on the roots of the disinterred rose bush. The blood from his finger is streaming down his hand, forming a macabre line of red tracing across his palm. It doesn't slow him. Lex can barely look. "Just because you're out on your own like a grown person doesn't mean you get to stay out all hours, doing whatever it is you want to do. You've got more responsibilities on your own, remember that."

Oscar is giving an unwarranted lecture, one of his favorites, to a son who barely understands why he's there. Lex squints at his father, trying to catch meaning from the words being tossed his way. Every other one eludes him and he counts himself grateful. He's understands that his father thinks he's trying to recover from a hangover, from a night of hard partying and heavy drinking. He probably credits the influence of his very good friend, Parker.

Lex debates correcting his father, telling him the truth. Telling him that he indeed has not been sleeping, but not because he's been out partying and drinking with who knows who. He considers telling Oscar that there are things happening to him in his place that makes him want to leave. Things that make him regret ever moving away. Of course, he can't exactly say this to the guy who'd practically cheered when he announced that he would be packing his things and heading out on his own.

The last thing he needs to hear is Oscar's other favorite lecture on how dangerous the city is and how he would do best to live somewhere safer. Like closer to home. Not too close to home, mind you, but close enough so that the stink of whatever happened in the city at night didn't rub off onto him so completely. How it had always been a bad idea to live in such a dangerous, unpredictable place with complete strangers from places unknown.

He keeps quiet, steadying himself so that his sway isn't as obvious. He thinks he's doing a pretty good job, eyes wide open and legs planted slightly apart, knees bent. He's not sure how much longer he can keep it up, but Lex is pretty confident that they're not going to be outdoors for much longer.

"Lex!" says Patricia from behind him. She sounds very happy to see him and, before turning, Lex hopes that she hadn't brought along mute, creepy little Trigger. "I was just telling Trigger how neat it is that you live in town, you know, brave. Adventurous."

Lex pivots to face Patricia just in time to see Trigger reach down and pick up a large, round pebble and stick it in his mouth. He worries briefly that the child will choke on the pebble until he reads the expression in the kid's eyes. Again, he's staring straight through Lex. He's pushed the stone through his lips, capping the expression in a dark, sinister grin.

"Patricia," continues Patricia, beaming. "You remember me, right? We were here for Halloween. Anyway, I stopped by a couple of times and you weren't here. I forgot that you didn't live here any more, that you were downtown. But, then I got to speaking with your lovely parents. Oh, hey there, Mr. Oscar."

"Patricia," mumbles Oscar without looking up. Rose bush twigs are falling all around him as he tugs at another stubborn root.

"I didn't even see you there," says Patricia. She waves as if Oscar were looking at her. She's completely ignored the boy at her side who's sucking on a pebble while staring holes into Lex. "How is Miss Lorraine doing?"

Oscar mumbles something as he stands and brushes the dirt from his knees with one had, tossing a handful of twigs and dead leaves in to the refuse bag with the other. He looks to Lex with a half-scowl before turning to Patricia, standing with her son, at the edge of the yard.

"She's doing well, thank you for asking," says Oscar. "And how are you doing today?" Lex knows the cordiality in his voice is forced. His father is never that involved, especially in other people's affairs.

Lex glances over to his father quizzically. He's sure that Oscar realizes what he's just done. He's engaged Patricia Holloway in a conversation where she gets the opportunity to give the long answer. Oscar shoots Lex a look that acknowledges as much. This must be part of some sort of penance Lex is being expected to pay while visiting his parents.

"Oh, you know," Patricia starts, resting the backs of her wrists on her hips. "I'm still waiting for that good-for-nothing to sign the papers. He's been giving me such a hard time this week, you know, not wanting to give me anything. I keep telling him, or at least my lawyers keep telling his lawyers that he can't just cut me loose without some way of helping a girl like me to get along in this big scary world."

Lex wonders how scary the world really has been to her.

"So they sent this delivery guy with my stuff, some of it was a little beat up and I let him know that I didn't leave my hair dryer like that when I left the house. I don't know what some of these people think sometimes, mis-handling other people's belongings as if we wouldn't notice. I get mad right now just thinking about it. But, I won't let it get me down. You know, all of these setbacks are just temporary. Lexington, you know about setbacks, right?"

Lex feels a twinge at the base of his skull and winces. He's certain she didn't notice.

"Well, this one is only temporary," Patricia says before taking a rare breath.

She looks from Oscar to Lex then down to her son, dribbling drool down his chin as he continues his one-way staring contest with Lex. A strange look flashes across her face and Lex is certain that it may be the dawning of a small degree of self-awareness.

The little boy stops staring at Lex as the stone falls from his mouth. He looks up at his mother and wraps his arms around her denim-clad leg. She looks a little blank, a bit lost. Her mind seems to be a million miles away. Lex doesn't think she's about to cry, but she's definitely a different person from the woman who was just filling them in on every little tedious detail of her life.

Even Oscar seems briefly taken aback. He displays a small hint of curiosity. He then huffs and turns back to his rose bush, pushing to try and straighten it.

Suddenly, Patricia returns. Life leaps back into her face and she looks down at the little boy hugging her leg. She smiles and pats his head.

"Oh, bless your heart," she says. "What is it, Trig? You ready to go back to Granny's? Give me just a minute, I need to talk to Lexington."

Oscar drifts toward the porch steps. Lex figures he's spotted an opportunity to remove himself from the situation. Lex wishes that he could join his father in the escape.

"Lexington, do yo mind if we talk alone for just a few minutes. I have something I want to speak to you about."

"Sure," Lex says after a few moments of silent tension. He's convinced that he could hear the hair on the back of his neck stiffen.

Oscar chuckles under his breath as he passes behind Lex and glides toward the porch steps. Lex quickly glances from the corner of his eyes and notes that Oscar's mouth is tilted in the mean grin he usually wears when he's about to let someone know just how right he'd been.

"Have a good one," Oscar says as he climbs the steps and pushes open the front door. He doesn't wait for a reply.

Lex can barely push down the fight-or-flight instinct and swallows hard. He stares at Trig who, for once, is not staring back. Instead, the child is hugging his mother's leg tight while staring at her chin. She barely acknowledges it with a hand resting casually on the boy's back.

"Lexington," Patricia says in a loud whisper.

"You can call me Lex," he interrupts.

Patricia flusters slightly and appears to blush. She looks at her feet for a moment before batting her eyes at Lex, smiling shyly. He doesn't like where this conversation appears to be headed.

"Lex," she continues. "That's so weird to say, I've been calling you Lexington for as long as I can remember. It's so distinguished. That's why I like it. Like you, so different. You know?"

She's fumbling with the elastic cord at the waist of her coat. It bunches in a way that makes Lex think it's not meant to be worn in cold weather.

"So I was wondering," she continues without really making eye contact with Lex, "if it was okay with you. I mean, you can say no, it's perfectly fine. I was just hoping, because we go so far back. We've known each other for so long and — I wouldn't just ask anyone this, I want you to know. I've always liked you, you know that, right?"

There's a pause where Lex thinks he should have said something. His mind is racing and he misses the opportunity. He regrets it immediately. He'll think later that he could have prevented the exchange from proceeding had he not missed his opportunity to derail the conversation, or at least stall it long enough that she would lose her nerve and not continue with what she was about to ask.

"Anyway," Patricia says, slicing through the moment. She's wrapped a bare thread from the edges of her coat around her finger. "I just was wondering if I could come stay with you for a couple of days. In the city. Just temporarily, you know, to get away from things here for a little while. To get out of the house. A bit of a staycation."

There are several things that pull at Lex's attentions in that moment. The first is how little Trigger has started looking around the sidewalk as he holds firmly to his mother's leg. He hasn't looked at Lex since Patricia started her little speech. In a way, Lex misses the distraction the kid provided.

The second is how nervous the woman before him is. The entire time. Her whole speech seemed simultaneously well rehearsed and completely impromptu. This makes him think that it had been rehearsed in the mirror repeatedly, that she'd waited, even lurked, until she ran across him during one of his visits to his parents'. He can't imagine working himself up to asking someone he barely knows to stay at their place.

The third and, for Lex, the most important thing pulling Lex's attention is the smile. It's a small, flirty smile. It's a smile carefully designed to accentuate a perfect row of teeth, the roundness of her cheeks, the size and shininess of the eyes. It's a manipulative smile that's meant to ensure she got her way. With men, specifically. He wonders how many times it didn't work.

"I don't think so," says Lex. The words tumble forward more smoothly than he'd expected. Relief. "That wouldn't be a good idea."

Patricia gasps. The gambit of the look seems to have failed and an undertone of anger is building. Trigger, sensing the change in his mother's mood, breaks from his scrutiny of a nearby hedgerow and resumes his laser focus on Lex. He's scowling.

"Don't get the wrong idea," Lex says. The knot in his gut tells him he should try to smooth things over a little. "You're great and I'd love to reconnect. Get to catch up with you again after all these years. I just don't think it's the best idea. For you."

Anger is beginning to spread across Patricia's eyes. A cold hatred turns her cute little smile into a small, disdain-filled snarl. In that moment, she's a woman who has clearly had enough of people telling her no.

"Never mind," she says quickly. She clinches the back of Trig's jacket, nearly lifting him off of the ground. "Forget I said. . .I've got to go. I left something in the oven and I need to go check on it."

Patricia turns down the street, the opposite direction from her parents' house. She pretends to straighten her hair, brushing some imaginary strands from her forehead before marching onward without another word. Trigger follows apace, eyes fixed on Lex as he goes.

Lex hears his father's laughter erupt from behind the closed front door.

20

"I SAID IT WOULDN'T BE A GOOD IDEA FOR HER," LEX SAYS TO HIMSELF AS HE stands at his kitchen sink. He's been talking to himself all evening, trying something new. He's growing accustomed to his own voice cutting through the silence of his apartment. The ringing dulcet tones, at least as he hears them, punching across the drip drip of the kitchen faucet or gentle whirr of the refrigerator.

Lex is thankful that his strange conversation had, for a time, taken his mind off of being followed, off of the odd feelings he gets whenever he returns to his apartment. A constant feeling of being watched.

He couldn't put his finger on it before. It's been a bur in the back of his mind for weeks, even before Felicia fell. He wonders how he's been able to ignore it for so long.

"She looked so disappointed," Lex follows. Again, the soft whirr of the heater fan answers. Lex laughs, thinking himself completely ridiculous.

The scene from the front yard plays itself over and over in his head. Lex considers the request, considers his own response. He thinks of how nervous she was, almost smitten. The way she'd been twisting the cord on her jacket, the small shuffles in her step, the subtle batting of the eyelashes.

He laughs again, more nervously.

He wonders how she could have simply asked that question. How she could have just built up the nerve to ask someone she barely knows, has barely ever known, if she could stay with him for a little while. What did that mean? Was she proposing a romantic entanglement? Was there a desperate grasp toward escaping whatever situation she's found herself? The logic of the whole thing strikes him as being off.

Then there's the kid. The boy with the odd name staring constantly. Lex thinks back to little Trigger, and can still feel his big brown eyes trying to probe into his skull. That Patricia doesn't seem to notice what her kid is doing seems odd. Trigger stands at her side, gripping onto his mother's leg, locking eyes with Lex whenever they're around.

Lex already thinks kids are creepy. Trig is a special case.

As he moves toward his refrigerator, Lex thinks about what it would mean to have Patricia stay with him. He wonders what she has in mind. He shudders when he thinks about the little boy roaming around his small space, head on a swivel to keep Lex in his sights. He frowns at the thought of sleeping on an air mattress in his designated dining room while he chivalrously concedes his bed to the down-on-her-luck woman and her small child.

"Who asks that?" Lex whispers, shaking his head as he opens the fridge. He closes the door to the refrigerator immediately, realizing that he's bored. He moves to the kitchen sink and leans back against the edge of the counter.

Looking over the entire place, slowly taking inventory of his possessions while picturing what it would be like to share it with a crazy person, he nearly dozes off. Eyelids are heavy, breathing slows and he begins losing feeling in his legs. Diffused sunlight is still peeking down into the alley, tinting the room a peculiar shade of blue. The color blue that wishes it were simultaneously purple and green. Lex yawns then smiles, understanding that his long, sleepless day might finally be over.

Shoving aside the recollection of the afternoon's absurdities, a plan begins to form. There's no time for delay and Lex moves as quickly as he dares. He doesn't want to lose such proximity to sleep.

Sleep has prowled the perimeter of his consciousness whenever he's on his commute to work, whenever he's journeyed afield to his parents. He's felt it in the distance while sitting and trying to talk with Oscar and Lorraine. It's close as he stares at the terminal on his desk in the office. It would stay away everywhere else, playing coy, pretending to edge nearer only to recede into the dark shadows. It had always left him exhausted and irritable, feeling himself drift further from the threshold of slumber. He relishes this opportunity, the first real chance to get sleep in over a week, and he feels the need to seize it.

Lex works his way from the kitchen to his futon, tossing off the hooded sweatshirt he'd wrapped around himself. He also brushes aside the beanie cap he'd left on. Whipping off his belt and tossing it to the floor in front of the television, he dives headlong onto the folded futon, scooping up a pillow for his head to land on.

Sweet bliss pours over him like a warm bath. Sleep was finally taking hold after too long an absence. His limbs begin losing tension, his eyes barely staying open. It doesn't matter to him that it's only six in the afternoon. He's certain that, he'll be able to sleep clear through until morning. While drifting off, he imagines paying a massive sleep debt. He sees himself at a bank counter with large, soft bags of sleep, shoving the bags across the counter to some bureaucrat-type with horn-rimmed glasses, and telling them to settle his accounts in full.

He laughs softly at such a cartoonish image.

He thinks of Patricia, that sly and practiced smile as she flirted with him. As she asked him an impossible question as if she were merely trying to find out about the next day's weather. In his mind, she steps forward, strokes his face as she pulls herself closer to him. She's offering the promise of herself. She moves closer in his mind and he knows the dreams to follow are going to be very pornographic.

He's drifting, almost floating away. His body aches as everything sinks into the futon cushion. He can barely feel the wood frame beneath the compressed foam. He doesn't care. The dark is taking over.

Until.

The pounding on the door is rhythmic. It comes in threes. Three firm, urgent pounds. Like the mallet striking an oversized timpani.

The first three knocks are sudden and abrupt. They do just enough to knock Lex out of the drift. He fights to hold on to the sleep that's lingered so close. He covers his head with a pillow and squeezes his eyes tight. He's already losing the feeling, sleep has already begun to retreat.

The next three knocks are more urgent. They're followed by small rattles as the door springs back into the frame. Lex squeezes the pillow over his head nearly suffocating himself. He holds it, wondering how quiet he can be and for how long. The offending knocker would need to leave sooner or later. He just needs to wait it out.

There are three more poundings at the door, more intense than the ones before. He waits. Three more and he waits still. There are three that sound as if the door frame is about to splinter away from the walls. No words, no calling out to whomever may be inside. Just the violent pounding on the apartment door. The next three sound like they're done by a battering ram.

He doesn't wait for the jackhammering knocks that surely will follow.

Lex tosses his pillow into the kitchen and swings his legs over the edge of the futon. The floating bliss of drowsiness has fled to the edges leaving an achy fatigue and heaviness behind. He blinks while his eyes readjust to the odd brightness of the room, dying daylight flooding through the windows. His legs cramp a little and he stumbles while trying to stand, trying grudgingly to come to his full senses.

Three jackhammering knocks rattle the door and Lex swears he can see the hallway light through a gap between the door's frame and the wall beside it.

Shaking his head, he strides to the door, straightening his shirt as he does so. One hand unlatches the locks as the other grasps the handle and he yanks open the door, not even bothering to look through the keyhole. He knows who its going to be and he's prepared to give that person a piece of his mind.

"Fuck, Merle, what the hell do you . . ."Lex shouts before the door has opened fully.

The words echo off of the empty hallway walls. A faint ringing pings back from the closed doors and tile floors. It's brighter in the hall than in the apartment, twilight being outshined by the cold fluorescent tubes above. The apartment behind him is silent, the hallway is humming from a dying ballast in the ceiling overhead. Distant street sounds are muffled, barely audible from the open window at the far end of the hall.

Otherwise, there's no-one there.

Lex takes a step back, closes the door, counts to three, then reopens it. He sticks his head out beyond the threshold and looks up and down the hallway again. Still empty, still silent. There wasn't even the benefit of his voice echoing off of the walls.

Fatigue slaps him hard across the face and he stumbles back into his apartment after closing the door. He stares at the door while the twilight deepens outside the windows behind him, bathing the apartment in a deep purple. The world feels heavy and he sways under its weight, but he stands there. Something leaves him, draining from the top of his head through his heels as they press against the wood floor. He feels at once empty and heavier.

It's a long while before Lex moves again.

21

PARKER LOOKS LIKE HE CAN BARELY CATCH HIS BREATH. HE'S BEEN LAUGHING for a solid ten minutes. He's turned a deep shade of purple that's spread from the tips of his ears all the way down his neck. Tears roll down his face and he lets snot dribble across his upper lip.

"It's not that funny, Parker," says Lex. He's sitting quietly, waiting for his confidant to collect himself and return to the conversation. "Do you need some water?"

Parker doesn't answer, his body racked with wave after wave of laughter. Lex is tempted to leave.

He doesn't like Parker's choice for lunch that day, anyway. The small, tight burger restaurant makes Lex feel like he's inside the color green. It's not just the decor that creates the effect, though it's a very large factor.

Every inch of the diner is covered in some shade of green. The four glossy hunter green booths are cozied up to speckled hunter green linoleum table tops rimmed in bright green metal banding. The solid mint green tiles on the floor probably hide all manner of stains and dirt, the sea foam green industrial wallpaper covering the walls do not. The green quartz counter is very close to the griddle top where two men labor over dozens of sizzling fatty beef patties, steam rising to the large industrial vent hood overhead. From the sound the hood's fan makes, one would assume that it worked at maximum efficiency, pulling the acrid stench of overcooked meat and singed cheese from the tiny space. Alas, the odors of fry grease and a well-used griddle-top lingered in the air, clinging to the clothing of all who are brave enough to breach the front door.

Lex knows that he's going to smell old, burnt grease on his coat for at least a week. He then wishes it was the most pressing of his problems, remembering that he's yet to speak another word to his best friend. He waits a little longer, sipping water through a straw from the mostly clean glass in front of him.

Parker had chosen a place at the counter, a spot closest to the deep fryers, when they'd first walked through the green-framed glass door. Lex stared at him, glaring as best as he could through sleep-deprived eyes. He's afraid the effect was more woe-is-me pathetic than you've-got-to-be-kidding-me irate. Either way, Parker changed course mid-stride and parked at an open booth situated at approximately the midpoint of the small dining room. They could see the two grease-soaked cooks laboring behind the counter, one flipping ten burgers on the griddle, the other pulling onion rings from the bubbling oil of the deep fryer.

Parker can barely hide that he's salivating, ready to shove whatever comes over the counter into his waiting mouth. Lex isn't quite as excited. There's a faint buzz around the edges of everything he sees and hears and smells. Every time he closes his eyes, they sting with green flashing stars and comets. Everything feels sticky and jagged, but that could also just be the air in the diner.

After wiping his face with a napkin, blowing his nose noisily into it and catching his breath, Parker looks red-eyed to Lex. The joviality in his face morphs slowly into an amused confusion and he takes a swig from his water glass, wincing as if he'd expected the contents to be different.

"You're serious?" Parker says. "That shit really happened?"

"I told you that," says Lex. He feels more tired than he ever has. The lack of sleep simultaneously increases the gravity in the room and corsets his spine, keeping him upright somehow. Every word he says rides from his throat on the backs of sighs. "It actually happened that way. That's exactly what she said."

"And you told her no?" Parker responds. His eyes say that he's still waiting for the punch line. "How could you have said no?"

"You can't think it's a good idea."

"Good idea? I don't mean to offend your sensibilities here, buddy, but it sounds like you passed up on the opportunity to have a live-in no-strings-attached."

"Who asks that from some guy she doesn't know."

"She was going to get to know you. Rekindle the old thing." Parker's grin broadens. He's not threatening to melt into another fit of laughter though there are tears beginning to trickle from the corners of his eyes.

"Parker, that was a lifetime ago," Lex sighs. His head dips as he tries to ease the tension at the base of his skull before it spreads to his shoulder blades. "There's no way she even remembers that."

Parker stifles another burst of laughter, wiping more tears from his eyes.

"Okay, so she probably does," Lex concedes. His mind is swimming and he wants nothing more than to lay his head onto the greasy green table. "I don't know. Maybe. That's not the point."

"Dumbass, that's the whole point," says Parker. He leans back, preparing himself to deliver his next lesson. "You two were each other's first little diddles, right?"

"I'm not going to talk about that."

"It was a young you and a young her in a blanket fort in your bedroom, right?"

"Parker, I'm not talking about that. We were kids. I wish I hadn't told you about it."

"That's not true," Parker laces his fingers behind his head, smiling like a prophet. "Your life is made better by telling me that. Why? I'm glad you asked. It's this kind of insight that allows me to shed some light on your next course of action. I'm your own personal guru, so let me guru to you."

Lex rolls his eyes before slumping into his seat.

"Lexington, Lex-man, Lex. Kid. It's all connected. Everything has context and the context of that hottie. . .she's still a hottie, right?"

Lex stares ahead silently.

"No matter. She's got a kid, only downside. Upside, she would be so readily available to be 'so completely grateful to you for your kindness and generosity and oh, by the way, funny story, was just thinking about that time under the blanket fort when we discovered what bases were, wanna do that again now that we're a little older.' Yeah, that's what'll happen."

"Please, God, make it stop," whispers Lex.

"That's exactly what I'm talking about," says Parker, pointing his straw in Lex's direction. "Only the opposite. You'd be begging for it to not stop, my friend. You'd get to change things up. You'd put this insomnia to good use, trust me."

"It's not insomnia."

"So you've been sleeping, then?"

"Well, no."

"But it's not insomnia."

Parker stifles yet another burst of laughter, covering his mouth with a fist. He holds this pose for almost a minute.

"Forget it," Lex says, "I'm not sure what I expected from you, anyway."

"You expected to learn the dictionary definition of insomnia," says Parker through his fist. "You open up the dictionary and it has a mirror there just for you, my friend."

"It's insomnia, but not for lack of trying."

"Okay, good point."

One of the greasy chefs casts a shadow over the table, a steaming plate in each hand. Lex regrets the angle at which he first regards the plates and hopes the top side were much more successfully cleaned than the bottom. The cook looks at the identical orders before sliding one in front of each man. Having done his waitering duty, he wordlessly shuffles back toward the opening in the counter that leads to his domain.

Parker dives into the pile of oily fries with one hand, grasps the crusty half-filled bottle of ketchup with the other. Lex's stomach performs a couple of cartwheels and he frees an angry belch from his throat.

"That's the spirit," Parker mumbles, mouth full of potato mush. He smiles as he chews.

"Take your time, Parker," says Lex as he pushes his plate away. "While I have part of your attention, let's square one thing right now."

"You're cranky when you haven't slept," Parker interrupts, spitting bits of chewed potato across the table.

"I'm not cranky. Look, Parker. Thanks for your wisdom, but you're not catching my point. I don't think things are working out the way she planned. That's the point. We're all just so fucked up, you know. That place, that neighborhood, those fucking people have us all so twisted that when we try to make things happen for ourselves, it just blows up. We come crawling back to try and get back on our feet."

Lex feels himself getting emotional and takes a sip from his water glass. Parker has taken another large bite from his burger and he chews slowly while staring at Lex.

"She's so desperate to get away from the curse," Lex pauses to let the word land. He hadn't thought of it as a curse before that moment, but he held on to the idea. ". . .that she asks a guy she barely knows anymore if she can come crash with him for a little while. She's in the middle of a separation. . ."

"A divorce," Parker asserts.

"Whatever, a divorce, and she has a small kid."

"Special-needs kid," Parker says just before chomping on another french fry.

"Eat your food. I just think it's all of us that lived on that street. Everybody in that neighborhood. The whole damn town. I feel bad for turning her away. I can relate."

Parker wipes his hands with his napkins and mocks a slow, sincere ovation. His brows are creased, his lips pursed, and he shakes his head slowly as he feigns being moved.

"You are such a fucking head-case," Parker says while maintaining his mock earnestness. "Don't fool yourself, though. You are not somehow persecuted because of where you come from. You weren't held back by a community that tried to push you forward. The shit that happened to you was because you're who you are. The reason you moved on was because you wanted to move on. You needed a break. There wasn't some kind of magical umbilical cord snatching your ass back to mommy and daddy's because life got too hard after making a few bad decisions and hearing a couple of stray accusations. There was a real human fucking tragedy."

Lex shifts uncomfortably in his seat and he looks around to make a quick exit. He can't breathe and the room is swaying like a funhouse.

"Hey," Parker leans across the table and touches Lex's sleeve. The derision on his face has been replaced by genuine concern. "Look, I get it. You're not ready for that talk yet. I get it, man. I just don't want you to think that what she's going through has anything to do with what you were going through. It's two divergent paths, buddy."

Lex sighs and closes his eyes as he leans back. He only feels a little dizzy and the nausea has retreated.

"Two divergent paths that could have been one big, sloppy, no-strings-attached path," Parker says settling back into his seat, crooked grin reappearing. His shoulders bob up and down as he grinds his hips below the table. "You know what I'm talking about, don't pretend to be too innocent to understand."

"You're a fucking idiot," Lex says. He can't fight the smile spreading across his face.

"At least I'm an idiot who sleeps. When's the last time you slept, Lex? The last time you actually curled into your lonely little bed and sawed off some logs?"

"A week ago yesterday, maybe." That realization makes Lex even more exhausted.

"You tried Ambien?"

Lex shakes his head slowly. Parker shoves another fistful of fries into his mouth while nodding. He thinks for a few seconds.

"I know a guy," Parker says after swallowing his food. "I think he does Ambien, I'll need to ask. I know he does. . .never mind what he does. I'll get you some either way. If he doesn't, he probably knows a guy."

"I'm not taking Ambien, Parker," Lex says. Things have settled enough that he braves chomping down on a couple of french fires. The saltiness snaps him back into the moment almost magically.

"You're taking Ambien, Lex." Parker smiles while nodding. He lifts his burger and takes another huge bite.

22

Lex stares at the small, clear plastic baggie bulging with chalky-looking oblong pills sitting on his desk. It feels like a loaded weapon to him, something that he'd hoped he'd never need. He leans closer, reading the neat little letters and numbers stamped into the sides of each pill. He pokes the bag with his index finger and watches it rock back, the overstuffed jewelry baggie of Ambien.

Parker promised him there were about thirty pills in the bag, enough for a month of, as he puts it, "lovey-dovey-sleepy time". Lex tried to back away, tried to avoid taking the unsolicited gift, but Parker shoved the baggie into his coat pocket just as they were parting ways.

It's tempting. A little pill that will let Lex sleep through all the oddities. Something that will perhaps slow his mind enough to relax and enjoy the absolute blackness of slumber. Even if he dreams, he would happily trade a night or two of surreal moving imagery for the torturous aches of having not slept for almost two weeks.

It's been two weeks. Lex tosses that idea around in his mind while fingering the zip top of the pill bag. He tries to remember the last time he'd slept a full night uninterrupted. He thinks back to the last time he'd placed his head on his pillow, closed his eyes before opening them again on a new day. Two weeks.

He rocks slowly side to side, his neck muscles a collection of knotted steel cables. He would try to catch a few winks here and there. He's gotten very good at sleeping on the bus without missing his stop. He sneaks the occasional cat-nap at his desk while waiting for something to load or for a response in e-mail. He's discovered how truly noisy the office can become when one tries to sneak in a cat-nap. There's always a sudden noise or nearby laughter ready to punch through the consistent sound of computer fans humming and buzzing fluorescent ballasts.

Two weeks since he's felt rested and aware. The world has grown darker for Lex and he's started seeing things in the deeper shadows. He catches himself jumping at the sight of some dark movement in his periphery, something running across his desk at work or along the sidewalk. He turns to see what it is every time and each time nothing's there.

Two weeks without hitting the reset button on his psyche. Everything is piling on top of itself. He's losing track of the days, overlapping encounters. He looks at people and gets a confused stare in return. "You just said that," or "we've already had this discussion" frequently ends whatever normal conversation he thought he was having. He's forgetting what it's supposed to be like to be normal.

Eyes closed, watching the after image of his monitor fade, Lex tries once again to focus. He's mustered all of his energy into tasks more than once during this ordeal. A quick count makes him realize that he's going for something akin to his twenty-third wind. At least twenty-three times he's tried to rally, refocus and simply get through this thing or that. He does so with the promise of the approaching night being different.

Perhaps he would sleep all the way through that night.

He opens his eyes to the sound of a throat being cleared.

"Mister Delaware," says Dean. He's towering over Lex's cubicle, coffee mug in hand, primed to deliver its payload. "I'm quite sure there are other appropriate times for sleeping."

Lex quickly and, in his mind, stealthily swipes the baggie of pills from his desk, palming them smoothly into the open backpack next to his chair.

"I wasn't sleeping," says Lex. He looks up at the bottom of Dean's mug and swears the tiny print indicating the dish's provenance is marching around in circles like fleas. He blinks hard. "Just thinking through a few things. I think better with my eyes closed."

"I'm not interested in your excuses," says Dean after taking a sip. He has the expression of the man who's accustomed to reprimanding teen-aged boys. It's all stern determination with an edge of admonishment and an undertone of someone who will actually do nothing but fill out a lot of paperwork. The bluster of the true believer.

"Sorry, Dean," says Lex. He tries to look contrite.

"Lexington, Mister Delaware."

"Lex is fine."

"Right. Lexington. You've been with us now for how long?"

"Seven months."

"Seven months. We hired you seven months ago because you're bright. You showed potential. We looked past your obvious lack of work history because you impressed us with your skills. You passed all of the tests. You started as a very hard worker, always going that extra mile." Dean sips again at the edge of his mug. "I've noticed, and believe me, Lexington, we've all noticed, that you've been a little lax in your, shall we say, professional vigor of late. You don't seem as enthusiastic as you once were. Not that we expect complete cheerfulness every day. We're not delusional. We're all humans with our good days and bad days."

Dean looks around the office as if trying to find an example of each, people to drive his point home. He catches sight of something near the executive offices, smiles and doffs his mug at whatever he sees there, then takes another sip before returning his attention to Lex.

"What I mean to say, Lexington, Mister Delaware, is that you seem to be slipping," Dean pauses to let his point land. Lex sighs and fights the urge to lay his head on his desk, riding out Dean's rambling rebuke. "The gild has left the lily. Are you familiar with that phrase, Mister Delaware?"

Lex winces each time Dean glances at the name plate on the outside wall of his cube and hisses "Mister Delaware". He's tempted to tell the oversized pompous asshole that Mister Delaware is his father and that if he were to speak to his father the way he's speaking to him now, he would be wearing a face shield to reset his broken nose the next day. He want's to scream to Dean, Mister I-don't-really-do-any-work-here, that not everyone is a lifer. Not everyone sitting behind their terminals, dutifully entering figures into soul-numbing spreadsheets, enjoys their time in the big, open brick and steel loft that some rich asshole has decided to make their office. He then wishes that he could simply stand, looking Dean in the eyes and explain how little sleep he's gotten in the past two weeks and that he's sorry if it seems to have affected his performance, but he is a fucking human being after all and not sleeping is why he can't seem to focus.

All of this flashes through Lex's mind as Dean continues to dress him down in a righteous tone, a drone that Lex now wonders if he could use to put himself to sleep.

Lex laughs to himself then quickly hopes Dean wasn't staring at him while in the middle of expressing a very serious point. He glances up from his keyboard in hopes that his little chuckle wasn't noticed.

"I'm glad you find bankruptcy amusing, Mister Delaware," Dean says. He was clearly saying something important, making a dire parallel to global market conditions and his inability to keep his eyes open at his desk. "We aim to keep you amused here."

"I'm sorry, Dean," says Lex. He breathes deeply and tries not to sigh. "Look, that was very unprofessional of me, I admit. You have every right to be angry.

Please understand that while it may seem that I'm completely disinterested, know that it's only a reflection of how excited I am to work here. I know how much of a privilege it is to be at this company."

Lex isn't quite sure where the words are coming from, but they're having the desired effect on Dean, whose posture is softening.

"All of this is very true," offers Dean.

"So, and I hope you don't mind my saying so, seeing that I consider you one of my role models here in the office, I'm very sorry to have disappointed you at all in my appearing to sleep on the job. Trust me when I say that I'm only trying to grasp a mental picture of how best to do my work. Here. For the company."

Dean smiles, an almost sinister, painful-looking smile that wrinkles the skin on his face in ways that Lex isn't quite prepared for. Lex knows he's off the hook, but decides to offer one more little nudge of kiss-ass.

"I trust that this doesn't tarnish my prospects here," says Lex. "I appreciate the position in which this company finds itself and I look forward to doing my part as we stride into the future. Meanwhile, I will try and use a more orthodox approach to things at my workstation."

"Well, Lexington," says Dean, "I'm glad to hear that you're trying new things. Just, try to run new procedures past us before implementing them into your everyday workflow."

With that, Dean nods to Lex, turns, and walks toward the far side of the office.

"Well done," says Carmen. She's staring at Lex from her desk across the aisle. She has her headphones around her neck and is actually smiling. "I didn't think you had it in you. Bravo."

"I honestly don't know where all of that came from," Lex says. He smiles back, much more awake than he's been all day.

"Doesn't matter, man. That was really impressive. I may have been wrong about you."

"People often are."

She lets out a puff of a laugh while reaching for her headphones. She nods a few times then turns back toward her terminal as she fits the headphone cuffs around her ears.

"We should hang out sometime," she says while staring at her screen. She's still smiling.

"Uh, sure, okay," says Lex. He looks around the office to see if anyone else was nearby. He quickly concludes that she was indeed speaking to him. "That would be great."

She reaches over to her phone and hits a button. The music is loud, sounds bass-heavy, and definitely drowns out anything Lex would have to say going forward. He turns back to his terminal trying to sort out the events of the preceding half-hour. He suddenly feels very tired again.

"Just be sure you actually get some sleep first," Carmen says without looking over. She's still grinning as she starts rapidly fingering her keyboard.

"I'll try," Lex mumbles. "But I think my apartment's haunted."

fifth

23

THE PACK OF PILLS LOOKS ORDINARY AGAINST THE WOODGRAIN TOP OF THE small dining table. They seem harmless. Lex barely touches them once he's taken them out of his bag. As if merely touching the plastic bag would have an effect. He uses the fingernail of his forefinger to gently nudge the plastic baggie from one end of the table to the other, thinking carefully about what to do next.

He's been sitting at his dining table for at least an hour, having gotten to his apartment after a long, drawn-out dinner at a very busy Mexican restaurant. He'd eaten his meal as slowly as he could manage and made the waitress refill his chips basket at least three times. He has a doggie bag full of them to prove it. He's tempted to just toss it in his trash, but he decides to keep them for an early-morning snack.

He still hasn't decided if he's going to take the Ambien.

Lex rises from the dining room table, the air in the apartment damp and heavy thanks to the humidifier he's brought from his parents'. His mother had insisted, claiming that it would keep the winter static at bay. He likes the soft hissing sound it makes. The idea is that one day, when things are far more normal, he'll be able to use the sound of the humidifier to fall asleep. That time seems so far away.

In the kitchen, Lex reaches into the cabinet and pulls forward a glass. It takes a while to select one as his world has taken a hazy, underwater quality that he can't shake. Everything looks like it's moving in slow motion, every sound comes to him through a liquid that he can't see. Even smells are muted.

He thinks about sitting in the tiny restaurant during dinner, a place he'd been several times before. Usually, he walks out smelling like fried corn and spicy meats. He hadn't really noticed those aromas that evening. He doesn't notice the lingering odor of them as he stands in his kitchen.

Finally, choosing the straight-sided glass he'd acquired during a brewery tour, he pours himself some water from the tap and leans back against the sink to drink it. The apartment is well lit, so he guesses it's fatigue that causes shadows to jump and dance before his eyes. Always in the corners, constantly just beyond view. He blinks slowly, swallowing another mouthful of water. The shades follow him behind closed eyes, floating across his vision as light gray shadows. He follows them more easily, watching them hover along the sides of his sight, resting at the bottom like the blobs suspended in a lava lamp. They swim and glide only to be stirred again to rise and float in formless blobs.

He opens his eyes and the room remains still, silent. On the table, the small plastic baggie filled with white pills sits next to a large white paper bag spotted with frying oil containing leftover corn chips. He thinks about how he should've gotten some salsa to go, but the thought is fleeting.

The fatigue Lex feels is heavy, the heaviest weight he's ever carried. He feels it in his shoulders whenever he tries to lift anything heavier than a sheet of paper. He feels it at the base of his skull every time he turns his head to look at something. He feels it in his back each time he moves. It's a relentless mass that increases as time passes, making everything around him move more slowly. It makes things harder to see, the world more difficult to hear.

Emotions are not immune to the leaden weight of insomnia. One moment he feels a blazing rage that he fears will never subside. Woe be unto the poor fool that stumbles across my path and tests my patience, he would think in those moments. The next moment he feels an overwhelming shame, wishing to hide himself away from the gaze of everyone around him. There are the momentary flashes of frustration, the pops of jubilant euphoria, the lingering dread. No drug, he's certain, has ever had such a potent effect on its user.

His favorite moments have been the fits of intense focus. Times when he's able to sit silent and still, attention sharpened to a fine point, and let time whiz by unnoticed. Everything makes sense, solutions present themselves naked before him, everything he does is easy. Those moments, like all the others, never last. They pass suddenly, usually when he's flying high on the solution for something that's previously confounded him. They're replaced by the weight of complete stupidity. He nearly weeps when lightness and ease vanish. In those moments, it's as if his head is made of so much raw meat.

He skirts on the edge of that clarity while standing with a giveaway glass half-full of water and staring at the pills on his table. He wonders if they will really work, if they will allow him to slumber through anything that may happen around him. Wonders if they'll shut his ears so that he's deaf to whispers and footsteps and running water. Wrap him in a bubble so that he doesn't feel cold or heat. Force his eyes closed so that all of the shadows that move from one corner of the apartment to the other disappear.

"What do I have to lose?"

He pushes himself away from the the counter and drifts to the table, glass of water in hand. Lex is having a moment of clarity. He knows exactly what must be done and is willing to take the steps to ensure that they're done properly. He passes the table and closes all of the blinds. He then moves to the thermostat, checking that it's set for a comfortable seventy-two degrees. He checks this three times. He eyes the thin strip of light trickling in from under the front door and considers it carefully. He decides to leave it alone instead of stuffing a towel there to block the hall light.

The apartment begins to resemble a cave, small points of light coming from the small desk lamp sitting on the floor next to the futon, from the clock on the oven and the microwave, from the small night-light plugged in over the bathroom sink, reflected in the vanity mirror. It all works to cast enough light so that Lex can make his way from one side of the place to the other without jamming his shin or toe against a piece of sensible Swedish furniture.

He stands in the middle of the room and spins once, a small check to see if there's anything he's missing. He's satisfied that, if the pills do their job, everything in the apartment is in proper sleeping order.

He sits at his dining table once more, bag of pills to his right, glass of water to his left, wrinkled paper bag of tortilla chips directly in front of him. He looks from one hand to the other, from the pills to the water, building his courage to move forward with Parker's plan for a night of blissful slumber. He reaches for the pills and stops himself.

"Dammit," Lex sighs as his hand drops to the table. "How many?"

His shoulders hunch and his head dips so that his chin rests against his chest. The brief moment of clarity has passed and he feels slow and dumb. His fingers are like small cudgels extending from a hockey puck. He feels fifty years older than he is, back and legs aching for no apparent reason. The question confounds him completely and he sits silent for almost fifteen minutes. He's stirred only by the shadow of a man standing just next to the table between him and the kitchen.

He jumps and turns to see who it is. No one's there.

His heart is pounding, but the stupid, slow feeling has yet to let go. He blinks, trying to understand what he's just seen. Or what he thinks he saw. He's just imagining things. The shadow was a combination of an eyelash and the way the bathroom night light bounced off the television with the arm of the futon acting to throw another faint shadow. It was in his head. He has a difficult time fitting all of these puzzle-pieces together. His brain fumbles around with them, forcing them into the wrong spots.

He closes his eyes and they sting. He feels dizzy. Opening them again, he confirms that he's still alone, no shadows, pills and water on the table. He shakes his head.

"Damn," he whispers to the empty apartment as he turns back to his task. Lex puts great effort into really thinking about what to do next. He's forgotten what question perched on his lips before he was distracted by the shadow of nothing. He blinks slowly, feeling drunk. Worse than drunk, he feels hungover without the benefit of having been drunk or high. He drums his temples with his fingers and tries to think.

Lex decides to retrace his steps. He looks around again and notices how cozy everything seems. He's ready to try to sleep, but doesn't know what time it is. The closed blinds have robbed him of the benefit of seeing the sky and he can't quite read the clocks in the kitchen. He feels too lazy to pick up his phone and look at it.

He reestablishes where he is, at his dining room table with the bag of pills to his left, the glass of water to his right, and the bag of tortilla chips off to his far right near the edge of the table. Something about this doesn't seem quite right and Lex waits for the answer to this puzzle to come to him. He's not sure what's wrong, but he knows that things don't feel right. He questions himself. Is it the fatigue? Lack of sleep? Why am I having such a hard time thinking?

He pushes himself back from the table and looks up, stretching his neck and his back. It eases the tension, makes him feel a little better. He raises his arms over his head and laces his fingers together. That stretch makes him feel even better and he closes his eyes to let himself drift into it. The muscles in his back and neck loosen, the tension working its way out with each breath. The slight pain along his spine as his muscles relax is a relief, as brief as it is.

He's jerked from his stretch with the sound of his glass hitting the floor and breaking. He opens his eyes to see shards of glass fly from the large pool of water on the floor, pieces making their way toward the kitchen and underneath the table. On the table, the bag of pills sits just in front of him with the greasy bag of leftover tortilla chips on its side near the far edge from where he's sitting. Lex scrambles to his feet, placing his chair between him and the table. Looking around, he notices that the blinds over the windows are now open and the night-light is off in the bathroom. The cool purple light from the windows casts deep, black shadows into the corners of the room and under all of the furniture.

"Right," he mumbles to himself. He's decided it would be best to leave, take a long walk through the city, perhaps find a nice, quiet bench to sit on and rest for a while until it's time to make his way back to his apartment and get ready for the next day's work. He scans the apartment once more to locate the things he'll need. Shoes are under the futon, coat is in his closet along with a scarf and gloves. His hat is on the floor next to the table lamp beside the futon. He nods definitively, glancing for a moment at the jagged pieces of glass surrounding a splat of water on the floor and resolves to clean it up after he gets back. He doesn't think, after all, spilled water and a broken glass will go anywhere.

He steps over the spill and stoops in front of the futon to retrieve his shoes. The dumb feeling has fallen away with a newfound focus. He reaches under and comes up empty. He looks under the futon once more and the shoes have shifted to the far back near the corner of the room.

Perhaps they didn't shift, he thinks. Perhaps they were there the whole time and I just saw it wrong.

He moves over and reaches toward the back of the futon and comes up empty once more. He doesn't have very much time to be confused by this as, without warning, the cushion leaps from the futon frame and drapes itself over Lex's back.

24

LEX REMAINS STILL UNDER THE WEIGHT OF THE FUTON CUSHION FOR A VERY long time. He's waiting for something else to happen, something else to leap at him without warning. He waits for the next sound to be the footsteps of someone walking around his apartment, looking for something else to make mischief. He hears nothing, sees nothing. His nostrils are filled with the slightly chemical artificial smell of the foam from his mattress. It's both comforting and a little nauseating.

Finally, he pushes himself up, brushing the mattress from his back as he does. The room has darkened, as if all the lights had been snuffed out. He glanced quickly to the kitchen to see if the faithful little clocks on his appliances were still visible through the darkness. There was nothing. He could barely make out the shapes of his refrigerator and the stove and the cabinets in the absolute black. Blinking doesn't make it better. Each time he opens his eyes, total darkness.

He feels his way around his immediate area hoping to somehow gain his bearings. He's lost his place in his apartment, being under the mattress for what's felt like an hour. He swears that the room has spun while he was weighted down, pressed against his hardwood floor. An arm sweeps ahead, the other arm propping him up so that he doesn't feel so utterly helpless. Where the futon frame should have been, Lex encounters nothing. He flails around just in front and still comes up empty.

It's disorienting how dark the apartment has become. It's a small room, but it's easy to get lost when all the lights are out and the blinds are closed. The place usually doesn't get so dark until deep into the night, even then the ambient light from the city outside finds a way to cast a faint glimmer into the apartment through the gaps in the blinds. He looks for the windows, for the glow around the blinds and can't see it. Can't see the futon frame that should be right in front of him. Can't see the bookshelves that split the room into functioning chambers. All he feels is the cold wood floor, all he hears is the sound of his palm sweeping across that floor searching for a familiar landmark.

Lex sits back on his heels and pivots his head from one side to the other. For a moment he thinks he still has his eyes closed. He tries blinking, hoping to reopen them and fix the stubborn dark. When that doesn't work, he raises his hands to try and pry open his eyelids. His eyes are open. The dark silhouette of the kitchen remains steady where he knows it should be. It's the only feature in the otherwise flat, black landscape.

With his hands held before him, Lex stands and starts to move to the kitchen. It's a voyage that should only take a couple of seconds, a trip of just under a half-dozen steps. He takes a deep breath to relax. Four or five steps into his journey and the shadow is not getting any closer.

It's not a large apartment. It's difficult to lose things within its cozy confines. Lex is familiar with how long it takes to get from one spot to the other. From the Futon to the kitchen is about five short steps. He can shuffle and make them last a little longer when he wants. To the closet is about the same number of steps, perhaps a little further. The kitchen is definitely six paces away from the divider bookshelf in the middle of the room. He's challenged himself when bored to see if he can make the trip in only four, but the steps become comically broad and impractical. This causes him to take for granted that the trip is six steps. Seven if he's being lazy.

The longest distance he's ever recorded is the fifteen paces he takes between the front door and the toilet. It's usually a very hurried set of steps, driven by the need to empty a full bladder.

He's thirteen steps from where he'd started after being smothered by the futon mattress to the shadow of the kitchen and he still hasn't reached it. He slows, confused. His diminutive apartment seems to have grown, stretched improbably in the oppressive darkness. He looks back, hoping to see the bulky form of the mattress slumped on the floor where he'd pushed it from his back. Perhaps he could catch a glimpse of the shadow of the futon frame or of his bookcase. Nothing stood out of the darkness. Even the windows, the three large, square windows that should have been directly in his line of sight were hidden by the shroud of inky black.

Lex should be standing in the kitchen. He should be pressed against the counter between the sink and the stove. The disorientation is acute and he begins to feel dizzy, vertigo pulling the dark around him like taffy. He looks again at the shadow kitchen, still steps away, still the only thing he can see in the dark.

Suddenly, there's a drip from the faucet in the kitchen. A large, forceful plop that echoes across the apartment. It rings in his ears strangely, a loud whisper that's pitched too high. He hears the drip of the water as if from underneath the surface of a deep pool. He leans forward, trying to make out what is different about that sound. It drips again, louder and closer. The drops of water start to fall more quickly, one immediately after the other.

The shadow of the kitchen fades away as a sudden wave of fog overtakes it. Lex is left standing, dumb, in what he assumes is the middle of his apartment. The dripping water from the kitchen faucet grows more earnest, more aggressive. It sounds as if there are three faucets dripping into the same deep pool. Then ten. Then a hundred, all slightly out of sync with each other. The rush of water comes overwhelming with each drop becoming indistinguishable from all the others.

It sounds like a waterfall, all of the drops from all of the faucets hitting the sink at once. The waterfall grows in intensity and Lex swears he can feel the mist rolling off of it. A cool breeze carries a fine spray of water across his bare arms and onto his face. It's a wonder the apartment isn't flooded and he hopes someone downstairs will call the super or the public utilities, get the water shut off before it floods the entire building. He waits for the trickle of water overflowing the sink to reach his bare toes.

The water never comes though the cascade, seemingly just in front of him, is getting louder. A faint undertone of sulfur drifts through the cool breeze. The white noise surrounds him, echoing off of the walls and ceilings and floors. Mirrored by an identical sound originating from behind the bathroom door. It's reverberating through Lex's skull and he tries to shut it out, hands on either side of his head pressing his ears against his scalp. It doesn't work and the rushing, falling water grows louder. The world is filled with it, becomes the very substance everything is made of. He feels as if he's drowning even though he's not. The unseen waterfall has almost convinced him that he's been shoved under water, that his lungs are lying to him.

Lex gasps, eyes open as wide as he can manage. He turns, or thinks he turns, to the windows. His arms are splayed open before him to warn him before careening face-first into a wall. Or a door. Or the windows. He tries to stretch his senses, tries to hear beyond the water falling all around him, tries to see through the darkness in which he's enveloped. He coughs and it sounds distant to his ears, like someone else is coughing through the walls.

An image leaps to his mind of a man thrown overboard at midnight in the middle of the ocean. He treads water in the inky black, not certain which direction is which. The sky betrays him, stars hidden behind dark storm clouds. There are no lights anywhere, nothing making a sound except his body against the surface.

Not being able to tell the immediate surroundings from the distant horizon. Flailing, trying not to sink, hoping to drift to shore before time and fatigue overtakes him.

Lex feels exhausted, wandering across his small apartment that has suddenly become so vast. The constant sound of water falling all around him has caused him to doubt his senses. He feels as if he's lost his hearing to an endless drone of white noise. He's certain his ears are bleeding.

He pushes forward for what feels like hours. His legs feel like they've become liquid, like they want to join the vast pools the waterfalls are pounding into. He wants to rest but fears death waits unless he can find the island of his futon. He needs to press to the limits of the apartment that he knows are there.

A thought flashes that he must be hallucinating. That the contact with the pills combined with total fatigue have joined forces to assault his sanity. He tries to remember if he'd actually taken the Ambien, if what he's seeing and hearing is just a part of a nightmare in paralysis driven by the drug. There's no way to check, no way to know for certain.

He keeps moving.

His hand brushes against a cool, hard surface. He turns to his left and brings his other hand around to verify. He feels along the shape of an outside corner that he hopes is the wall that leads to his bathroom. He chooses a side, the one to his right, and begins to feel along the wall in search of the door. He's blind, working his way along the wall by touch. He tries to imagine where he is based on the number of steps he takes and how much of the surface passes beneath his finger tips.

By what he knows about his apartment, the distance between the kitchen and the bathroom door should be less than two steps. He can usually make it to the bathroom door from his kitchen in one giant stride, pivoting to round the corner toward the toilet. The distance he experiences with all of his senses otherwise occupied is far more vast. It feels more like a long, cold corridor than a quick turn to an adjacent door.

Finally, his hands run into the wood trim framing the door to his bathroom. He fumbles about, searching the surface of the door for the doorknob. He finds it with his right hand just where it should be, about hip height. The small victory causes a faint wave of relief. He grasps the knob, turns, and pushes open the door to his bathroom, hoping to escape the suddenly vast expanse of the waterfall-possessed apartment.

The sound of the water falling grows to an angry growl.

He's greeted by a spray of fine mist in his eyes. The water is salty and warm and smells like iron. A hand reaches up and wipes his eyes clear leaving a fine, tight layer of rime. No matter how much he blinks, the feeling will not go away.

The fine spray will not cease.

He can't seem to clear his eyes. There's always a fine film where he wipes. The liquid is thick and sticky. It somehow makes the the darkness deeper. Lex wonders if he's sweating, if the remaining film on his face is the result of the water from the falls mixing with his own perspiration to create a sort of paste keeping his eyes from opening. He blinks and feels his eyelashes cling to each other, his eyelids struggle to peel themselves apart.

Suddenly, the water stops falling. There isn't a stray drop, a lingering plop or reassuring slosh of liquid. The tap to the vast Niagara filling the small apartment has been turned off and the water obeys without further complaint. The most obedient of servants in response to some almighty request for silence.

That silence fills the room far more than the continuous din could. Lex's ears ring with the memory of being flooded with the most painful of white noises. Silence and the high-pitched whine of a frequency dying, leaking away from his auditory nerves. The silent room pitches about, a dry ocean to float in.

One final, earnest effort finds Lex wiping his eyes with the heel of his palm, pushing in to get the most liquid he can manage. He blinks, opens his eyes, and blinks again. He can see. The bathroom is flooded with light, almost blinding. He doesn't remember flipping all of the light switches, but the vanity and overhead lights are pushing out massive volumes of stark white illumination. He can't move. The sudden restoration of sight is shocking enough. When pared with the onset of silence, the world takes on a hazy, dreamlike quality.

Add to that the sight of blood covering every surface of the bathroom, and the desire to leave is only magnified.

25

The bathroom as Lex remembers it is white. White tiles with dark grout and a light gray ceramic tile floor. The walls of the bathroom have a tidy black and white tile accent border at around elbow height. The toilet could almost get lost in all of that white, the bathtub adding its own weighty block of white porcelain to the scene. On a good day, it's as pristine a place as one could find, the shiny surfaces of the polished porcelains glistening in the incandescent light. It's a sterile and forgiving sanctuary, key to any place that a person would want to call home.

The room that has revealed itself to Lex is not that place.

The prevailing color of the room is red. The texture is wet, sticky, glossy. The air is thick and smells like iron with an undertone of rotting meat. Chunks of a deep red, almost black, flow slowly down the walls in rivulets of a lighter crimson. Every vertical surface is covered and oozing. Every horizontal one is coated in bulbous layers that build by the moment. It creeps forward toward the door, toward Lex.

He retches then catches himself. He can see his reflection through the scarlet glazing over the mirror, distorted and macabre. The red-tinged lights show he's covered in a fine spray of it, head to foot. He fights looking down at his hands or at his clothing for fear that what he's seeing is true. He retches again and is able to resist, staring at the blood-coated toilet and the amount of the burgundy liquid lining the floor between him and it.

The light flickers, sending red and black and purple shadows pulsing across the bathroom. He hears a faint buzzing and popping as the lights fade, fail, then flair. The darkness is absolute, the light is blinding and harsh. Under the buzz, there's a rasping that sounds like breathing. It's jagged and rapid, gasping and spastic. A moan rattles the air of the entire apartment as the breath is expelled. Someone is exerting a great deal of effort in pushing air from their lungs.

Lex is frozen. He doesn't want to move for fear of seeing how much blood surrounds him. He fears it's crept across the rest of the apartment, that as soon as he turns he'll see all of his belongings coated in it. Dripping with the stuff. He can sense it behind him. His heart pounds inside his chest, causing the ringing in his ears to fade in, fade out. It almost drowns the faint dripping sound coming from behind his bloody shower curtain.

The lights flicker once more, strobing between blinding red and white and inky black. The popping grows, accompanied by a buzz that sounds like a large, angry hornet. The buzz lingers over, the pops add emphasis and the lights blink out on the macabre scene. Lex expects to be plunged into absolute darkness once more. He's steeled himself for whatever's next. The dark is quickly replaced by a hazy, greenish-purple glow.

He dares a look around. Carefully. He turns very slowly so that he doesn't catch a glimpse of himself, fearing that he's still covered in the fine splatter from the blood-mist. Part of him screams that he shouldn't turn his back on the bathroom. That small part fears what the room has become, an impromptu unkempt abattoir, will yank at him violently, thus ending his story once and for all. That tiny, fearful voice begs him not to ignore what might be behind the closed shower curtain.

He quiets the voice with a grind of his molars, the throbbing and ringing in his ears taking care of the rest. Once Lex stands fully in the bathroom doorway facing into the apartment, he sees a weak, greenish purple light and is puzzled. Enough so that his feet unstick themselves from the bathroom floor, their soles peeling away from the sticky substance beneath them. He ignores it and takes two steps into the main room.

The entire space seems restored, the shadowy forms of his furnishings and belongings apparently in their places. The large lumpen form of the mattress still lies beside the frame like a dead body. A small shock ripples across Lex's tongue before he remembers what it truly is. The cool, weak light dribbles from behind the blinds. It feels uncertain of itself. It doesn't go far on its own and bounces languidly off of the white walls, the polished wood floors.

There is a faint popping sound as the soles of his feet are peeled from the floor. A thin film of something persists around the edges of his toes. His heel rolls, then drags across the hardwoods as he eases from the bathroom door, head panning to both sides while he scans as much of the room as he dares.

Not a lot of light, but enough to see shapes.

His nose stings, holding tight to the odor of iron and flesh and something tinged with sulphur. The ringing and throbbing in his ears has eased, allowing him to focus on the faint crackle of his footsteps across the floors. Theres a subtle tick hiding in the background, the sound of metal cooling or wood adjusting to a change in humidity.

Lex blinks and his eyelids fight to part ways. He blinks again and can feel the crust forming in the corners of his eyes near the bridge of his nose. There's an urge to wipe it away, to dig his palms into his eyeballs and clear the gunk. He hesitates, then does nothing, afraid that he will only make it worse. That he will only add the slime from his hands to the slime on his face.

He's unsure if there is slime on his hands. He hasn't had the courage to check. Everything feels like it's been smeared in grease and mud, but he begins to wonder if it's all in his mind.

Staring at the futon frame a few feet away, he wonders what caused the mattress to pounce on him. He tries to remember why he was on the floor in the first place, sprawled on all fours in front of the sofa. It was something urgent, something that he desperately needed to do. The urgency of the moment has departed, replaced by a dread that has resigned to never be resolved. It isn't helped by the faint ringing, fading slowly with each passing moment. It's somehow made worse by the strange light rippling across the apartment. It isn't quite moonlight, isn't quite street light. It's the light the night gives off when it has filled itself with secrets and begs to keep no more. It's the glow cast into the air by foul deeds long forgotten. Filled with the unease of things left behind.

He continues to stare at the empty frame, rigged to hold itself upright. The dark forms underneath in the far corner near the wall resemble shoes that have been placed neatly, carefully. Something about shoes. He leans in, trying to remember why shoes are so important. He understands he's barefoot, that his feet are still sticking to the floors. He's puzzled, caught in a limbo of craving more information and fearing the very information he craves. Why will he not look at his own body? Why is he afraid of the sticky substance he's absolutely convinced coats every square inch of him? Why are his shoes so important?

Something moves off to his right, something large and fast. He turns his head, looking into his kitchen to catch sight of the thing in his periphery. The space is empty, forms of his kitchen appliances resting in the shadows. Something else darts through the edges of his vision, making its way behind him. He spins again, glimpsing the rest of the apartment as it's bathed in shadow. He sees nothing. The open door of the bathroom whizzes by, then the closed door of his closet, and back around to the empty frame of his futon, mattress lying crumpled at its feet.

Shoes still in the far corner, next to the wall. Waiting patiently.

Ringing has faded in his ears, far in the distance behind the flat whistle of his breath through his nostrils. The breath sounds out of control, wild. He can feel his heart pounding in his chest, the veins pulsing in his neck causing him to flinch with every thrum. He's frightened, but neither fight nor flight feel like options. He can move, but not quickly and not far. He feels constrained by sheer stupidity. He's unable to reason what is happening or what to do next. His mind goes back to his shoes, waiting under the futon frame. He forces himself to ignore another shadow, racing past toward the front door.

His mind jumps to what Parker would do if he saw Lex standing there, dumb and inept. "Fuck you and your goddamned lame ass," he would yell between sips of something with the aroma of turpentine. He hears the voice in his mind, closes his eyes to focus on it. "Why aren't you going anywhere, you pussy? You got two choices from. You can either get the fuck out of there and go somewhere, snuggle up to someone soft and forget the rest of the world exists or you can tell whatever poltergeist motherfucker that has its claws wrapped around your dick to get the fuck out of your house and leave you the fuck alone. Then you go and find you someone nice and soft to bring back to your place and make your self-imposed isolation worth something."

There's some truth to what his mental image of Parker says. He needs to do something. Lex feels he needs to let go of whatever it was he's trying to recall and move on. He shakes out some cobwebs and opens his eyes. Shoes still nestled in the corner of the room. They would stay there. He would leave and go somewhere safe. Somewhere he could rest and recover. Someplace to hole up while he worked out how to leave the apartment for good. He would come back in force, with several people or perhaps some movers and get all of his stuff. He would figure it all out later. He needed to make the move to exit, make the move to end the torment.

Lex immediately forgets this plan, startled as he is by the sudden flood of loud screaming issuing from behind his closet door.

26

THERE ARE FIVE THINGS LEX KNOWS ABOUT HIS APARTMENT. THE FIRST IS that it's tiny. Weighing in at only four-hundred fifty-two square feet, it was the most he could afford given his spotty employment record. Typically, landlords in the city like to see a long line of work where the applicant has steadily increased their income. This means that not only did Lex need to talk his way into convincing the building's owner that he was reliably employed, he needed to lie about the reasons his work history failed to reflect this fact on paper. He recalls spinning a tale that somehow ended with his rescuing a toddler from atop a telephone pole in rural Namibia in the midst of a little-known war four months prior. The details, as far as he's concerned, are inconsequential.

The second thing he knows is that the building, at one point in its history, was used as a boarding house for men who, for whatever reason, couldn't get into housing elsewhere. These were men with checkered pasts, men without families willing to take them in, men who, were it up to the wealthier citizens of the day, would be laboring gratis in the advancement of society. There were never stories or reports of anything foul happening inside the building during those days. No tales of missing call girls or nefarious drug rings being operated from within the halls. It was difficult, however, to find records of the men leaving, advancing to better places after their time was done, after they'd supposedly gotten back onto their feet. Then again, Lex had only done a cursory amount of research, an afternoon spent in a library while he built up the courage to return home.

Third thing is that it took the current owners of the building a very, very long time to renovate the property to ready it for its modern batch of tenants. It struck

Lex as odd that, given the redevelopment momentum in that part of town, the renovation of this building was unusually slow. It's been covered rather broadly in all of the local redevelopment blogs. Local students calling themselves podcasters followed the progress of the area greedily, asking quite loudly "what's up with that building on Eighteenth near Lawrence?" It's the type of question that Lex, while still finishing school with hopes of changing the world someday, found himself asking his peers just before getting high on some quality weed.

The building eventually wrapped renovations quietly. The owners seemed to want to dampen some controversy they'd stirred by cladding over the elaborate red stone facade with vast sheets of faux gray marble. They called it an acquiescence to market forces. Critics call it shit.

Fourth, Lex knows he forks out far too much for the amount of space he's been given. He wonders how much above "market rate" he pays, then stops wondering out of sheer depression. He can't bear to think that he's getting cheated in a building that no one in their right mind would live. Then he remembers all of the mailboxes have names pasted to their fronts and figures that he's lucky to have a place in such a hip, cool neighborhood at all.

He knows that Barnes' Alley isn't as cool, hip, and transitional as everyone would like to pretend. Odd word, transitional. It's filled with promises that may not be kept. He knows the area's ultimate success hangs on a razor's edge and that anything, a string of violent crimes, a sudden fluctuation of the market, the discovery that one of the marquee buildings is possessed by demons, would throw values in that block and others into a severe tailspin.

Leading to the fifth thing he knows about his apartment. It's something that he's confirmed though he'd suspected it from the moment he tossed his backpack into the corner after getting his keys. He knows that his apartment, possibly the entire building is, perhaps, possessed by malevolent etherial spirits. Headcount pending.

The myriad of screams issuing from behind his closet door only serves to reinforce this hypothesis. It's something he can point to and say, "hey, here's evidence that my place is bona fide, one-hundred percent possessed of some sort of malevolent spirit." He finds it comforting considering his circumstances.

He looks around the shadowy twilight illuminating the apartment in search of a confirmation. Disappointment finds that he's completely alone. He wonders what comfort he would find with a cohort, someone to compare notes with. Someone to confirm that he's having a very fucking weird night. Then there are the shadowy figures darting in and out of his periphery. As his remaining focus shifts, another glides past from the kitchen moving toward the windows. He half-waves at it as it passes, resigned to the idea that he's only scratched the surface of understanding that he involuntarily shares his home with something.

The screams themselves are terrifying. There are multiple voices, all at different pitches. They all sound like they're in agony, tortured by something that has touched them to the very core of what defines pain. The screams are breathless, no pauses taken after the lungs have emptied. They are continuous, agonizing.

Lex's breath quickens as he stands mute while the sound of the screams behind the door fill the room. They initially hit him with the force of a child's sneeze. That force grows until it begins to feel like he's standing at the edges of a hurricane. All the air in the apartment moves past him, sucked toward the closet door. Toward the screaming voices.

At least they've drowned out the persistent ringing in his ears. He thinks that's the only good to come from uninterrupted, tortured screams pushing into the apartment. After almost a minute of bathing in the shower of sound blowing across his face, he's certain he'd prefer the ringing.

After five minutes of standing frozen, five minutes of screams filling the corners of his auditory landscape, five minutes of not being able to catch his breath, Lex stumbles backward. The sound is making its way into his memories somehow. He's beginning to have trouble remembering a time without a chorus of tortured screams flooding his senses. All of his senses. He can taste the torture, smell the pain drifting from behind the door. He can almost feel pinpricks across every inch of his skin. He fights the urge to join the screams. He even checks himself, his hand drifts under his jaw to check that it's not open, that he's not screaming in tune to the chorus.

He shuffles away from the closet out of instinct. Every fiber of his being tells him he needs to escape. He knows he's next. The dread is palpable and he can taste the bitter bile coating his tongue. He fights off the building sick, but that only adds to the pain that's been filling his lungs. The grinding he hears behind the screaming is quickly explained by the sudden taste of blood in his mouth. Lex tries to stop grinding his teeth.

One more step away from the closet door, another step in trying to escape the madness somehow contained within and Lex stumbles backward over the corner of the mattress he'd forgotten was crumbled on the floor. He barely misses hitting his head on the corner of the futon armrest and slams his back fully against the window ledge. The room brightens briefly as the pain flashes along his spine. His head whips back and taps the blinds, causing them to shudder and sway. It doesn't change the quality of light in the room, only works to prove to him that the light is something else, its own thing that doesn't need a source.

He lands awkwardly on his tail bone, his palms taking the brunt of his weight. The pain that shoots up his wrists joins the throbbing sensation pulsing from his spine. Together, they begin to approach the sheer agony behind the voices screaming from within his closet. Lex is winded. He sees spots of bright yellow among the pale blue-green shadows of the apartment, dancing and swimming through the air like sea creatures adrift after a storm.

They also remind him of the little embers that would drift from bonfires during boy scout camp, tiny motes of dying ash drifting on the updraft. He smiles a little through the pain, the remainder of sanity he'd been holding surrendering to the wanderings of a mind submerged in nothing but pain. He wonders where the fire is and if whoever set it brought marshmallows. The blinds tap him on the back of the head to make him snap out of his delirium.

Lex does a quick check, wiggling his toes and fingers. After that succeeds, he winces as he tries to push himself up onto his feet, his palms and wrists burning a little from the effort. Everything he moves hurts and the voices behind the closet door pitch upward as if to punctuate the pain. Lex nearly stumbles, his elbow buckling underneath him as he is finally able to move himself around, resting himself on all fours. The shadows deepen briefly and he wonders if it's a sign he's about to pass out. He squeezes his eyes closed and lets a wave of dizziness pass through him before opening them again.

There's a moment, resting on his hands and knees, that Lex realizes how ridiculous he must look. How, if observed from the kitchen, he would appear to be an insane primate, grimacing, prone on the floor next to a bare futon frame, the mattress folded haphazardly on the floor before him. It's a scene out of the worst surreal comedy he could imagine. Were he not living in it, he would probably walk away from his own performance thinking it too high-concept for his tastes.

The idea punches through the spreading madness. It's the only thing, he realizes, that will save him from the final collapse of his already fragile mind. He knows he needs to find some way out of the apartment. The volume of the screams increases in approval. He closes his eyes, feeling that they would be no use in trying to find his way out. They've betrayed him once already and he needs to eliminate the possibility of being fooled again.

Shoes. That's the thought that punches him directly in the forehead. He'd been on the ground, feeling about underneath the sofa for his shoes. Shoes that had somehow found themselves in the far corner. He feels the bulk of his current issues started with the need to get the shoes and debates if it's worth the possibility of deepening his woes by going for them again. After a very brief consideration, he decides to leave them. Perhaps it was that the tone of the screams pitched higher still.

He couldn't hear his own voice inside his head telling him to move. Screaming, actually, which he finds oddly appropriate. Screaming over the screams, one voice trying to drown out a tortured chorus. He would laugh, but would probably not hear that, either.

The pressure of the dense air, the sound making it heavier, makes Lex's limbs feel like they're carrying a ton. He goes to push himself upright from his crawl and can't seem to manage the leverage. He tries several times, failing to make it past his knees. Arms shaking, thighs burning, and back tensing from soreness, he decides that he must crawl his way out. If the increased gravity allows it. He pants and groans, trying one final time to stand only to be pushed back onto all fours, winded and aching.

He wonders if opening his eyes will help. If the addition of sight will help increase his strength. Feeling completely ridiculous, he opens his eyes to the gray-green shadow world of his apartment. He sees something dart just behind him as his eyes adjust to the room. He ignores it. His sanity can only take one blow at a time and keeping the screams from melting him like an ice cream cone is taking every ounce of his focus. He's staring at the futon mattress directly in front of him and reaches a hand out to use it for leverage. Something in the back of his mind screams to use the frame instead of the cushion, but the voice is drowned out by the sound issuing from the closet.

He scoots himself forward just slightly and places his palm on one of the larger folds in front of him. Eyes open, help from the mattress, he makes a last-ditch effort to hoist himself to vertical. He gets as far as bringing his knee up to his chest before, exhausted and with a shooting pain running through his shoulder, he resigns, falling face-first into the cushion. His legs lose all resolution and splay behind him causing his ankle to contact the leg of the frame squarely.

He's sure he screams out in pain, the wooden frame slamming into his ankle at the joint. He's quite certain that it was a loud scream, full of the agony and frustration of the night's proceedings. He's not sure, however, because its being overwhelmed by the other sounds in the apartment, the sounds that are forming a mass that keeps him close to the floor.

He feels the rough texture of the uncovered mattress on his cheek and in the palms of his hands. He's beginning to think that he's going to die there on that spot, sprawled spread-eagle on the futon cushion. It's not a picture he likes. He imagines someone coming to the door, perhaps Merle in his manic impulsiveness, banging on the door once too many times causing it to fly open accompanied by the metal splinters of a hinge that had just given up. Merle would gasp in horror, seeing poor Lex prone on his futon mattress, his shoes in the far corner of the room. He would turn around and run screaming from the room, banging on other doors, knocking them in with his bear-like strength.

That would be in Lex's obituary, found by a concerned neighbor, collapsed on the floor of his apartment with the imprint of the mattress's fabric deeply engrained on his face.

He shakes off the image, still trying to work out how he's going to make his way across his own floor with all of the added gravity. Crawling is his best option, but he still doesn't like it. He supposes he'll be able to make it to the door, stand using the door frame as support, then make his way haltingly to get help. Or to find a place to sleep. Or perhaps a place to simply disappear. He hasn't thought that far ahead. First, he wants to get away from the oppressive noise now wrapping jagged claws around his mind.

First the left hand, then the right and he pushes himself up onto his knees, hands planted on the mattress. The shadows in the apartment have taken a deeper hue, have become more abrupt. They're the paintings of shadows as described by a child. The faint blue-green light interrupted suddenly by a thick line of absolute black. He can see a path to the door, beyond the mattress, beyond the bookcase. He can shuffle past the kitchen in a direct line, reducing the agony he'll feel fighting the heavy air of the apartment.

Left hand moves, then right hand, right knee then left.

He begins a shuffling crawl, ignoring the twinge in his hips and the pinch of pain shuffling up his spine. His shoulders feel weak, like he can barely keep his own torso aloft. He wills himself forward, anyway. Tries to ignore the shaking of his limbs, allowing the ceaseless cries to do part of that work. He focuses on the ground directly below him, the woodgrain behind a layer of polish on the floors. He's barely able to lift his hands, barely able to gain enough height at his knees to pull them forward. His breaths are shallow and thin, pinched at the back of his throat as if a hand were there.

Left hand, right knee. Right hand, left knee.

He feels the tops of his toes drag along the floor past the mattress. He's getting closer to the kitchen and turns his head to spot the TV stand. He's like a tortoise pulling his heavy body along, scanning from side to side for obstacles that may slow him further. Tortoises have the advantage, however, of hiding in a shell should something go wrong. There's no place to hide, no place to ride out any added blows. Teeth clinched and face set to a grimace, he pulls himself along with agonizing effort. The weight of the air on his back seems to grow with each hard-earned inch. It's getting more difficult to keep his head up, to keep scanning his path.

Right hand, left knee.

He is keenly aware of the seams in the floorboards in his knees and on his feet. The smell of sulphur is easing but he fears he's simply beginning to become accustomed to it. He thrusts his hips forward to try and gain more distance with each crawl. He doesn't look up, but feels he's close to his dining table. This means he's close to the door. He's close to getting out. He lifts his left hand and stretches it forward, balanced on his right palm. Fireworks of pain explode across his eyes as his left hand comes down on a jagged shard of glass.

27

Lex collapses to his side, pulling his right hand into his chest. His chest hits the floor at an odd angle, freeing what little breath he still holds in his lungs. His hip lands with a thud, sending bolts of red-yellow pain up and down his spine. His toes go numb for a few seconds. A thought flashes briefly in the remaining space that says he's just broken something and will never be able to walk again. It's a fleeting thought that fades as all of the agony returns to his feet and hands and back.

The apartment looks like a different place on his side. He loses track of where he's supposed to be for a moment. The air is a little less heavy while he lies so close to the floor. There's no force pressing down, forcing his body into the creases between the boards. He wonders if he could just stay there, simply rest and let his body heal. The throb in his palm gives him the answer he needs.

Out of the corner of his eye, he can see the small pool of liquid forming beneath where his hand landed, just below his chest. The puddle glistens just slightly. He wonders if he's hallucinating, if the combination of blood loss and mind-erasing screams have finally worked to confound his remaining senses. He doubts that all of the pain is real. He's unsure if there really is a large shard of glass, slightly curved, jabbed into his palm. Looking down at it, the first time he's looked at himself since leaving the red-smeared bathroom, he sees the jagged fragment protruding like the dorsal fin of a shark.

"Fucking glass," Lex mumbles as he lifts his hand toward his face. He wonders how much of the glistening liquid he sees on the floor and on his palm is blood and how much is the water he'd been trying to drink earlier.

As abruptly as they'd begun, the screaming stops. The apartment is silent once more. A blood sacrifice has been offered and accepted. The ringing in Lex's ears, however, has returned with renewed vigor. It's taken a slightly different tone and feels like it resides as much in his sinuses as it does in his ears. He fights the urge to bang the side of his head with his pierced hand.

Instead, he freezes, unsure of what to do next. He's again forgotten where he was going, why he's sitting on his floor in the dark. Ears are ringing painfully and he fears that he's permanently lost a lot of his hearing in the past couple of hours. He's not sure if he'll ever be able to appreciate music the same way again.

The apartment gets darker somehow. The cold shadows are getting colder and deeper and are spreading. He feels the air lighten around him, no longer pressing against his back and shoulders. They're pushing themselves out of the corners and from under things, no longer kept at bay by the chorus of screams. They're fingers reaching toward him from across the void. It's fascinating, the way shadows can play across shadows, moving without the apparent movement of a light source. He's caught mesmerized for a little while, watching shadows chase each other from the edges, joining and separating like ink spreading through molasses.

Lex finds himself turning and sitting up. He's sure that there will be a very ugly bruise forming on his legs and hips and shoulder. He wonders if he still has blood on his face, splatter over the rest of his body. He wonders if the blood streaming around the shard of glass in his hand has started to congeal. None of this matters at the moment as he's become rapt by the slow, steady, balletic movements of the dark. He makes it as far as sitting upright, his spine curled so that his shoulders sit suspended above his hips. He stares ahead, the faint whistle of his breathing breaking the steady tweet of failing auditory nerves.

He has, at least, remembered not to rest his left palm on the floor.

A strange curiosity creeps through his mind. Now that the air has lost its density, now that the sounds of screaming has abated, he wonders where it really came from. He tears his attention away from the shadows, joining and separating slowly, and regards the closed closet door. In the shadows, it looks like a kind of portal into some deep place meant for horrors. The only way he can really tell it's still closed is that he can still make out the doorknob. It's the shiniest thing in that area. So shiny that it glistens, like the pool of blood which is forming beneath his punctured hand. He stares and thinks about reaching for it, about opening the door to investigate.

None of what's happening seems real.

He finds himself on his feet. One moment he's sitting, hunched, staring at his closet door. The vantage point has become familiar and he feels a little safe on the floor at a distance. The very next moment, after a blink, he's on his feet, swaying like a branch in a light breeze. He's keenly aware of his feet beneath him, bare and aching from where they've scraped the floor. Both ankles sore, both knees weak, both hips feeling like they're out of joint. He looks down at his hand and sees the blood pouring from the gash over the glistening sharp shard. He reaches over and pulls out the glass, clinching his left hand into a fist to stop the blood that's been dripping into a pool by his left foot. He feels a little dizzy but ignores it.

He checks around his feet, making sure that none of the glass has migrated to where he needs to step. There's a clear path through shadow, past the mattress and futon frame to the gaping dark of the closet door. The gravity is also normal, nothing pressing down upon him to prevent him from moving. He can look up to the ceiling which is darker than it should be.

The shadows seem to have taken dominion overhead.

Lex looks again at the closet door, blinks, and is standing before it. Startled, he checks around. The spot he'd been occupying is marked by a small pool of blood, glinting weakly on the twilit floor. His wounded hand is still clinched at his side. There's no trail of blood, at least not one that stands out in the semi-dark. Another small pool of blood has begun to form at his feet just before the closet. Shadows pull themselves and sway, some darting across the walls in a fast twitch, others languidly creeping along the seams of the wood floor.

Lex's head is pounding. The fear is getting to him. The constant reminder of all he's heard is the steady high tone in his ears. The reminder of his encounters lives in the discomfort and agony of limbs and a body that has been badly bruised. He's not sure if he's dreaming and wonders if pain is any indication that he's awake. There are stories he's been told, articles read, movies absently consumed that tell him all about how the sensation of pain immediately jolts one from their slumber, no matter how deep. His world has become so strange, the movements of everything around him including time doesn't conform to what he's known to be normal.

The closet door is dark and silent. In the full light of day, it's an old-style panel door painted white. It's not heavy, which means it's new and not very expensive. The knob is a silvery metal with manufactured swirls to give the appearance of quality and craftsmanship. Very much in keeping with the idea that the building owners want to give their tenants the trappings of authentic antiquity, without laying forth the costs of the genuine article.

Standing inches away from it in the shadows, he can see the panel details built into the door. The doorknob still glints weakly. All of these features, however, seem to have been dipped in pure shadow. There's no sign that the door is white, but the trim still stands out in faint contrast, taking on the cool color of what little light he sees.

He takes a step back, careful not to trip over the arm of the futon frame as he does so. He edges right up to it, feeling it with the backs of his knees. His eyes dart back and forth between the closet door and the bathroom door adjacent to it. Around his peripheral view, he sees the shadow fingers flexing and crawling and darting across the walls. Those fingers dart over and around the bathroom door, providing a little contrast to its white surface. The closet door, with its void-like appearance, devours all of the shadows that try to pass.

"The light's playing weird tricks," he thinks to himself while staring at the door. It seems hazy around the edges and he's having trouble focusing on the details. He finishes taking in the dim-lit scene, white door to the left, black door to the right. Both are shut, both basking in the shadow light. He sighs and takes a step forward taking his place directly before the black door.

Proximity doesn't help bring the door into sharper focus. He grasps the doorknob and leans toward the door, straining through the ringing to hear what may be on the other side. He edges closer, placing his damaged hand on the shadow-colored surface. It seems to rise slightly to meet his fingertips.

It's warm to the touch. Warm and soft like flesh.

He brings his face closer to the surface of the closet door. He hears a slight hum. There's energy here, another mystery to add to the growing list. Closer still and he can hear something beyond the hum. It's faint and distant, fading in and out. He leans closer, ear nearly touching the warm surface.

The door feels like its responding to his presence. As if it's almost leaning toward him. He could swear the door is breathing. He can feel puffs of air from underneath the door on his toes. A moisture hangs in the air accompanied by the smell of musk. Lex loses himself in it and closes his eyes, leaning ever closer to the door. The sound of a heartbeat in the distance seems to match his own. The sound of breathing blends with the soft thumps. Underneath all of this, somehow distinguishing itself, are faint whispering voices. Lex touches his ear to the door. It responds in a soft caress along his cheek. His breathing matches the nearly imperceptible rise and fall of the door's surface. The room gets darker.

The whispers aren't urgent. They're muffled as if the speakers were far away, across another room on the other side of the door. It reminds Lex of listening at his own bedroom door when he was a child, while his parents threw parties with their friends on the first floor. They would assume that he'd gone to bed, that he was sound asleep tucked tight under his race car bed sheets. His mother would always say goodnight, always kiss him on the forehead as if she were saying farewell. She would slip out, watching him the entire time and close the door behind her, smiling in the backlight. Little boy Lex would wait, watching shadows pass beneath his bedroom door for a while. Then guests would arrive, each one ringing the doorbell, each one being greeted by the high-pitched laugh of his mother. Joy filled the house, wafting up from the downstairs living spaces and packing the second-floor hallway with a communal energy. The energy of family. It refilled a house that didn't generate that energy on its own. It was intoxicating, the flood of love coming from the people arriving at the house to visit with his parents on whatever joyous occasion they were celebrating.

Lex would climb out of bed and shuffle slipper-less to the closed door and press his ear against it. He would listen to varied adult voices, some in intense conversation, others casually demonstrating something they'd deemed impressive. The authoritative baritone of his father's voice intertwined with the laughing crowd. The feather-light lilting laugh as his mother gossiped with friends she'd not seen in weeks. Lex would put all of his weight against the door, pressing his cheek so deeply that it would leave an imprint of the woodgrain that lasted through the following morning.

This is what he thinks as the room darkens further, as the shadows take over the already shadow-cast room. He presses his face deeper into the warmth of the black closet door. It responds by pressing back gently, like a parent's palm caressing their child's face. All tension falls away from Lex's shoulders, his back, his legs. He leans more into the door and closes his eyes tight. The whispers are just beyond comprehension. He doesn't care. He's stopped trying to understand what they're saying and is content to let the vocal tones wash over his ear.

He realizes he's stroking the door with his damaged hand. He doesn't mind. His legs move forward on their own, pressing the rest of his torso and his hips against the door. The right hand hasn't released the doorknob. Lex stands pressed fully against the door, lost in the feeling of total bliss and warmth.

The whispers on the other side of the door get louder. Not clearer, just more pronounced. There are five voices. Perhaps seven, Lex loses count. He just listens. The whispers are easy, smooth. Like a group sharing a secret. Like they're practiced at whispering. It's a language all its own. It draws him in just like the conversations his parents and their friends had. Lex feels as if the door is drawing him closer to the speakers. He lets it happen, lets himself lose his feet.

The door seems to lift him from the floor. He doesn't open his eyes, only feels his heels drawn aloft. Then his toes. He feels himself leaning forward. Right hand releases the doorknob and works its way up the warm surface of the door. It feels like there are hands pushing through, working their way across his body. Palms press themselves against his, fingers run along his brow and down his cheek. The whispers are just on the other side of the door. Immediate and so very close. The voices reach out and stroke his earlobe. Move across the ridges and into his ear.

Underneath the nonsense words he begins to hear something repeat. It's so far away, mixing with the breathing. He plucks it from the rush of whispers and recognizes it. Repeating rarely and randomly at first, he then catches it in a slow rhythm.

"Empty," the whispers repeat underneath everything else. It punches through then recedes. His fingertips clutch, body tenses to focus on the word and its meaning.

"Empty."

It repeats more and more. Urgency increasing with each cycle. Voices closer. Like they're all in the same room, Lex and the whisperers. There are dozens of them. The word passes between all of them in turn.

"Empty."

Lex repeats it after them, feeling the need to join the chorus. He whispers it at first, uncertain. Slowly, more air pushes behind the words and his whispers grow louder.

"Empty."

His lips tremble and he repeats after each voice in turn. Finally, he finds his full voice and says it without any hesitation.

"Empty."

He opens his eyes as something grabs him and throws him sideways across the room.

28

Darkness envelops him as Lex flies through the air. He has only the sound of the wind passing his ears, drowning out the ringing. Taking over for the whispers that had him held aloft in a state of euphoria. Panic pushes back. Uncertainty of where he'll land.

The sensation of speed is intense and he thinks it's probably an illusion. He cannot see anything. He feels nothing beneath his palms or underneath his feet. His body feels like it's tumbling over itself, gravity shifting constantly. Head pointed down then arm then shoulder then feet then head again as he tries to gain his bearing. It's useless without his eyes. He tries blinking, and feels his eyelids stick as he reopens his eyes. The surrounding blackness abides.

It's an odd sensation, tumbling headlong through space when there's no visual point of reference. You have no idea if you're traveling at all. The sensation is like swimming at night. Floating through an inky substance with the constraints of gravity temporarily suspended. Nothing lasts forever, especially not untethered flight across a gravity-filled space.

Nausea creeps forward, the result of moving too much without context. Vertigo is a given, but it's somehow intensified. It becomes his default state. More than mere dizziness, more than a simple churning of the stomach. It makes him question his very existence, make him wonder if anything he's ever experienced in his life was real. Wonder if stability itself was a myth.

The euphoria of the closet door is a faint memory. He's only aware of two things. First, he knows that he's traveling an impossibly long distance for the size of his apartment. The tug, the toss was strong to yank him away from the door. He guesses that he's traveling at a pretty good rate, sailing more quickly than he could walk. Second, he knows that when he reaches the other side of the apartment, the collision with the wall is going to hurt. Badly.

He tenses, bracing himself for the eventual impact. The fresh tension adds a new layer of pain to his back, to his legs. It temporarily colors his world in a cool white light, flashing before him before fading into the deep shadowy darkness.

It smells like flowers and fresh-hewn lumber. The air is cool, like the fresh breeze of an early April morning.

The sound changes, the increased pitch of the whooshing past his ears becomes more menacing.

Something is about to happen.

Lex tries to adjust his body so that his back is pointed in the direction he thinks he's going. He pictures the videos he's seen of skydivers changing their positions in mid-air. He imagines himself forming crosses and ells while flying across the room. He can only go by what he's trying to tell his limbs to do. Spread-eagle, flex an arm to the side, try and bend and twist. He thinks he has a handle on it.

He's spent too much time in the air. The promise of the painful landing that is, in his mind, rapidly approaching causes him to tuck his head against his chest and cover it with his arms. He counts.

One-Mississippi.

Whooshing pitches higher.

Two-Mississippi.

Breathing becomes more shallow.

Three-Mississippi.

Absolute silence. Even the high-pitched tone that has accompanied him since the ceaseless waterfall takes a breath.

Four-Mississ. . .

A sickening crack echoes through the room as his shoulder crunches into the wall first. The arm guarding the left side of his head hits next, cushioning his skull. There's no time to cry out, no time to assess the damage as the rest of him slams into the wall, emptying his lungs. Stars fill his vision and he feels a second hit as his body crumples to the ground.

He's having trouble catching his breath. It's dark and cold and the taste of blood fills his mouth. Something feels broken, but he's not sure if it's in his arms or legs, torso or back. Everything is screaming in agony. Nothing feels like it's ready to move properly. He gasps, trying to refill his lungs. They burn with the effort, his throat straining to open as much as it can.

Lex has never suffered a broken bone. Not even the time he'd set an old, weather-eaten sheet of plywood onto a couple of crumbling cinder blocks to form a stunt ramp for his new roller blades. Lots of bruises and cuts resulted from that stunt as well as a partially dislocated wrist, but not a single broken bone. He has no context for how a broken bone may feel. He suspects, however, that he has a few broken ribs after being thrown across his apartment. Each breath is fire. Each movement sends sparks of pain through the rest of his body.

All of the occurrences of the evening have become lost. Everything has dissolved into the roiling torrent of agony. He can only think of getting out. Of leaving the apartment somehow. He knows he's not walking away. He's not sure if he has the strength to call out for help. He's stuck.

Meanwhile, the shadows around him shift once more. The inky black recedes and shapes begin to reveal themselves as the familiar forms of his apartment. The nearest of the shadow forms is the table and chairs that make up his dining room suite. The scene would make a great set for an independent movie were it not for the occupant lying crumpled at the baseboards nearby.

The room fades a little as Lex tries to take another breath. His head swims and he's sure the room continues to move though he's lying still. The front door is just a few feet above his head, but it could easily be miles away with the way he feels. His arm cradles his ribs as he unfolds his legs. More stars of agony and the room fades slightly once more as he blinks back unconsciousness. He tries to take another deep breath and the burning in his lungs intensifies. He thinks of coughing and decides against it, knowing the resultant pain would likely cause him to pass out cold.

The apartment resolves itself after he shakes off the latest wave of near faintness. Lex pushes himself into sitting, back against the wall. It hurts to breathe, it hurts to sit. It hurts merely to move and the act of pulling himself upright nearly causes him to cry out. Instead, he grunts unevenly as the room rights itself with the floor below him and the ceiling above.

According to the color of the room and the glow of the windows, it's still early evening. He looks over and can see the warm lights from the alley below trickle over the slats of the blinds. He sees the movement of the lamppost shadows as cars and buses pass the opening onto the street. There's even the faint echo of a distant car horn bouncing around the stone and metal facing the alley. It seems late enough for the windows in the building across the way to be completely dark, not late enough for all of the street traffic to have died down for the night.

Looking across the small space, the improbable abnormalities of the previous few hours seem ridiculous. The apartment has become the plain, boring abode he's lived in for months. He wonders what it says about him that he thinks his apartment is boring. Wonders what it means that he doesn't think much of his decor choices. If he subconsciously thought that his lodging there was temporary. He wonders if he has a concussion.

He takes a breath before lifting his hand to his face, checking the injuries from earlier. There's an angry red-black gash, jagged and raw, in his palm. The rest of his hand is covered in dried and drying blood, all running down to his fingertips and terminating in fat crimson teardrops. He tries flexing his fingers but they've grown stiff and swollen. He hopes it looks worse than it is. His examination moves past his hand to his legs, stretched out like a pair of pontoons before him. The pants are ripped, though not shredded. The knees are nearly bare, the left pant leg is torn up to the thigh and the right hem has been reduced to threads.

Lex laughs, takings stock of his entire person. He's not in such awful shape, all things considered. The ringing in his ears has mostly stopped and he can hear the fan of the heater kick in. There's a slight dripping in the kitchen sink, indicating that he's again neglected to fully shut the tap. It's far too calm, too normal for the things he's seen and heard. He glimpses down at his bare feet and thinks how all of his troubles started with the desire to put on some shoes. He'd already made the decision to leave. Time had come to do so.

He pushes himself up, with assistance from the wall, until he's standing upright. Well, mostly upright. He's a little wobbly, and waits a moment with his back pressed against it. The door is a few feet away, doorknob almost within reach. He could lean to his left just a little and open the door. He considers it then looks around, hoping his intentions aren't overly obvious.

He waits in silence, holding his breath in anticipation for some kind of reaction.

He can see the naked futon frame from where he's standing, the mattress crumpled just in front of it. There's a small circle of blood just next to it with a trail leading to the closet door. Everything looks almost as it should. The khaki walls trimmed with white. The white doors to the bathroom and closet with their cheap brushed aluminum hardware. The kitchen appliances stare outward, their green LED clocks reflecting a subtle time warp, each one displaying slightly different times. Then there's the broken glass and puddle of water near the end of the dining table. A bloody handprint reveals where he'd come down fully on one of the larger shards.

One final look around the apartment that tried to murder him or, worse, drive him insane. Lex has resolved that he'll never return to this place again. Nothing is so valuable that he'll even risk coming back to retrieve it. Everything will be abandoned happily, a fair exchange for whatever is left of his senses. His resolve stiffens and he moves to leave, barefoot and short-sleeved.

He freezes as his phone rings, vibrating across the table, playing a ringtone that he hadn't heard in almost two years.

sixth

29

THE FIRST TIME IT HAPPENED, IT HAD BEEN THE MOST AMAZING, MOST OUT of character thing he'd ever done. The small candid photo he'd taken of Natalie as she stood smiling, wrapped in about four layers of sweaters and coats, scarf looped around her neck three times. She was wearing a big, knit beanie that covered most of her forehead, blue-dyed hair sprouting from underneath the edges. She smiled with her entire face and it beamed through the layers of winter wrappings. It had been a windy day at the beach and she'd insisted on walking near the water, saying that low tide meant the winds would be weaker. He'd let her go ahead a little, kicking the damp sand toward the unsettled ocean, giggling the whole time at their little inside joke. She turned just as he snapped the photo, big wave swelling up just over her shoulder, wind blowing a few loose strands of hair across her nose.

A moment preserved in digital amber.

He'd set that picture to her caller ID accompanied by a small snippet of the pop hit from the nineties they'd been listening to repeatedly during their long road trip from campus out to the islands. It was an upbeat song, full of the optimism that had become so fashionable to mock.

It was a moment of underdeveloped romanticism that caused him to change his cell phone settings immediately upon returning home. He'd had second thoughts, the constant doubt that rattles a guy's mind when there should be other concerns like earning passing grades and advancing a nascent social life. It was easy for him to mistake friendship for something more, so he'd taken the approach that every encounter he had with a female classmate would be undeniably platonic. All the way down to his "no contact" rule. To his reckoning, if there were no hugs, there would be no mistaking the intent of either party. This rule lead to a lot of nights spent alone pretending to do homework and more than a handful of nights spent verbally consoling whatever girl happened to be crying near his shoulder.

With Natalie, the feeling of affection had overwhelmed him immediately. She would joke that the only reason they'd started dating was because she'd been the only girl on campus he would touch. She would point out that this was a fact observed by more than a few young women who'd orbited through his social galaxy for months.

So the move to give her a custom ring tone and modify his screen so that she would appear each time she called could be seen as a major breakthrough. Seeing her face every time he heard the song made him smile. Side effect, he gained an irony-free affection for the song, even dancing to it whenever it was played on an oldies radio station. Lex, after all, had always been a person who did not dance under any circumstance.

The song catches Lex off guard and he nearly stumbles as he crept toward the door. He doesn't immediately turn to look to his phone. He knows precisely where it is, sitting at the far side of his dining table next to the bag of leftover tortilla chips. He knows that it's probably sitting on the table face-down, a habit he'd developed to keep himself from constantly looking expectantly at the face of the phone, hoping for a reassuring telephone call or sympathetic text message. Perhaps even an apology. The last thing he wants is to turn and see the phone vibrating across the table, screen glow pulsing around the edges. He's afraid it will make everything he's just been through, up to and including that moment, real. He's really hearing that song. She's really calling him.

Lex tries to move his feet, tries to resume the momentum he feels he's earned. There's no mistake that he should be long-gone. By his reckoning, he should have left that apartment weeks ago, back when things were getting weirder. All of the clues are there and glaring and he's looked past them. Finally, the scales had fallen away from his eyes, he sees the place for what it truly is. He has every right to simply leave, to continue with his plan of never turning back.

His phone continues to ring and his paralysis persists. Each jostle of the phone as it vibrates on the table chills Lex's spine. He tries to shut it out, but there's no ignoring the conditioning his emotions have gone through in reaction to the song. His fists clinch, sending a thread of pain through his palm and wrist as his fingernails dig into the fresh gash. The phone continues to ring long after it should have stopped, well after the caller should have been sent to his voice-mail inbox.

Lex takes a deep breath. The apartment smells like new polyester and laundry detergent, faint undertones of pine and dish soap. He's so close to the door he can feel it vibrating from the sounds of the air exchange units above the hallway, the compressed air between him and it quaking against his eyelashes. All he has to do is leave.

The phone vibrates more, the ringtone repeating over and over.

He turns to face the table, staring at the small dark rectangle shaking on its surface. His heart is racing and he takes more deep breaths to try and calm himself. He knows he'll only be able to move in one direction. He knows he must retrieve his phone, verify the caller ID. His feet will not go anywhere until he sees the lighted image on the phone's glass face.

The snippet of the song repeats again.

He blinks and finds himself standing next to the table, looking down on the surface. Grease-stained bag of leftover tortilla chips sitting upright, the lip of the bag folded over just enough to hide the contents of the bag. He stands over the phone for a moment longer, watching the edges dance as the screen glows against the table's surface. He flexes his damaged hand once more, letting the pain keep him present. With the other hand, he reaches down and grabs the edges of the phone, feeling the pulse shiver up through his fingers.

All it takes is a flick of the wrist, one simple movement and he is face to face with the screen. His fingers temporarily lose their strength, nearly causing him to drop the phone. Lex recovers and stares at the glowing image of Natalie, smiling that smile, with her name floating just below the scarf. A small confirmation that the face above belongs to the word below. He slides the green button to one side and slowly lifts the handset to his ear.

"Hello?" Lex asks. He pauses, clears his throat, then takes a deep breath. "Hello? Who is this?"

There's the long drone of static and a few pops and clicks. The connection sounds poor, strained. He presses the phone against his ear, trying to discover if the other sound he hears is breathing or crying. His heart pounds inside his ribcage.

"Nat?" Lex whispers. "Is that you Nat?"

"Lex?" The voice that answers sounds distant, muffled. The static cuts out some of the high tones, but he recognizes the voice immediately. "Lex, where are you?"

For the first time the entire evening, Lex relaxes. He hears the voice, Natalie's voice, and is immediately calm. His hands are steady, even after stretching the one with the gash. He blinks once.

"Natalie," he says. His voice is a dry rasp, but he swallows hard and continues. "Where, ah. . .where have you been, Nat?"

"Lex, is it really you?" The voice sounds desperate, on the verge of tears. "I can barely hear you."

"Can you tell me where you are, Nat? Where have you been?"

"Lex. . .so empty here. . .come get me."

The voice breaks among the static and distortion. There are more pops and clicks than silence. A faint whistle comes in under all of it.

"Come get me, Lexington. . .please. . .come. . ."

Lex doesn't react, doesn't move. Simply presses the handset against his ear and listens. He waits and listens. The voice grows more faint, the static more pronounced.

". . .get me. . .empty. . .please. . .get. . .come. . ."

"Okay," Lex whispers back. "Okay, I will."

There's a long, static-filled silence. His thoughts fill with images of darkness broken by a single orange shaft of light. At the bottom of the light sits a naked girl with bright eyes, shivering in the cold. She's crying into her hands, elbows protecting her torso, ankles crossed under her. He sees large motes of dust floating through the air across the shaft of light, drifting upward and sideways. The image in his mind's eye stays fixed and he tries to blink it out. It persists each time he closes his eyes.

The phone cuts out, the silence sudden and absolute. He pulls the phone from his face and looks at the screen. Cold and blank. He presses the side button to turn on the screen's backlight and nothing happens. He tries repeatedly and still nothing. The battery, it seems, has died.

30

"You should have charged it before we left," says Oscar, wielding the steering wheel of his pickup like a broadsword. He's pulled at one side of the wheel with both hands, making the effort appear more involved than it should have been. It's as if he'd turned off the power steering, chosen to drive about caveman-style.

"Charges faster in this beast," says Lex. He winces as he pushes the charging cable into the USB port in the center console. The phone lights up, green battery accompanied by a lightning bolt verifying for him that everything is in working order. He looks at his bandaged hand, small red dot at the center indicating that he still has quite a bit of healing to do. At least he's gotten the good painkillers, the ones that require the prescription and pages of warnings from various medical watchdog groups outlining the potential for abuse and addiction. Apparently a stitched hand and deep bruises along the length of his body warrant such attention.

"As long as you don't drain my battery."

Oscar seems particularly grumpy. Sure, the sight of his bruised and bloodied son at his doorstep at what he calls "all-hours" begging to "crash out for a few days" hadn't been accounted for in his plans on how he was going to spend his Thanksgiving holiday. He'd worn an expression on his face that told Lex, were he not Oscar's son, he would have been shot dead on sight without so much as second thought regarding circumstances. As he'd put it, Oscar's tolerance for raising his only child had reached it's natural limit and any time or resources spent in continued support of that adult child should be considered pure charity.

That night, Lex shrugged, winced, and pushed past his father and slinked up to his old bedroom.

"I'm not going to drain your battery, Oscar." Lex is thumbing on his phone through all of his old contacts, people he hasn't spoken to or heard from in the years following his downfall. Lex had been fond of saying it had only been months since hearing from many of them, but once those months stretched into the dozens, he stopped deluding himself. He thought about simply deleting a lot of the contacts, lose them forever to whatever digital scrap pile existed. His thumb would hover over the delete button, hesitate just long enough for him to really look at the names, think about their context before cancelling the delete action. He tosses the phone onto the console in frustration. "Just get us there so we can get back home."

"Oh, we're in a hurry to get back home, huh?"

"You know what I meant."

"First time I've ever heard of you being eager to get back to YOUR home. You know, one that you're actually paying for."

"That's not. . .you know what I meant, Oscar."

"And would it kill you to call me dad every once in a while?"

"No, Oscar. No it wouldn't."

Oscar had taken the long way to the supermarket, calling it his own special back way. The route may have been faster when Oscar was a child, but the advent of modern road construction combined with widening of what were previously tractor paths have resulted in an efficient route that's eight whole minutes shorter. Lex has pointed this out to his father on more than one occasion and is usually greeted by scorn and disdain. He's since grown tired of the exercise and just lets Oscar go whatever the hell way he wants.

The truck rolls into the parking lot, jostling over curbs and taking speed bumps with abandon. The suspension was soft and bouncy which always led to a sort of delay between cresting big bumps in the road and the passengers feeling it in bouncing, rolling waves. Oscar didn't really need such a large, workman-like pickup, especially as an everyday driver. He wasn't a contractor or some sort of delivery guy. Oscar worked insurance, so the large, unwieldy pickup was a vehicle of pure vanity.

After finding a parking space in one of Oscar's favorite areas, a small strip of spaces near the back of the store near the loading docks, the two climbed from the cab and made their way to the entrance. They exchanged a quick glance, acknowledging that they were both present and accounted for.

Oscar hadn't spoken much to Lex since that night. Lex had the feeling that he was waiting for the story. As grumpy as his father was, he had a difficult time masking a degree of concern. He wouldn't ask directly what happened, leaving such direct inquiries to Lorraine. He would simply hover, waiting for his wife to extract all of the necessary details.

His mother had been her usual, accepting self. She didn't say a word as she washed his bloody hand and wrapped it in a bandage of gauze and elastic tape. After that, she put a hand to his forehead the way she did when he was a child and she needed to check if he had a fever. She stroked his cheek then left him alone, saying only that they would go to the clinic the next morning to get him checked out and to get him something for the obvious pain. She cooked all of his favorite meals, never questioning his prolonged presence or his pronounced silence. Lex didn't reveal much, only that he needed some time away from his apartment, that since the holiday was right around the corner, he may as well stay with them at least until the week after Thanksgiving. She smiled and nodded to him, threw a stern look to Oscar, then checked on the soup she'd been making.

This exchange and others like it clearly frustrated Oscar. One thing Lex knows about his father, however, is that he becomes more stubborn the more his truth is challenged. His truth is that Lex is taking yet another opportunity to freeload, to shirk adult responsibility as long as he can. Lex knows that, since his father holds so closely to this opinion, nothing he could say, no matter how truthful, would change it. So, he keeps his mouth shut.

He's tempted to tell his mother what happened that night, about the torments and impossibilities. He comes close to telling her everything, including the phone call with Natalie. It's this last thing, that phone call, that keeps him silent. He knows the looks he'll get when he mentions her. He knows the response even those who love him will have, given the very rough string of months they'd endured after he'd left school. He can't bear to subject himself to those reactions.

He's made up a different story that will go down easier with his parents. It's a story that fits more snugly with Oscar's world view. He's told the harrowing tale of how he was on his way back to his apartment after a fun night out at a Tex-Mex place with a large group of co-workers. Of how, after a margarita too many, he'd neglected to pay attention to his surroundings and was assaulted by a pair of burly gentlemen in masks demanding the contents of his pockets.

He failed to account for the fact that he retained possession of his cell phone, but that was a hole in the story that was never quite explored.

He's told of how he complied with the request only to be beaten by the muggers. His story included a shattered bottle which accounted for the gash in his hand and steel-toed boots for the bruises all over his body. His story didn't account for how the blood-thirsty muggers managed to miss his face, but Lex guessed that it wasn't as much of an oversight as the phone thing.

The story ticks all of the boxes for Oscar, how the area surrounding his apartment always has been and always will be dangerous. The story also allows Lorraine to take his side when he'd announced that he was uncomfortable returning to his place for a while. She even offered to send him to counseling to help with the trauma, but he's told her he was willing to deal with it on his own time. The previous stint in months of counseling had armed him with enough catch phrases that he could get away with it.

He'd similarly shut down talk of going to the police, adding that the muggers would be difficult to identify as it was kinda dark and he was kinda drunk.

Oscar suspects something more, but Lex keeps his mouth shut on the matter and lets his father stew. So the two walk into the supermarket, Lorraine's shopping list in hand. She's told them she doesn't need much to complete her prep for the big meal in a couple of days. Lex volunteered to go and Oscar, looking for any clue he can find, insisted on driving.

"You go grab the canned green beans, I'll head to the freezer section," Lex offers as he grabs a basket. Oscar looks at him sideways.

"Faster if we stick together," Oscar grumbles.

"I'm not going to escape. Just meet me at the meats. First one there gets the smoked turkey."

Lex walks away toward the stack of coolers near the middle of the store before Oscar can raise another objection. He's wearing a knit cap and thick, sherpa-lined sweat shirt and he pulls the cap down over his forehead while pulling the drawstring of the hoodie, closing the neck opening around his chin. He knows everyone is scrambling to get some holiday shopping done before it's too late, many of whom are familiar with his family. He wants to cruise through unseen while savoring the time away from his parents' house. He makes it to the frozen dairy cooler without so much as a close call and he's grateful.

He slows to a stroll, taking in the product being kept frozen behind the tall glass and metal doors. All of the frozen dairy treats fascinate him in ways they never did when he was younger. He notes how all of the really bad stuff, the most decadent, unhealthy items had the most wholesome packaging. Inviting the consumer to release their inhibitions and indulge in a bit of caloric hedonism. Meanwhile, the lighter fare, stuff that's intended to fool the buyer into thinking it's somehow healthier, uses plants and loopy lines on their packages. He laughs as he passes something called a diet fudge bomb topped with whole-grain sprinkles. He doesn't see Patricia until he runs right into her as she stands deciding between flavors of a very fancy gelato.

"I'm so sorry," he says before he truly means it.

Patricia jumps back, looks him over from head to toe somewhat critically, then stares him directly in the eyes. The expression on her face morphs gradually from startled outrage to stunned surprise through several stages of emotional turmoil before finally landing on tear-filled pity. Her mouth hangs open and a half-breathless sound that somewhat resembles an old, creaky door.

"Lexington!" she says. She drops her own basket, placing her purse carefully on top, and throws her arms around Lex's neck. "Oh my god, I keep meaning to come by and see you. I heard what happened and its so awful."

"It's okay," he replies. He tries to hide the immense discomfort he feels with her draped around him. He's careful to keep his bandaged hand away.

"How are you feeling?" She holds on a little longer before regaining her composure, pulling herself away. "Oh, I'm so sorry, you're probably still hurting a little bit, huh?"

"Yeah, that's fine. I'm fine. Just healing up a little."

"Well, good. I'm so glad. I'm so sorry about what happened to you. I couldn't help but think about when you tried to warn me about this kind of thing. I didn't catch on at first. I just thought that I'd done something wrong, something to make you hate me or made you mad a me. But, no, you were just trying to protect me. Just like you've always done. You've always looked out for me and I'm just sad that there was nobody there to look out for you when you needed help the most. I still can't believe that you got jumped by ten guys with baseball bats."

"Excuse me?"

"My mom told me all about it. Heard it from your father, that you were mugged by a gang of thugs on your way home from doing charity work or something. It's such a shame when bad things happen to the best of us. It's just like they say on the news, you never know who the next victim is going to be. It's so random."

"It wasn't quite like that."

Lex spots Oscar at the far end of the aisle just as Oscar sees who he's talking to. His father stops, smiles, turns, and walks back in the direction from which he'd approached.

"Well, listen," she says. She steps closer, nearly pressing herself against him. He can't help the erection that starts to rise and he tries not to look her in the eyes. She's intimately close and grabs his non-bandaged hand in hers. "If there's anything I can do to help, anything at all, will you let me know? Even better, I'm taking you to dinner and you can't say no."

"Okay," escapes Lex's mouth before he has a chance to process what's happening in the frozen dairy aisle.

"Good." She squeezes Lex's hand, smiles then backs away. She stares at him the entire time as she lifts her shopping basket onto one arm while whipping the strap of her purse over her shoulder with the other. He notices her basket is loaded with several packages of frozen corn and a bright pink bottle of wine. "Don't make any other plans for tomorrow and I'll swing by. Gotta put Trig down, so it'll be around eight-thirty."

The confidence with which she makes the date stuns Lex into an awe-struck silence. He simply nods and tries an innocuous smile. He's sure he probably looks like the Joker.

"Dress comfortably," Patricia says as she backs away. She gives a little head tilt with a smile, waves with her fingers, then turns and rounds the corner toward the dairy section.

"Huh, you were right," says Oscar, appearing just over Lex's shoulder. "We both got more done by splitting up."

31

Lex holds his whiskey glass like it's a life preserver. He's earned his buzz and he doesn't want to let it go. The world has lost a little bit of its edge, the blurring of the harsh angles and aggressive lines have become a comfort. Especially at the extremes of his peripheral vision where the small but vocal crowd occupying the tables around them have faded into congregations of soft, foggy puffs. It even filters everything he hears through a nice, melodic tune. Everything sounds great and there's no memory of anything before five minutes ago.

Patricia has put maximum effort into her appearance and it's worked to completely disarm him. He thinks she looks wholesome but dangerous. It's a look that professional models seem to have perfected, the appearance of being angelic and accessible, perfectly flawed. Lex is in awe of the effect and has tried to drink as much and as quickly as he can to dull it.

His senses are as dull as a fist.

They're sitting inside a very nice restaurant, the kind that has massive floor-to-ceiling windows that look out onto the street. The patio is closed, tables stacked on each other at the far corner. Lights are strung under a canopy, casting a warm glow that mixes with the lights strung over the "old", narrow, brick street. The neighborhood looks ancient but is only a few years old, a shopping center built to resemble a well-worn brick-lined streetscape. All of the facades are unique and distinct, but hide a continuous building of modern concrete and drywall and metal. The designers had gone out of their way to make the patrons forget that they're drifting through the middle of the ultimate evolution of the suburban ideal.

For Thanksgiving eve, it's surprisingly full. It's not "mid-Summer date night" full, but it's not too shabby. Lex half-expected for them to be one of the few people in the restaurant, adding a layer of awkward to something that was already promising to be uncomfortable. He'd been prepared to order a whiskey and have the bartender leave the bottle with him. It hasn't come to that. Yet.

The restaurant seems to sway and Lex is feeling pretty good. He stares down at the ice cubes in his nearly empty glass and smiles. He's rather fond of the brown liquid he's been throwing down his throat. It's a relationship that he's interested in exploring much further.

"So I told her that she didn't see it coming which is why she'd peed herself a little when it buzzed by her ear," is what Lex heard when he realized Patricia was still talking. She'd been telling a story about her time in Texas. Perhaps it was a story about her living in Oklahoma. Either way, it involved a life of living lazily among other housewives while their husbands fucked women from their offices. He gets the impression, based mostly on the tone of her voice, that she'd thoroughly enjoyed her time among her tribe of home-bound mothers. Most of her words, however, point to the idea that things weren't as amazing as she'd hoped.

She also seems to be very happy relaying her story with limited interruptions from Lex. She clearly doesn't need any sort of encouragement to continue. He isn't sure if she is willfully ignoring that he's not really paid attention to her the past half-hour or if she truly hasn't noticed, enrapt as she is by telling her own story. He doesn't really care.

"I'm sorry," she says after laughing and touching Lex's hand across the table. It snaps him back into the moment. "I've been monopolizing the conversation the entire time. That's what happens when I get going, just plow forward, right through the walls of manners. So tell me, why are you so secretive about your place in the city? I would bet it's so amazing, having that kind of freedom in a place with so much possibility."

She finishes her sentence in a whisper, like she's trying to let Lex know she's in on the secret.

"Oh, it's not really all it's cracked up to be," says Lex. He's stunned at how truly pretty Patricia is in the soft, hazy light of his inebriation. She smells nice, too. The combination of the two is making him dizzy. He puts down the drink and braces himself against the edge of the table, hoping she hasn't noticed the slight sway in his spine. "I'm really not sure how long I'm going to stay there, to be honest."

Patricia didn't take that statement as Lex intended.

"Look at you," she says. "Moving up in the world so quickly, already thinking of trading up. What are you thinking? A riverfront condo? One of those industrial lofts with all the exposed brick and metal?"

"No. I don't think so. Just somewhere other than the place I'm in."

Lex feels drowsy and fears he won't be able to keep up with his end of the conversation.

"Okay, Mister Bigshot!" she smiles and sips the pink liquid in her wine glass. She winks as she does so. "You don't have to tell me anything. I'm just happy for you. After all that bad business with. . .well, I wasn't going to bring it up, but I just think you were treated so poorly when that girl went missing."

Klaxons are blaring in Lex's mind as the conversation ceases being innocuous.

"I don't think I really want to talk about that."

"Oh, I understand. I just want you to know that I was always on your side when all those people were saying all that nasty stuff about you. Mother would keep me posted and I would tell her that you were as innocent as an angel. She wanted to know how I knew and I told her that I just knew your heart and that you weren't capable of anything like what they were accusing you of."

"Thank you, but can we change the subject?"

"And to think, that your name was just dragged through the mud up and down main street. Mother said you couldn't leave the house for almost a year. There you were, trying to start your life after school and you were being hounded for something you couldn't have done."

"Patricia, I don't think. . ."

"Vultures. That's what they were. Circling vultures trying to get a piece of a salacious story without regard for who's life they were destroying in the process. I told my son, I said, 'Trig, don't you ever go and try to be a bully. You'll ruin other peoples lives that way.' I just hope he listened. That's kinda why I wouldn't mind if you two spent some time together, you know? Get to know each other. He could really use someone to look up to, someone who's been through it."

"Can we please. . ."

"They never found her, did they? She just up and vanished into thin air without so much as a see-ya-later. You know what I think? I think she just took off. She wanted to be somebody else, somewhere else. Can't blame a girl, really. I understand the temptation. Sometimes I just want to leave Trig with my mother, pack some underwear in a duffle bag and just take off. Assume a new identity. Somewhere far, far away. I bet that's what that girl did. What was her name? Natasha or something like that?"

"Natalie."

"Natalie, that's right! I bet that's exactly what Natalie did. She got tired of being around everybody. No offense. She was fed up and she just took off. She didn't tell anybody because she didn't want anybody to try and stop her. She just flew off into the wind, never to look back. And there you were, sitting up in your parents' house, completely innocent of what they were accusing you of doing. All that talk about you being unstable and her being all innocent. I didn't buy that for one second. Trust me, I was on your side the entire time."

"Do you want to see my apartment?"

It just tumbled out. Lex couldn't stop himself. He's not sure where it came from. Up until that moment, his head was a beachball in the middle of an ocean during a hurricane. He'd lost track of what direction was up and was certain that he was continuously falling backward. It wouldn't end. His stomach was turning over on itself, spinning in the opposite direction as his head.

He'd been unsure how things would turn out once they did finally escape. Would he yell at Patricia, scream at the top of his lungs in hopes that she would finally get the point that he wanted her to shut up? Would he burst into tears, becoming a useless heap of blubbering, sobbing sorrow? He hadn't expected to be able to speak, much less speak those words. In that order.

"What?" Patricia asks. She seems as shocked by what Lex has said as he is. She's frozen, her face creeping into a half smile as she replays the memory of his seven words over and over.

"My apartment," Lex says. There's no walking it back, the invitation. There's no un-ringing the bell, as they say. His only choice is to plow forward in hopes that it goes nowhere. "Would you like to see the apartment?

"I didn't think," she stutters. She then blushes, takes another sip from her wine glass, then collects herself. "Well, of course I'd love to see it, silly! I didn't think you were. . .you sounded like you were going to be at your parents' house for a while. It is only downtown, but. . .yes, let's go check it out."

So much for going nowhere. A headache begins to form at the base of Lex's skull, the kind that will spread slowly over the next few hours, culminating in the inability to look at any light brighter than a candle. He tries to decode what malfunction occurred within himself to have all of his building angst manifest itself in an invitation to go to the very place he's sworn never to return. His ears ring at the very prospect of hearing falling water or ceaseless whispering.

"I warn you," Lex starts. In the second involved in taking a breath, a part of him hopes that he will say something that expresses the sheer terror he feels in going back to such a horrible place. He wants to say something that will make her change her mind, something that will dissuade her from going. "It's not the cleanest place you've ever seen. I'm pretty sure I left some dirty dishes lying around."

Were he able to without seeming unhinged, he would have punched himself squarely in the jaw for what he'd just said. Lex strains to fight back the spins which have grown in intensity since his mouth has decided to take over without assistance from his brain. There's a certain disconnect that he will, if he remembers, look into at some point.

"Don't worry about that," Patricia coos. Lex can see that she's completely forgotten about expressing her opinion about his prior travails. "I won't judge you on a few dirty dishes."

32

"It's a really cute building," says Patricia, shivering on the sidewalk a quarter block from the main entry door.

Lex has yet to discover the correct deterrent, the thing that will keep Patricia from wanting to proceed with her examination of Lex's independent life. He doesn't want to tell her about the occurrences in his apartment. That, he thinks, would be a bridge too far. He wants to discourage her, not turn her against him completely. He still needs her to drive him back to his parents' house.

He fails to square what will happen when they reach the fifth floor. Wouldn't preparing her for the eventuality that something inexplicable will happen once she crosses that threshold be a kindness? Let her steel herself for the evil that lurks in the shadows waiting to pounce. Even worse, what if nothing happens? Nothing at all.

"It's been covered over. Used to be brick and marble. Very ornate. Very old."

"How old?"

"Pretty damn old," Lex looks up and down the block. There's no foot traffic, no car traffic, not even the occasional passing taxi. The emptiness of the city on Thanksgiving eve has a palpability. He can sense it in the air, the idea that everyone should be safe and sound, at home with their loved ones. The chill air even smells like it wants everyone to be indoors.

He doesn't want to set foot in the building. His face reflects this sentiment, screams it. He's leaning away from the building as they approach. The closer they get, the slower he walks. He's stalling, hoping to come up with some sort of excuse for them to not go inside.

He's telling her about the history of the neighborhood. The history that he remembers, at least. He's recounting how he'd found the apartment in the first place. Online classified ad that seemed too good to be true. He tells her about his commute to and from work. One bus, direct shot, twenty minutes on a bad day. He even makes up a few details about the neighborhood based on remote rumors he'd heard via some drunk guy at the mall. He has no way of knowing if they will indeed renovate the old cardboard factory into a shopping complex with a cinema and bowling alley.

Patricia appears to be very impressed. She looks like a person who is close to achieving their ultimate goal and cannot believe it's taken so long to do so. Her face is fixed in an expression that's meant to convey how impressed she is with everything she's hearing. She's eating it all up, every word that he pours out. She nods like a bobblehead, making little approving moans with each one. She's almost where she wants to be.

By the time they've reached the main door of the building, Lex is out of ideas. He could tell her that he's left the apartment keys at his parents' but for one annoying little physical tick that would belie that idea. The entire way into the city, he'd twirled the keys around the forefinger of his left hand. It's something he does when he's trying to ease a little stress as the keychain is capped by a large industrial ball bearing he'd found after his shift working some mind-numbing high school job years before. It was shiny and unique, standing out among all the other garbage strewn about the ground. It seemed a good idea at the time, make it a part of his keychain. That way he would always have something to fidget with whenever things got too intense.

He'd fidgeted with the damned thing most of the way over.

Lex looks at her and she looks back, smiles on both their faces. Lex picks the right key and inserts it into the lock.

"This is so exciting," she says. It doesn't make things any better.

"I hope your expectations aren't too high. It's just a tiny little apartment in a walkup building."

"But it's in the city. Everything is so much better in the city, right? It's so, I don't know, cosmopolitan."

Click, and the door opens into the lobby. He hears a small squeak from her as he holds the door open and she steps through. The expression on her face changes suddenly and she freezes.

"You okay?" he asks. The way she stops, like a mime before a wall, causes him to nearly fall into her as he moves to escort her up the stairs. She's straining to hear something and it's caused hair to stand on the back of his neck.

"What is this?" she whispers. She's leaning forward, frozen where she stands.

"I don't under. . ."

"Shhh!" She's shaking, one hand rising almost level to her waist. He thinks he's swaying, a new wave of the swims pushing him to one side. He dares not make a sound.

Patricia leans forward before stepping further into the lobby. Like she's being called from afar and she's carefully moving closer to better answer. She looks back to Lex who trails just behind her shoulder. Like she's searching for something. An answer to a question that sits unasked between them. He stares back, feeling stupid.

"You hear that?" she asks. She seems to have grown more pale since they left her car. The chill air that had flushed her cheeks has clearly worn off and she stands, unmoving, just inside the building's entrance. Her lips part and her mouth holds open for a moment before she continues. "That wasn't you, but who was it? Is somebody playing a prank?"

"I don't hear anything," Lex answers. He strains against the silence. He realizes he's holding his breath as she stares at him, searching for something.

"Are you sure," she whispers, gasping for breath. "It. . .it's your voice."

Lex's stomach drops just as he hears something. It pulls his gaze away from her and down the hall toward the staircase. His eyes focus quickly as he leans into the door, listening for the gurgling sound coming from somewhere beneath the staircase. A sound that he remembers from his first day.

"I haven't said anything." He can feel his balance shift, all drunkenness forgotten. She hasn't stopped searching his face and he's only barely aware of it. "I've been here the whole time, haven't said anything until now."

"You're still speaking," she says. She's shivering and not from the cold. Lex stops leaning toward the loud gurgling down the hall and meets her eyes again. There are tears forming there. She's shaking her head slowly, lips parted slightly as if she's trying to sing along to a song she's just hearing for the first time. "You're saying. . ."

The world begins to spin and Lex grasps the door frame to try to stop it. His guts aren't in the best condition to be spun and he forcefully pushes himself away from the lobby. All he can manage is one word. "No."

"How could you say?" Patricia looks down the hall as if she can pinpoint the source of the voice she's hearing. "You're saying such awful things. Why?" A large tear rolls down her cheek, hanging on her jaw before falling to the tile just inside the door. She gasps as Lex grabs her wrist and pulls her away from the door as he stumbles back toward the street.

He pushes her away from the building rather roughly and pulls the door closed behind him, leaning against the glass. It feels warm despite the chill in the air. They're both breathless. She has an expression of shock frozen on her face. He stands with his mouth wide open trying to suck in enough air to try and ground himself. Hands on his knees, he gathers the saliva that will not stop building in his mouth and tries to spit. He barely saves himself at the last moment, but turns toward the building anyway to avoid the ultimate shame should his supper have other ideas. He slowly starts to feel better by taking deeper breaths, though the faint sound of the building's gurgling guts still linger.

Behind him, Patricia doesn't fare much better. He hears the sounds she makes as she tries repeatedly to suppress her own gagging. She drags her feet as she shuffles away from him toward the curb. She coughs then spits then coughs again, sighing and whispering something to herself as she paces across the sidewalk. Lex turns to see her, pale and fanning herself, pacing then bending over as if she's wrestling with her stomach. Finally, she stands straight, tilts her head back and takes a deep breath.

"Are you okay?" he manages to say after she's clearly collected herself. She has her back to him, looking up the block at the empty streets and shuttered storefronts. The entire city feels as if it's gone out of business. She waves without turning, without really moving anything else but her arm, her elbow, her wrist.

He wants to tell her that it's not normally like that. That the sound in the lobby is highly unusual. Then, he thinks, he would need to tell her that the building itself isn't as bad as the apartment he rents. Follow that with the events of the previous week and he decides just to leave her be, let her collect herself, decide if seeing his apartment is still high on her to-do list.

"We should go," he offers instead.

"What was that?" she says. Her voice bounces off of the stone and brick facades around them.

"I wish I knew. I've never. . .I have no idea what that was."

She turns to face him, tears ruining her makeup. She's shaking, causing her earrings to sparkle even more in the streetlight.

"But you live here," she says. "This is your home."

"It's not always like this."

No, he thinks, it's much worse.

"We should leave," Lex offers again. "Go back and call it a night."

"Are you going to stay here?" She hasn't moved, standing about six yards away from the building's door.

"Definitely not," he says. He takes a step toward her, driven by a wave of remorse. As horrible as he considers his own situation to be, he pities her in that moment even more. "I'm sorry."

She blinks, tries a smile that fizzles immediately, then nods. Her expression is unreadable as she walks to him and puts a hand on his shoulder. She starts to say something, but words fail as another large tear rolls down her cheek. The hand on Lex's shoulder pats the spot as she moves past him, heading to her car.

33

"I CALL BULLSHIT, MOTHERFUCKER!" PARKER'S SMILE IS SINISTER. HE HAS A look in his eyes that reminds Lex of a death-metal album cover he'd seen as a child which scared the piss out of him. "You tried to smooth-talk, didn't you."

Lex holds his forehead in both hands and shakes his head. It took every ounce of restraint he had to tell Parker the details of his Thanksgiving eve. He left out some of the less flattering details, of course. He did leave in the vomiting if only for effect and to drive home the strangeness of the experience.

"Fuck you, asshole," says Lex. He sits back away from his bowl of pho. He pretends that he's offended by what Parker has accused him of, but really he simply wants to let the bowl of boiling-hot broth cool before he tries to eat any more of it. "I was hoping for a small bit of empathy. Perhaps a 'things aren't so bad, Lex'."

"No empathy here, baby!" Parker ignores the volcanic temperature of his own soup, taking greedy mouthfuls of brown broth and swallowing them eagerly. "You made that mess all on your own."

"There's no way we should have even been at that building. I should have just called it an evening and slept off the whisky spins. Better yet, we should never have been out in the first place."

"You were hoping for a little fun, that's why you agreed to it. You like to pretend you're all innocent and nice, that you aren't driven by the same base desires as the rest of us, but we're all just the same."

"Parker, the only reason I have these ridiculous lunches with you is because I want to be reminded of the person I don't want to be."

"Bullshit!" Parker picks a noodle from his bowl and flings it at Lex's face, sending droplets of broth flying toward the table behind him. He knows better than to duck, taking the brunt of the impact on his cheek. The woman sitting the next table over, however, brushes the back of her ear and looks up to see if there's a pending storm of beef broth overhead.

"You're about to get us kicked out. Again." Lex wipes his chin.

Parker's expression changes, becomes darker and more intense. He leans forward over his bowl.

"Seriously, though," Parker says. "She brought up Nat? On your little lame excuse for a date, no offense, she brought up the Natalie thing?"

"Yeah, she really did."

"What the fuck, man? That shit is out of bounds. I would have punched her right in her fucking jaw on the spot, dude. Chick is lucky I don't know where she lives."

"Calm down. She was just running her mouth, caught in the effort of bringing the conversation back around to herself. She didn't know what she was saying."

"All the better reason, Lex. You just don't bring that shit up. I don't care what kind of bullshit she was trying to spin about being on your side. Of course she's on your side. You didn't do anything."

"I just think she was trying to flirt, but couldn't quite get it right."

"That's fucking lame, Lex. I know I'm doing the same shit, but at least I know what I'm talking about when I bring up how jacked-up it was the way you were treated when Nat left. They assume that just because you're fucking a girl before she vanishes. . ."

"Dammit, Parker!" Lex slams his spoon onto the table.

"It's true. They're all fucking jealous. They see you in the pictures with her and you're both smiling and happy, a brown face and a pale face, and they think they know jack shit about you. They don't know shit and they know it and they treated you like a fucking Manson anyway. Dragging you through the shit like they did."

Lex pushes his bowl away, shaking. He looks around the restaurant, a small place with a counter at one end. There are photos of Vietnamese celebrities, at least Lex assumes they're celebrities, shaking hands with the same thin guy in white with a white cap and a scar running down his left cheek starting just below his eye. It's the same thin guy in white wearing a white cap with a facial scar who's shouting orders at a haggard-looking young man who never quite looks him in the eye. The menu boards on the walls are in Vietnamese with English translations scrawled in black marker just below the calligraphy. It's a colorful place, mirrors on the ceiling and on the walls helping make the place seem bigger than it truly is.

He takes a deep breath before looking back to Parker who has been waiting wordlessly for the conversation to resume.

"My bad, Lex," Parker says before taking another spoonful of broth. "Look, sooner or later, probably sooner, it's not going to be so bad, you know. Soon, you'll be able to put all of this shit, all of the horrible treatment and the looks and the doubts, all of that will be way behind you. You're going to be fine."

Lex sniffs.

"Now," continues Parker, "let's talk about this gurgle you claim made you throw your chunks. You know what I think?"

"Wouldn't know where to begin," says Lex.

"I think you just got too goddamn drunk on whiskey and couldn't hold it any more. You made up a story about hearing something weird, convinced your little school friend that she heard it, too. Your stomach probably churned a note or two, contributing to the auditory hallucination."

"You're sick."

"Not as sick as you were."

"Why in hell would I do that? Tell me that much."

"Aw, that's super fucking easy. You realized on the way back to your place, thinking about all the nasty stuff you were going to do to young mommy. Planning how you were going to finish that game of doctor you started all those years ago."

"It wasn't like that at all, Parker."

Lex can feel himself blush and tries to hide it by pulling his bowl back under his chin and trying to take another spoonful without scorching the roof of his mouth.

"No, not at all, you innocent little motherfucker. Literally, you tried to. So, you start to get to the penetrating act. Spinning her around, pulling her onto you, grabbing the back of her head to get a little more support. Next thing you know, you're wondering if you brought condoms, trying to figure out if you've got enough sleeves to get you through the night. Then you remember you left all your condoms in your other pants."

"Other pants?" Lex is smiling.

"Yeah, the other pants where you keep your balls, stud!"

Parker erupts in a large, boisterous laugh that echoes off of the walls of the restaurant, causing the other diners to stop what they're doing and stare. Parker doesn't care, letting his percussive hoarse bark of a laugh loose freely. Lex is torn between being embarrassed, apologizing to the diners all around, and joining him with a wide-open laugh of his own.

"You're ridiculous, asshole," says Lex.

"You know I'm right. You left them at home like an idiot and you plotted your escape using some kind of sound effect, you know what I mean? A trick of the ears."

Lex wants to tell Parker about the building. He wants to tell him about the last time he was in his apartment, the waterfalls and the closet door. The phone call from Natalie. He wants someone to share the burden he's been carrying, understand why he hasn't slept well in his bed since he's gotten a place of his own.

It's not lost on him that he's unsettled at his parents' place, so he gets his own place only to become unsettled yet again. It's a cruel joke. Whenever he's tried to get his life going, tried to get things on track and plant his feet underneath himself, something holds him back. Something has happened to knock him in reverse. He can't seem to stay on his feet and it's becoming more and more frustrating. It's all out of his control and that makes things worse somehow.

He wonders how Parker does it, gets himself up everyday and succeeds. There's no self-loathing or doubt, at least not any that he can see. He strides across the world without stopping to ask permission. He thinks of Parker's reaction to being told that the latest reason Lex can't get started, can't get his shit together, is because he's moved into an apartment that may very well be haunted by malevolent spirits intent on driving him mad. Yeah, that would be a successful conversation.

"You seem lost, my friend," Parker says, tone of voice shifting again. "I'm not sure what it is, but you seem so lost. It's not just the loss of confidence, buddy. It's that you just seem to be driving from one place to another. Without really wanting anything."

"That's not true," says Lex. He speaks in a whisper. "There are things I want."

"I don't think so. Not really, anyway. You just go through the motions of wanting. You don't really, though. Not like the rest of us. We all go around here trying to be something. Trying to be our best. We go from one place to another to another, trying to scratch the itch that we've all been told we've always had."

Parker pauses to think about this for a moment, staring down at his nearly empty bowl. He grabs a piece of warm beef, dripping with broken bits of noodle and scallions and tosses it into his mouth. He swallows it after three chews. Lex simply watches, not sure what to say.

"That's the way we all get along, Lex. We all need to want something to move us ahead. We need to want to stay young or be pretty or have great sex or eat good food or do the best drugs chemistry has to offer. We all want shit to make sense of the world. We want so that we don't have an empty void in our fucking lives, making our very existence seem fraught of purpose. And that's what you lack. You lack want."

"But I don't need want."

"Of course you do. We all do. Haven't you been listening. We all need want. It's an essential part of who we are as human beings. We're human wantings.

All of us but you. Ever since that fight with Nat, ever since she vanished. You've stopped wanting anything. At all. It's not healthy and it's starting to wear on you. I can see it in your eyes."

"What about you, Parker? You don't want anything and you seem to be doing just fine."

Lex is getting warm around his ears and can feel his pulse in his neck. He shifts in his seat after feeling a sudden pinch in his hip. His foot taps almost on its own.

"That's where you're wrong. I don't just want something. I want all the things. I have very large appetites and want to fill it all with everything I can. You see the difference? I've got enough want to get me through several lifetimes. There will never be a time where I stop and simply drift about. I'll never be satisfied, I don't think. There's just so much out there. I'm not missing any of it."

"Well, that's not me. I'm not the insatiable type. Never have been."

"No, but this drifting business is new. You're not the same guy I met trying to pick up a waitress in a pool hall because you thought she was nice."

"She was nice."

"She works for tips, Lex."

"I know that."

"She's nice to everybody."

"I know that."

"Especially to her girlfriend who was tending bar at the time."

Lex pulls his hands into fists as he leans back. He realizes that he's trying to control his breathing, deep breaths in through one nostril, out through the other. It's a trick he's not quite perfected though he'd spent most of his teenage years trying.

Parker downs the contents of his water glass, then does his own magic trick, summoning a server with a simple wave of his hand when there appeared to be no servers anywhere nearby. She appears with a full water pitcher and refills both glasses. Parker whispers something to her and she smiles before handing him the bill.

"This is on me. Happy Thanksgiving." Parker says as he pulls a wad of cash from his pocket and slaps it onto the table without counting the bills.

"Thanks," says Lex, knuckles turning white.

"Look, I do this because I care. Believe me, I hate to see you look like you haven't a friend in the world."

"Of course I have a friend. I have you."

"Damn, you sure as hell do, you fucking emo bastard."

34

Carmen is late getting to her desk, a rare occurrence. Especially the week right after a holiday. She'd been dragging the week before and Lex had noticed. He didn't want to let on he'd noticed, that he even cared about the comings and goings of a coworker who seemed to barely tolerate him. He couldn't help it, though, as she rushed down the aisle and sat in her chair noisily, tossing her bag and keys onto her desk.

Lex stares at his screens, trying not to notice that she'd been crying. He then tries not to let on that he's noticed she'd been crying. He shifts his weight and types a little too earnestly on his keyboard, hitting the delete key more than any other. He fidgets as he tries to mind his business, but he sees out of the corner of his eye that she's just sitting at her desk, staring at the blank screens.

It's out of character for her to show so much emotion and he really wants to say something, connect with her somehow to let her know that she could talk to him if she wanted. He's not sure how to broach the subject without her becoming offended. Suppose there was no problem and he was simply projecting his own subconscious state onto her. What if she were just sitting at her desk clandestinely typing a text message into her phone? He shakes off his own self-consciousness and braves a look across the aisle.

It looks much worse than he'd been able to glimpse indirectly. Carmen is at her desk, hands folded neatly in her lap. Her computer screens are dark, her keyboard and mouse sit unmolested. Her bag is crumpled in the far corner of the desk having knocked a Rubik's cube off of its stand and displaced several vinyl figurines which had been lined up like a tiny army. There are no tears on her cheeks, but her eyes are clearly puffy. She keeps blinking, staring straight ahead at the screens.

He looks away quickly as she starts to turn her head toward him, his fingers skittering across his keyboard forming a series of nonsense words, fodder for his delete key. He hears a sniff and movement as she arranges her keyboard, moves her mouse around, and starts to work.

The room gets a little warmer as guilt takes over. He's not sure why, but he's sorry he noticed how unhappy Carmen seems as she sits at her workstation. He's sorry he didn't offer to help in some small way.

Then he thinks he could have done more harm in his current state of mind. He'd probably just depress her, dragging her into the mud of his own self-doubt. He knows there's nothing he can do, no true insight he can provide no matter the problem. Nevertheless, the guilt persists, leaving him with a sickening pit in his stomach.

Shaking his head, Lex turns his attention back to his work, transferring the figures from a text document into a worksheet that can then be used by management to make more money, increasing their bonuses. He decides to try and lose himself in the grids, ticking down the minutes until the end of the day.

The rest of the office is relatively quiet. Most of his co-workers have music wired directly into their ears with various headphones and earbuds. There's an almost gentle wave of white noise caused by dozens of pairs of hands working rapidly over mechanical computer keyboards. The drone is occasionally interrupted by a random cough or sneeze, people adjusting to the rapidly chilling late autumn as the city plummets headlong into winter. There are surprisingly few telephone conversations happening and the ones that do are transacted in rushed whispers, the speaker not wanting to give away any hint of the subject matter. A cell phone vibrates across someone's desk and is rapidly silenced. The office, as a whole, is in the zone.

Lex tries to push himself in the same way, focusing on his job, brushing away the sick turn of shame he's cultivated from his earlier non-encounter. He's finally able to settle into a groove, fingers dancing nimbly across the number pad when he gets a chat notification at the top of his screen. His eyes blur as he pulls his focus away from the monochromatic window of tiny rectangles and up toward the soft blue notification bar that tells him NGUYEN, CARMEN has started a chat message session and awaits his response. He stares at it for a moment, wondering if it's some sort of mistake. Wondering if perhaps she's sent a message to him which was intended for someone else in the office. He chances a glance to her desk and sees that her posture is fixed, giant headphones over her ears, fingers gliding over the keys of her keyboard.

He opens the chat window.

CARMEN: (9:42 AM) Hey, Delaware. Was anyone looking for me?

He's frozen, unsure how to respond to the unsolicited query. Sure, she's been much nicer to him in the recent weeks leading up to the holiday break, but he didn't realize they were on chat terms. He fought back the grin creeping across his lips. Another message pops up.

CARMEN: (9:45 AM) Never mind. Not important. Sorry.

Lex glances over at the woman who appears laser focused on her work. She reaches up, adjusts her headphones, then resumes typing, clearly wanting to put all distractions behind her. He clicks on his chat window and begins typing.

LEXINGTON: don't be sorry. nobody came by. you're safe.

He sits for a moment, finger hovering over the ENTER key. He thinks, perhaps too much, about what his message means, how it could be received, wonders if he should add in concern about her obvious distress. He wrestles with the last part. You're safe. It strikes him as heavy, unnecessary, awkward. He hits the delete key fourteen times and presses enter.

LEXINGTON: (9:51 AM) don't be sorry. nobody came by.

Before he knows what's happening, his fingers type another message on their own and press ENTER.

LEXINGTON: (9:51 AM) is everything okay? noticed you seemed a little preoccupied. didn't seem yourself. sorry to pry.

Another rush of blood rises to the tips of his ears and the temperature in the room became almost unbearable. He searches quickly for the unsend button then slumps a little in his chair when there clearly isn't one. He almost says something, almost apologizes out loud for the message. Perhaps, he thinks, he can blame it on the idea that he'd meant to send it to someone else. Perhaps he can pass it off as being a message intended for Sarah, one of the analysts who sits across the office. Would work better in practice were it not obvious that Sarah barely knows his name. She'd once circled the office three times looking to deliver an envelope for him that was accidentally dropped off at her desk.

Just when he was about to clear his throat, another message notification. Click.

> CARMEN: (9:53 AM) Thanks, Delaware. No, it's fine. Just wrestling with some ghosts.
> LEXINGTON: (9:53 AM) i get it, trust me. just wanted to make sure there wasn't something i could do.
> CARMEN: (9:54 AM) Appreciate it. Just some shit that won't let go. Doubt you could relate.

That last line stings a bit, he admits. He's getting a clearer picture of how he's seen around the office, like some lost little puppy that's barely been through anything at all. He doesn't like it.

> LEXINGTON: (9:56 AM) you would be surprised. i have tons of experience wrestling ghosts that won't let go.
> CARMEN: (9:56 AM) LOL
> LEXINGTON: (9:56 AM) truly
> CARMEN: (9:57 AM) LOLOLOLOL
> LEXINGTON: (9:57 AM) google natalie ambrose missing. i'll wait.
> CARMEN: (9:58 AM) . . .
> CARMEN: (10:12 AM) HOLY SHIT!
> LEXINGTON: (10:13 AM) yeah.

Lex's heart is racing. He's not sure why he chose to out himself. As if out-dueling her own horrors would somehow make her feel better. He thought he'd dealt with his past, that he was beyond it enough for it to no longer matter. That it has come roaring back so suddenly and so completely over the course of a couple of weeks tells him he's not as strong as he'd thought. It tells him that he'd simply buried it and not very well.

He can't look over to Carmen, the shame is too present. He can hear the blood pulsing through his ears and he wants to get up, to catch some fresh air or get some water. Anything besides stay in his chair at his desk while a colleague gets her turn to pass her own judgement on actions he didn't take.

CARMEN: (10:14 AM) Shit, dude. That's fucked. I should be asking if YOU're okay.

Something releases in Lex's chest and he begins to breathe again.

LEXINGTON: (10:15 AM) it was a long time ago. those ghosts have been in my face a lot lately, so i can relate.
CARMEN: (10:15 AM) Literal ghosts?
LEXINGTON: (10:15 AM) literal, actual, physical ghosts, yes.
CARMEN: (10:16 AM) LOLOL

CARMEN: (10:21 AM) Holy, shit. Is that why you haven't been sleeping? Fucking ghosts?!?

Lex's fingers type out the message before his brain can debate if the truth in this case is a good idea.

LEXINGTON: (10:22 AM) that's exactly why i haven't been sleeping. they didn't bother me until i got my own place. something there doesn't want me to sleep.
CARMEN: (10:22 AM) Something? Voices?
LEXINGTON: (10:22 AM) to start. voices, noises, weird shit with the size of the apartment changing, growing, shrinking. smells, shit moving on its own.
CARMEN: (10:23 AM) Only when you're alone or have other people seen it? Any apparitions?

There's a moment that occurs in Lex's mind where the relief of telling someone the thing he's carried around all these months blends with the surreal feeling that he's making a connection over something that most people would consider impossible. Or, at least, only experienced by the truly mad among us. It's a strange sensation where everything takes on a light gray sheen. It passes and he continues.

LEXINGTON: (10:24 AM) others have seen it. sent one person screaming out of the building. i've seen movement and figures and weird shit, but only out of the corners of my eyes.

He decides that Carmen doesn't need to know about poor Felicia and the result of her encounter with his apartment.

> CARMEN: (10:25 AM) Solid or shadowy? Have you been able to see through them, the figures? Male or female?
>
> LEXINGTON: (10:36 AM) are you messing with me?
>
> CARMEN: (10:37 AM) I could ask you the same question. Do you really see that stuff in your apartment?
>
> LEXINGTON: (10:38 AM) yes, i do. i really want it to stop. haven't been back there since before the break.

He hits ENTER on his keyboard and goes back to staring blankly at a section of cells that all have the same four numbers out of some random coincidence. He feels eyes on him, someone staring, on the side of his neck. He looks over and Carmen is staring directly into him. She seems to be sizing him up, trying to read him more deeply. It's an intense stare that gives Lex a strange feeling in the pit of his gut.

She doesn't blink and barely moves. Her shoulders rise and fall with each slow, steady breath. The effect of the stare is somehow intensified by the pair of large headphones flanking her face, making her head seem much larger.

Lex shrinks in his chair, shifts, then throws a small, awkward smile her way. The churn in the pit of his stomach is getting stronger and he's breathing faster than he was moments before. He can't quite take the intensity of the stare, the kind of gazing deeply into his soul that only police detectives and sociopaths practice. His smile shatters like thin ice over a frozen lake and he turns back to his screen. His breathing begins to slow. He no longer feels the intense stare and is in the process of forgetting the entire conversation even happened. He mouses over to the chat window and, just before he clicks on the red x to close the window, a new message pops up.

> CARMEN: (10:59 AM) You're taking me to your apartment. Sounds like something I might be able to help with.

seventh

35

Lex has never been the type of person to go into a liquor store, ask for a fifth of vodka and a paper bag, then proceed down a side alley to down half the bottle in greedy swigs. He's considered himself possessed of more class and will than to then stumble from said alley, having downed half the bottle, and lose his lunch next to a trash can a block away from his apartment. Yet, there he is.

He feels a little better but no less apprehensive, standing on the scantly-trafficked sidewalk in a biting chiller of an evening.

He gathers himself, clutching his half-empty bottle under his arm as he pulls his collar up around his neck. The liquid sloshes softly against the glass and the paper bag crumples as he dusts himself and pulls the strap of his backpack up closer to his neck. He's as ready as he's ever going to be, so Lex directs his feet to his building, keenly aware that it'll be the second time he's broken his vow that he would never return to his small abode.

As he approaches the building, Lex sees Carmen on the sidewalk staring up at the gray stone facade. She's still wearing her work attire, a pair of loose khakis that drape in a straight line from her slender hips, and a pale blue collared shirt that's covered with a puffy silver parka. The bright red cord leading from her headphones disappears into the pocket closest to his approach. One hand is shielding her eyes from the glare of nearby streetlights, the other is holding a plain brown paper bag. For a moment, Lex thinks she's also elected to brown-bag her beverage. He gets closer and realizes that her bag isn't bottle-shaped nor is it crimped at the top.

His is and he twists off the top and takes another generous swallow. He approaches her while coughing, trying to catch his breath.

She looks at him, then down to the bag in his hand, then back to him. Smirking, she looks back up at his building.

"Did you bring enough for the whole class, Delaware?" she asks while still focused on the upper floors. He sheepishly offers the bottle. She laughs. "I was kidding. Finish it or put it away. We've got a flat to tour."

He debates the merits of finishing the bottle before tightening the top on the remaining liquid and tucking it into an outer pocket of his pack. He checks himself quickly to make sure he hasn't soiled himself or stepped through anything before returning his attention to Carmen, who has opened her own paper bag. Immediately, he's struck by an earthy, organic, almost manure-like smell, mixed with the scent of dying herbs and rotting flowers. It reminds him of when he would bag leaves and grass clippings in the autumn rains. The bags would burst before making it to the curb and he would be the one tasked with re-bagging the putrid remnants.

The smell from Carmen's bag is much stronger, the essence of those fall chores concentrated in a small package. He steps back as she pulls out a fist-sized sachet. It's made of a rough, open-weave material, sewn closed on one end and tied with a hemp string at the other.

"Hold out your hand," she says.

Lex does so and she plants the bag firmly into his palm. She holds it there for a moment before letting it go. The bag is heavy for its size. The contents feel substantial, but there's no sense that they'd escape from their confines. She reaches into her paper sack again and pulls out an identical sachet before crumpling the bag and tossing it into a nearby trash bin.

"Mojo bag," she says as she grips her sachet in a fist. "Whatever happens, you've got to keep yours with you. They'll protect us from whatever we might find up there."

"It stinks," Lex says as his stomach takes another turn. He has yet to close his hand around his own packet, afraid of what might be inside. He wouldn't be surprised if, when squeezed, a brown-black liquid would come streaming out like the evacuations of an old, saturated sponge.

"You're kidding, right?"

"No, it smells really bad."

"Get over it. It's a lot better than the alternative. You wouldn't want to get possessed or become the victim of a poltergeist, would you?" She does a pantomime of ghostly hands shaking by her face, which has gone wild-eyed and spooky. She drops the act as quickly as she'd assumed it. "Hold on to the bag."

Lex begins to close his hand around the bag and promptly opens his palm once more. He cannot bring himself to fully grasp it.

"It really stinks," says Lex, face scrunched in an expression akin to a small child trying steamed broccoli for the very first time. "What's this thing made of?"

"Don't worry about it," says Carmen. She looks like she regrets offering to help.

"So, hold on to it?"

"Put it in your pocket if that makes you feel better. You've got to keep it on you, though. No matter what, keep it on your person. Do you get what I'm telling you? It has to touch you. At all times."

"I get it. Constant companion."

Lex gingerly pockets the sachet, making sure not to squeeze or grasp it too firmly. He doesn't want whatever it is to spill on him more than it already will. He feels the bulk of it against his butt cheek and mentally works out how to walk without compressing the package. He figures it'll be easy on level ground. Simply keep one leg straight at all times, the back pocket will barely distort. Up the five flights of stairs, however, will be a challenge. He's sure that he's going to feel something damp at some point in the evening, but concludes it's better to feel it in the back pocket than in the crotch.

"Just don't lose it, Delaware," says Carmen. She's staring at the front door. "Your life may depend on it. Not meaning to be dramatic about it and all, but —your life really might depend on that bag staying with you. No joke."

"Got it," he says, pulling his keys from the front pocket of his backpack. He brushes against the bottle one pocket over and is tempted to take another gulp. Instead, he frees the keys from the bag and fumbles for the one that unlocks the main entry door. He tries to do so while holding his breath, fearing what they may encounter. He hesitates.

"Any day, now, would be good," says Carmen. She's standing just over his shoulder and, via the reflection in the glass, looks like she's on the verge of departure.

Lex turns to face her. "You may want to hold your breath or —" He pantomimes holding his hand over his face. He catches a whiff of the sachet, the smell having transferred to his palm, and he coughs. "Good god, what is in that bag?"

"Old family secret, don't worry about it," she sighs, rolling her eyes. She then adds, "Just make sure you keep it on you once you've finally decided to open the damn door."

"I just want to know if it washes out or if I maybe need some bleach —"

"I've got other places I can be."

"No, sorry," says Lex. He turns the key in the lock, pulls the door open and waits. The hall stretches before them, mailboxes to one side, the stairs straight ahead. Light dribbles across the floor and walls from sconces and overhead fixtures shaped like glass blisters, little nickel nipples at the apex. He realizes he's been holding his breath ever since he'd grasped the handle. He's not sure if it's safe yet to exhale and sample the air. He looks back to Carmen, trying to read any expression on her face. She seems at the edge of a very generous limit.

"What is it?" she asks, glancing at her watch. She doesn't seem to notice anything out of the ordinary with the door now standing wide open, both of them standing within the frame.

"Nothing," he replies after taking an unexpectedly deep breath. He half expects to choke, half expects to pass out from oxygen deprivation. Nothing but silence. Neither a whisper nor a gurgle. "Just checking something. I'm making sure everything is safe for the most part."

"What aren't you telling me?"

"You know everything. I'm just nervous. You understand, right?"

He steps through the door and makes his way toward the stairway, inhaling deeply through his nostrils every few steps. He realizes he's not being followed and turns to see Carmen standing just inside the door, one hand propping it open just a crack. She's frozen, staring intently at Lex. Her eyes are searching, trying again to read his intentions.

"I'll ask you again," she says without changing her posture. "Are you serious right now? Do you have some kind of weird, sicko game planned?"

She opens one side of her jacket to reveal a very large knife fit securely to a holster threaded through her belt. She keeps her stare pinned directly at Lex as she does so, continuing her read of his reactions, his movements. He shifts, feeling the intensity of her stare from his chest to his hips. The light glinting off of the knife's handle makes an audible ping that Lex realizes only he can hear.

"Carmen, I swear to you that this is no game," he says. He chooses his words carefully, pulling his thoughts through the thick muck of his mind. "There is some very strange shit going on in this building. If you don't want to do this, fine. I'd rather never step foot into that apartment the rest of my life. I'll go back out to Bayport and you can go to wherever you live and we'll wave to each other at work and life will go on. Trust me, I do not want to go up there."

They stand at opposite ends of the hall, regarding each other for a few beats more. Carmen blinks, closes her jacket, then walks into the hallway while giving her sachet a quick squeeze.

"Lead the way," she says with a nod. He turns and they head up the stairway to the fifth floor.

36

There is nothing that will make you feel more out of shape than trying to climb four flights of stairs at a steady pace while your heart is already racing in anticipation. Lex is winded by the time they reach the door to his apartment. He tries to hide it, hoping to mask his counter-athleticism. The vodka doesn't help. He's sweating and swears he can smell the Stoli seeping from his pores. His vision begins to blur and he feels that he's perhaps about to faint. This makes his heart pump faster, the inevitability of complete embarrassment so close, the pending collapse of any credibility. He recovers and hopes Carmen doesn't notice.

"You'd better not faint before we've even gotten there, Delaware," says Carmen from just over his shoulder. "You should maybe get into an exercise routine. Do some sit-ups or something."

"I'm fine," says Lex, whispering to disguise that he's still trying to catch his breath. "It's just been a while since I've been up. That's a lot of steps."

"Right," she says as a final word on the matter.

They're outside the apartment door and he pauses to look at her. She looks like a billiards player trying to anticipate what the next three shots may hold, all while focusing on the shot before her. Her eyes are open, clear, and focused beyond Lex, beyond the door.

He takes his cue from her and puts a hand against the door, resting his off hand against the frame next to the lock. His breathing has steadied, heart rate almost back to normal. He leans in, trying to listen at the door. He wants to be ready for whatever may lie in wait on the other side. He strains, thinks he can almost hear air flowing just inside. Did he leave the windows open? Is the apartment still there or has it become a gaping hole into the void? He listens more closely, trying to identify a sound that he's sure means they should turn back. His ear pressed against the door, he closes his eyes. The metal door is cool against the side of his face.

He relaxes as he realizes why the faint sound is so familiar. He pulls away from the door, realizing that what he'd heard was the blower fan for his furnace. Deep breath, and he looks back to Carmen who still seems to be working through a strategy.

"Did you say Bayport?" she asks flatly, eyes suddenly focused on his.

"What?"

"Downstairs, you said go back to Bayport? Have you been commuting all the way from Bayport?"

"Yeah," Lex says. The embarrassment he'd been avoiding has returned with a fury and he looks down briefly at his shoes as he tries to make what he's about to say sound cool. "Staying with my folks until all of this stuff is sorted out. No big deal."

Nailed it.

"Right."

He reaches into his pocket and drives a fingernail into the edge of his phone. He half-grabs and half-throws his phone as he pulls his hand from the pocket, sending it flying across the hall. He checks his finger to see if it's bleeding under the fingernail, a selfish gesture considering his phone is sailing toward the opposite wall. There's a small bruise forming underneath his middle fingernail and there's the unmistakable sound of a glass screen cracking as it hits the ground.

Carmen sighs heavily before turning her back to gather herself. Lex swears softly to himself as he turns to pick up the dropped device. Three cracks are spiderwebbed across the face when he flips it over to take a look. He checks to see if it still works. It does and he shoves it into his back pocket alongside his mojo bag before shoving his finger into his mouth to stop the nail from bleeding.

"That was unfortunate," Carmen says as she turns to face the door. She's been laughing quietly to herself, tears forming in the corner of her eye.

He smiles, looks up and down the hall, to her, then stands again before the door. He doesn't bother to put his ear against it. In one motion, much like he'd gotten accustomed to in the barely-eventful weeks he'd regularly come home, he unlocks and opens the door.

It's dark inside the small apartment, the late autumn sunset having taken hold of the city's darker corners. The alley beyond the windows is glowing with the amber light of the street lamps, reflected inward toward the ceiling by the partially opened blinds. Otherwise, he can see the forms of the table just a few feet to his left, the bookcase to the left of that.

He feels along the wall and flips the switches. Warm light fills the space and the two fans begin their lazy cycle. He blinks as his eyes adjust to the sudden flood of light.

Everything looks strangely tidy. Lex isn't sure what he'd expected, returning to his flat after more than a week-and-a-half's absence. He flashes to moments of that last night; broken glass on the floor, being thrown against the wall, futon mattress tumbled over the side of the frame, crumpled on the floor. He expects there to have been even more chaos after he'd left. He'd thought perhaps he would find that the bookshelves had all been emptied, their contents strewn in chaos across the hardwoods. Perhaps the meager contents of the refrigerator would be tossed on top, providing a layer of organic rot. There should be glass everywhere, from the television screen to the dishes in the cabinets, the destruction must be complete. He even expects perhaps an inch or two of standing water overflowing from the bathroom and kitchen sinks.

When he guides Carmen through the door to his dining table, none of this is the case. Not everything is exactly as he'd left them as he fled. Everything, from what he sees, seems to have righted itself. It's cleaner. There's no glass on the floor between the bookcase and the futon. The mattress has been placed on the frame, pillows neatly tucked into the corners. The chairs are arranged around the table invitingly, almost like a photograph from a homemaker's magazine. He even notices the faint smell of patchouli, as if someone's been burning incense. Even the bag of leftover tortilla chips is gone, replaced by the big, industrial-looking candleholder he'd acquired at a flea market.

"Nice place, Delaware," says Carmen. He'd almost forgotten she was with him and her voice startles him. He turns to see her looking over all of the walls peering into the corners between them and the ceiling. "How much do you pay for rent?"

"This is weird," he says.

"I agree. You've made a tiny place look almost palatial."

"No. This place was a chaotic mess when I left. There was stuff everywhere." He gestures with his palms as he turns a full circle. He expects to find something out of place, but sees nothing. Just a neat and orderly home. Very inviting. Extremely unusual.

"How much of a mess?"

"A very big mess. This looks like someone's cleaned up."

Carmen roams the small place looking along the edges of the base moulding, up and down the walls paying extra attention to the corners. She's kneading her mojo bag like a stress ball, mumbling something to herself that doesn't sound like English. Frowning, she stops in front of the futon, staring at the closet door.

Her lips are still moving. Knuckles are turning white from the fierce grip on her sachet.

"That's where things really got weird," says Lex. He hasn't moved past the table, searching the apartment for anything out of place. "All of the screaming and getting thrown."

Carmen doesn't react, finishing whatever prayer or chant she's been mouthing. She holds the sachet out before her face, taking a deep breath, then looks at him as if suddenly noticing he's in the same room.

"How long have you lived here?" she asks, shifting her weight subtly from one foot to the other.

"A few months. It hasn't always been, you know, active. Why?"

She pauses as if she's trying to put together the best words. She gives up and simply blurts out, "you can't stay here. You had it right, you gotta go."

"I know," he says. There's a sense of relief that someone understands what he's been going through. In that moment, he feels a deeper connection with Carmen. "I've felt that way for a while, I just haven't been able to act on it, you know. Like, what would I tell people? That I'm just abandoning the apartment that it's taken me so long to get for myself?"

"Stop," she says. There's genuine fear in her eyes. "You've gotta go right now. Get out."

The room suddenly gets colder and the light shifts. There's no sound, not even a whoosh from the overhead fans. The air seems liquid, everything has suddenly become heavier. Carmen's look of fear intensifies and she slowly starts to move toward the closet door.

Just as she rounds the end of the futon, a familiar song erupts from Lex's phone. His heart sinks and he feels a little nauseous. Mouth dry, he tries to say something to Carmen. She seems to understand and nods subtly back to him. He reaches into his back pocket and pulls out the phone, photo of his missing girlfriend smiling on the screen. Heart racing and hands shaking, he stares at it. The song blares louder. He can feel the vibrations in his palm and the phone dances, the vibration motor seeming stronger than he ever remembers. The screen's glow only adds a coolness to the surrounding light.

"It's Nat," he whispers after what feels like hours of staring at the ringing phone. He swallows over the enormous lump in his throat and fights the tears welling along his bottom eyelids.

"Don't answer it," she whispers.

"It's just going to keep ringing."

"Do not answer that phone. You need to get out. Now."

Lex stares at the green circle hovering just below Natalie's smiling chin. All it would take is one swipe of his thumb. The last time she called, the last time he was in his apartment, he promised he would help her.

"Stop," Carmen says. She's reading his face, reading the desire to speak with the vanished girl once more and the fear in her voice grows more desperate. "Delaware, look at me, please. You need to drop the phone and walk out of the door. That's all you've got to do, but you've got to do it right fucking now."

The swear comes out of her mouth awkwardly, punctuating that she clearly believes Lex is in trouble.

He doesn't look up, doesn't seem to hear Carmen's plea. He simply stares at Natalie's face as it smiles at him through cracked glass from across time. His hand moves almost on its own, pressing down onto the screen, swiping the little green icon to the right. The song stops but the photograph persists. It seems to be darker somehow. The screen's brightness is persistent, but the tone of the photograph seems to shift. The shadows are deeper. It makes the highlights in the background pop more. Her face feels different, more sinister. Her smile seems to be changing as he stares at the static photo. The phone begins to move toward his ear.

"Not a good idea," says Carmen. "Stop and listen to me. It's not going to be her. Drop the phone and grab your mojo bag. It'll help, trust me."

Her voice is shut out by the faint static coming through the earpiece as Lex presses the phone against his cheek. He focuses through the noise, trying to hear clues as to where the caller is. The static fades in and out, pitches wildly like a failed morse code transmission. Far in the background, he can hear breathing. He's certain it's not his own.

"Nat?" he says into the microphone. He can't hear Carmen pleading to put down the phone. He hasn't heard her snap her fingers toward him. He only hears the faint breath behind the pulsating static and whistles in the connection. He leans forward, as if trying to pull himself through the cellular connection to see where the other side lands. There's a sharp gasp on the other end that makes him jump.

The lights fade in the apartment which finally seem to pull Lex's attention away from his phone. He looks up, device still planted against his face, and glimpses Carmen's look of increasing discomfort. She's looking up at the ceiling so Lex follows her gaze.

One thing Lex has always liked about his small place is that it has high ceilings. The ten feet of space from floor to ceiling makes him feel better about the other, smaller dimensions of the flat. As if he counts volume in his calculation for size. He's certain that, if he'd wanted to, he could have lofted a bed against the far wall to increase his living space by about twenty-five percent. It's a tempting prospect, sleeping up high with plenty of headroom above while surveying the confines of his living quarters.

As he stands, cracked device still covering his ear, he looks up to see that high ceiling receding. It's disorienting and he feels dizzy watching the crown moulding and ceiling fans and flat white drywall creep away from them. He looks back to Carmen who is staring at him, saying something he can't quite make out. He's not worried, the static pouring through the earpiece somehow relaxes him as he waits for Natalie to speak.

37

Carmen's lips are moving, she's clearly saying something to him, but Lex can only hear her general tone. It seems urgent. He observes her increasingly frantic gestures in the fading light in a detached, clinical way. It's almost as if he's watching a very good 3D movie of someone trying desperately to warn future victims. She moves toward him without ever really reaching him, a growing look of fear mixed with frustration lining her face. He presses the phone more firmly against his face, listens for a sharp sigh and for Natalie to speak to him in the fading light.

He closes his eyes and imagines a beach in a storm, waves crashing and running along the sandy shore. It fills his chest with an aching nostalgia, a strong desire to be there with her. He waits for her voice. There's a faint breeze that he believes he can feel against the back of his neck. The sun is setting behind storm clouds and he's sure the night will be a rough one. That the rain will not let up and only get more intense as the winds pull chill air off of the ocean. He still waits for her voice, to speak with her. He doesn't care that it'll be dark soon. He can almost see her in the distance, feet licked by the salt foam rising from the inky depths.

Lex feels something else, a hand against his elbow and he opens his eyes. The room has gotten darker, the cold light sprinkling through from such a seemingly vast distance. There's a faint chill underneath, like weak tendrils creeping slowly across his neck. A firm tug at his elbow, then another as a hand grasps his wrist. He looks down as Carmen succeeds in pulling his phone away from his ear, her small hands wrestling with his arm and hand to free it from his grip. She has her sachet clinched between her teeth in a menacing determination, eyes blazing.

He feels a brief flash of anger as he considers pushing her away, fighting her efforts to free him from the phantom phone call. His emotions are a torrent swirling around the cracked piece of glass and metal and plastic in his palm. His thoughts are dark. Violent. He catches himself, seeing the fear in Carmen's eyes and starts to relax. He lets her pull his elbow, freeing his ear of the phone. He immediately feels more at ease, his shoulders dropping from around his ears.

Carmen continues to pull at his elbow, the hand she'd placed at his wrist moving toward the device. He looks at her, heart rate slowing, breath easing. He swears he hears what sounds like laughter coming through the phone just before it cuts out, screen going black.

The room continues to get darker as the ceiling recedes. That's the impression he gets as he collects himself. He barely remembers why he had the phone against his ear. Something about the sound of the ocean. Something about breathing, although he couldn't be sure if was his own or if it was someone else's. Carmen wraps her hand around the phone in his. He chooses to let it go. The moment he releases the device, he feels like himself. A fog lifts and an odd ache sits along his neck and shoulders just at the base of his skull.

Carmen doesn't hold the phone long, tossing it into the kitchen. It lands with a loud clank into the sink.

"Where are you?" she asks. By her tone, she's been asking that question or something similar for a little while. "Can you tell me? Where are you right now?"

He's a little confused by the question. It's an odd query to someone who, admittedly, has been a little distracted. He's never been confused, however, about where he is. He's known he's in his small, demon-possessed flat. He's not seen any actual demons, but that's the explanation he's settled upon. The question that really would have flummoxed him is an even simpler one; who does he think he is? Even in the best of times, that one always trips him up.

"I'm in my apartment," he answers, a slight edge to his voice. "I'm fine, I promise."

There's a pause, shadows deepening across Carmen's face. It makes her seem much more deadly, but he's sure that much of the darkness in her expression is already there.

"Fuck you, dick!" she says. She takes a step back, glancing between him and the ceiling. She begins to knead the mojo bag in her hand once more, working out what to do with both their situation and with Lex, standing there useless. "You should really just leave. Whatever this is is connected to you. You're feeding it somehow."

"What are you going to do?"

"Help you. Like I promised. Believe me, it'll be better for both of us if you go. While you can still find the door. Before it gets too dark or before your phone rings again."

A small laugh drifts through the air as the room gets darker.

"Wasn't funny," says Carmen. She is on edge and she's no longer trying to hide it.

"Wasn't laughing," says Lex.

The air gets cooler. A swirling breeze flits through the apartment raising goosebumps on Lex's arms and the back of his neck. The sweet smell when they first entered has been replaced by a faint sour with an undertone of rot. He can barely make out Carmen's silhouette even though she's standing right next to him. The sound of laughter is unmistakable. A female voice in a faint chuckle. He can almost hear the menacing smile behind it, the grin with hungry eyes.

"Leave. Now." Lex feels Carmen's hand against the side of his elbow, pushing him toward the bookcase at the center of the room.

"No," he says in an act of defiance that surprises even himself.

There's a faint click and the room is suddenly flooded with a stark, cool light coming from the television. There's no movement, no flicker as the futon side of the apartment is thrown into sudden illumination.

The laughter continues around them and seems to drift from the television's speakers. It's faint but clear, far in the distance, carried by echo.

"If you're going to stay," says Carmen in measured tones, "then you need to take your mojo bag out of your pocket and hold on to it. Do not let go of it, no matter what."

She's staring at the television screen as if trying to read a hidden message among the pixels. Lex notes it's the same expression she wears when she's deep into solving an issue on her screen at the office. Her face is relaxed, all of the tension and effort shown through her eyes. She begins mumbling something to herself again, just below her breath. He can only make out vowel sounds among the hiss passing through her lips.

Lex, having decided to see things through, reaches into his back pocket for his sachet, holding his breath as he does so. He's not looking forward to adding the earthy, rotting herbal smell to the bouquet of odors drifting through the air, but he'd rather play it safe. He has nothing to lose and feels the bag may help after all. He shoves his hand into his back pocket and comes out empty. He tries his other pocket with the same result. He feels along his backside across both pockets. They're both empty. Trying the front pockets yields identical results.

He feels a faint tug at his ankles and looks down. The floor beneath his feet seems to be moving, crawling over itself like an infestation of insects. There are ripples, waves moving across the floor away from the television toward the kitchen. Peaks reach up and lick his ankles, offering a small tug at the hem of his trousers. They settle down, rippling faintly around his feet only to increase in intensity once again, tugging at his heels. He almost stumbles backward, catching himself by planting his feet further apart.

"Bag! Hand! Now!" Carmen has not looked away from the screen. Her own sachet is secured firmly in her fist, knuckles turning bone-white. She resumes whispering, words coming faster and more breathless with each passing moment.

Lex searches once more across his waist and hips to find his pockets empty. He looks across the rippling floor, waves and bulges beginning to take the shape of a vast quantity of something scurrying just beneath the surface. The collisions with his feet become more frequent and more forceful causing him to shift his weight constantly to keep from being thrown. He looks around the room and across the floor. One spot catches his attention. Near the door is a patch of floor that doesn't move. All of the lumps are scurrying around a flat swath of floor, giving the bag at the center a wide berth.

He looks back to Carmen who is still focused on the lit television screen. The rest of her body is stiff as she holds a position that seems to be part of the magic she's trying to work. The hand with her sachet slowly moves in circles at her side giving the illusion that her whole body is swaying to some unheard music. The laughter has stopped and there's a faint hum in the air as the light from the television begins to pulse subtly. He then looks at his own sachet lying on the floor, creatures forming an oval around where it lies. Under his feet, the waves become violent, the floor resembling the surface of boiling water in a pot. He finds it more difficult to maintain his balance and knows he has to make a move for his sachet.

"I dropped it," he says. He doesn't look at Carmen. "I see it, I need to go get it."

"Get it or get out," she answers. Her voice is a growl escaping between her teeth.

He nods and takes a step across the bubbling surface of his hardwoods. Just then, with a loud snap, the television shuts itself off. They are plunged into an impossible darkness that causes Lex to lose all sense of direction. The black is so absolute that he cannot tell if he's still standing or has fallen. It's the kind of absolute darkness that makes him question if light ever existed.

The rolling under his feet has intensified, as if whatever has been beneath the surface is breaking through. The lumps and waves he's felt underneath his feet are starting to roll over his toes, over the tops of his feet. He feels things crawling along his heel and up his ankle. Thousands of tiny legs searching and creeping, feeling their way up his legs toward his waist. Pinchers and antennae feel along his hips and begin orbiting his body just below his navel. His heart is pounding and he's fighting to control his breathing, telling himself that none of it is real. That the darkness is playing tricks on the rest of his senses. There's no way, he thinks to himself, that there are millions of insects encrusting his lower extremities. He places his hand at his hip and can feel the slick, round bodies of something dance beneath his fingers. He feels them grab hold and creep along his fingers, hundreds of hard, smooth pebbles with legs and antennae creeping along his fingers and across his palm toward his wrist.

The scream catches in his throat as he frantically shakes his hands to clear them of the infestation. He finds he cannot move his legs and feels something pulling at his waist trying to force him onto the ground. A faint pressure pushes at the backs of his knees, another pressing at his hips and thighs. A force tugs at his calves, urging him to his knees. He fights it with every ounce of will he has left.

A wave of sound approaches from the distance; the sound of something crashing, glass shattering, water pounding rocks beneath an enormous waterfall, bones grinding. The noise is moving quickly and he knows it will fill the room in a matter of seconds. He loses the fight against the onset of panic and begins to hyperventilate. He feels the weight of panic in his chest. He knows that he will be overwhelmed by the approaching sonic onslaught. Warm tears run down his cheeks and each breath is fire in his lungs, released with a moan each time.

A hand grips his wrist in the darkness. Another hand grasps his hand, the rough surface of a sachet pressed into his palm.

“Hold on, Delaware,” whispers Carmen. Her voice is gentler than he expects or feels he deserves. “It’ll pass in a moment, just hold on.”

38

The cacophonous roar doesn't hit as hard as Lex expected. Like a wave that loses most of its energy in the approach, the sound washes around them, filling the air without knocking them off their feet. Carmen's fingernails dig into Lex's palm just a little, but he finds comfort in it. She smells faintly of fresh straw and lemons and he closes his eyes to focus his senses on that. He can't hear it, but he guesses that she's still whispering to him from inside the roar of the room, still reassuring him that it will pass soon.

The insects around his waist begin to fall away, trickling down his hips and legs and over his feet. He wonders if she feels them, too, the millions of hard, smooth bugs that tried to pull him into the floor, tried to yank him into oblivion. He wonders if she truly knows how close he was to being lost, how she saved him. He tries to move closer to her, but her firm grip on his wrist keeps him planted in the blackness as the waves of sound deaden. His breathing finds its rhythm, his lungs feel less strained.

The darkness abides, absolute.

The sounds of bones grinding and metal twisting, then crumbling gives way to the steady fall of water. Even that fades and Lex can hear his own breathing. The light ringing persists for a little while, but that too fades and he can hear Carmen's voice faintly in the foreground.

"You're still here," she says. "It's passing, everything is going to be fine."

He still can't see her even though she must be a few measly inches away from his face. He tries tilting his head this way and that, tries to find something to focus on.

"Lights are still out," she says as if she were reading his mind. "Don't think this dark will let up as quickly, but we'll manage."

"You were crying," Lex says. He doesn't know why this is the first thing to enter his mind. His voice is rough, words croaking from the back of his throat. "Yesterday, when you sat down to your desk, you'd been crying. Why?"

"I don't think our friendship's there yet, Delaware," she says. Her voice hasn't lost the gentle rounding she'd applied before. He finds it soothing. He wishes she was always this way, the kind-sounding, nurturing person pulling him back from the edge of the abyss.

"We're companions on a road trip through Hell. I think we're good to share."

She laughs and he can hear her take a deep breath before answering.

"Let's just say that not everybody who should has your best interest at heart."

"Boyfriend?" He flushes at the presumption. "Girlfriend?"

"Big sister. Sometimes she does things to emphasize to our father that I'm different. That I'm not the nice, traditional, little Vietnamese daughter that she is. Sometimes I try to throw it back at her and it always blows up in my face."

"Is she the favorite kid?"

"Not really, that honor goes to our baby brother. But I'm definitely fourth in the rankings of four kids. The others don't really care what I do, they've got issues of their own. But my older sister, she's made it her life to constantly pull the rug out from under me. I don't know why I get so surprised when she does. You'd think I would have learned by now."

"That sucks, needing to be on your guard around family."

"It's just par for the course with my family. Do you have any siblings?"

"No, it's just been me and my folks. There was a sister before, but she was already gone by the time they had me."

"Shit. Well, consider yourself lucky that you grew up alone. That you had your parents all to yourself so that they could actually get to know you for who you are and not in context of their ideals."

"You wouldn't say that if you had to grow up with parents who were perpetually in mourning."

Lex realizes that they haven't needed to shout over the sound of falling water. The noise is still present, filling in the gaps they leave in their conversation, but it's not dominating the space around them. He also thinks he can see. He's not sure if his mind is playing tricks or if he can really see Carmen's head in faint silhouette against the aggressive darkness around them. He blinks and the faint shadow is there when he opens his eyes.

"I think we're getting some light back," he says. He almost pulls away from her, taking his hand out of her grip. She tightens the hold she has around his wrist and digs her fingernails deeper into his palm, pressing the sachet they're sharing more into his hand.

"I see that, but stay put for now," she answers. A confident edge has returned to her voice as she resumes giving commands. "It's passing, but it hasn't passed yet. Let's be cautious with how we proceed."

"Do you know what it is?"

"No clue, Delaware. Not even a hint." She laughs and it makes him smile.

"How did you learn about all of this? The mojo bag, the chanting you were doing under your breath."

"I wasn't chanting," she says. He can definitely see the shadow of her head moving. He thinks she's looking around the room as they speak, searching for the source of the light that's creeping into the apartment. "I was asking for help."

"Praying?"

"Nope. Asking for help. Bà doesn't understand English and she doesn't like loud talkers, so I was quietly trying to convince her to help us through whatever the hell has wrapped itself around you."

He's not quite sure he understands, but Lex goes with it anyway. After everything they've just gone through, he's willing to accept that there will be many things he'll never quite understand.

"Did she help?"

"Are you dead?"

"Point taken."

"You should really learn to listen to people when they're trying to help you. I kept telling you to leave and you just stood there like a post in the road just waiting for a runaway car to mow you down."

"I didn't want to leave you alone with whatever this is."

"Bà would take offense to that."

"Well, I don't mean to offend Bà. Who is she, anyway?"

"My mother's mother. She came over when my oldest sister was born, but was my biggest ally my entire life. Even after she died. You have her to thank for the bags. Her recipe, her design."

Lex looks down at the shadow of her hand in his, sachet wedged in between.

"Can you see anything other than my outline?" she asks.

"You are a dark shadow against the darkness," he says. He looks into where her eyes should be, hoping to see irises and pupils in the middle of white orbs. Her face, her features remain in shadow. "I couldn't really tell you what part of the apartment we're in."

"I have an idea, and you're probably not going to like it."

"I don't like it already."

"Well, while I feel we've gotten closer and all, spending so much time together in your apartment, there's a limit. You're nice, but not really my type, and I don't want to spend the rest of my evening standing in the dark holding your hand."

"We could just walk out like this. Together."

Carmen's shadow shakes its head.

"We're already using up this one too quickly. Only meant for one, not meant for such a long time against something so strong. I need to go get the one you dropped."

"How do you plan to do that?" Lex's anxiety is rising.

"Before everything went dark, did you see where you dropped the bag?"

"By the door. Carmen, it's too dark. You'll never find it in this dark."

"Your place isn't that big. I'll be fine."

Lex clutches the sack more firmly, feeling her fingernails more deeply than ever. It feels like the middle one has pierced his skin. He tries again to pull her closer and again she leverages her hand around his wrist.

"Don't get stupid on me, Delaware. Or, at least don't get more stupid.

"The light's coming back. At least wait until we can see a little better, then I can go get it myself."

"I think we're in as much light as we're going to get. I'll be fine. Bà won't let anything happen to me. I'll go over grab the thing, come back, then we can plan our escape."

With that, she releases his hand, leaving him with her sachet. He's about to complain further before thinking better of it. He knows that she's probably got a better shot at finding the bag than he does. The dark is very disorienting and he's looking forward to being able to see normally again. She's released his wrist and, with sole possession of the bag, he feels a sudden lightness.

The fading falling water, he realizes, had been pressing on his spirits heavily. His shoulders had been rounded, hunched over with the constant onslaught of travails. With the bag resting in his palm, subtle aroma of rotting herbs aside, everything seems to be improving. He can't help but to smile and sigh, overcome with the feeling that everything was finally going to work out, that they would escape whatever oddities the sadistic spirits around them could throw their way.

39

LEX HAS ALWAYS BEEN MORE COMFORTABLE IN SMALLER SPACES. WHEN confronted with vast, open areas, rooms that stretch across great distances, he finds himself shifting his weight from one leg to the other. His palms begin to sweat, his tongue and throat get itchy, he wants to scream. At times, he's even found a restroom stall or some other tight space to sequester himself to calm down, to grasp hold of reality.

When he's been given no choice but to confront those vast, open spaces, he's developed a few techniques that help make the experience more manageable. Sometimes, he'll cup his hands to either side of his eyes, creating blinders to close off his peripheral vision. If he can sit, he'll gather his knees to his chest, and try to contain his own personal space by making himself even smaller. It's a technique that shouldn't work but does, calming himself in a matter of seconds.

Finally, when all else fails or if the space is unyieldingly massive, he'll simply start talking to himself. There's not a word or phrase that to repeat. He doesn't chant or start slinging around mantras and self-help quotes. He'll usually just walk around, eyes down, holding a conversation with the self he imagines is walking right beside him. It's taken lots of practice to make it appear that he's not crazy, that he's not a madman holding a conversation with someone other people can't see. The advent of bluetooth earbuds has helped. He'd once simulated an entire conversation while walking across the main train terminal just by having a pair of wired earbuds in his ear.

The way Carmen left, barely whispering to her Bà as she made her way through the darkness, reminds him of this. He could hear her and he thinks this is intentional. Her silhouette disappears almost the moment she lets go of the bag. He hears her mumbling as she moves toward what he thinks is the front door. He gives the mojo bag in his hand an extra squeeze as he tries to follow her through the shadows.

There's a loud crash and Lex knows the sound of knees crashing into the wooden futon frame, sending the lamp on the far side table crashing against the wall. The sound is surprisingly clear. He can hear every note of the crashing lamp, the clear percussive tone of the wood frame as it's struck by Carmen's foot. She swears in Vietnamese and that comes through very clearly.

"Wrong way," Lex says, trying to help.

"Stop trying to help," Carmen whispers. "Keep quiet, Bà thinks your voice sounds stupid."

Clearly, Bà has a horrible sense of direction and an even worse sense of humor. Lex guesses that being dead will sour even the sweetest person. He tries his best to think of something else.

A cool blue creeps into the room in thin streaks across the ceiling which still seems twenty-five feet too distant. He looks around to see if he can catch any other details of the apartment. He hopes that he can start to make out other things around him. He looks for the futon, looks for the bookcase that should be nearby. He hopes to spot the doors leading either to the closet or the bathroom, strains to find Carmen, who is feeling her way through the apartment. The moment he can begin to see things, even in low contrast, the sooner he can be put to use, helping to find the sachet he'd so carelessly dropped.

The darkness becomes like another massive room, space that has no visible limits, and he realizes his anxiety is growing. He wants to make his space smaller again. He wants to limit how far his view stretches. With absolute darkness, every place feels as vast as the expanse of space. Nothing has context and the only way he knows he's standing is that he can feel his feet beneath him. His balance tells him that the universe hasn't tilted while he's waited in the abyss. He must, however, make the room smaller.

He chooses to have a conversation with both of his parents. He pictures them standing in front of him, looking down at him pitifully . They're always larger than he is, no matter how old he gets. He always feels like their child, the lessons from earlier in life learned all too well.

He's not sure why Oscar and Lorraine pop into his mind in this exact moment, a moment of budding terror. He thinks to himself, if Carmen can talk to her Bà, then he can talk to his own folks, ask for his own guidance.

He begins with Lorraine. She's always easier to talk to. He tells her about his day, tells her about all of the stupid little blows he takes to his ego while making lots of money for other people. She asks him if it's jealousy he feels or something different, some sort of longing. He explains to her that there is very little longing left in his heart, that it's all been squeezed from him. She laughs a tiny laugh, then sighs and tells him that he's wrong. She tells him that he's nothing but longing and pain and always has been. That he's always felt things more than he's ever been able to say.

Oscar interrupts and tells him that he shouldn't keep things so close to the surface. That all of those feelings of desire and inadequacy, his phrasing, are just weakness and that if he keeps them out and open for everyone to see, he will be taken advantage of. Lex tells him that there's no way of knowing how people will react. He want's Oscar to understand that those feelings are what makes him who he is and he feels them fading everyday. He fears that one day he will cease to be because he can no longer feel. Oscar groans and, though Lex can't see it, he hears the sound of his father frowning and shaking his head.

Lorraine resumes control of the conversation, saying that he can never disappear as long as he has people who love him and care about him. He asks if she means he will be fine because she and his father love him. She tells him that she's always been there and will always be there for him. That she's proud of him no matter what he chooses to do. That all of the troubles he's gone through will be worth it someday, that they're building him into a strong fortress of a man.

Lex asks Oscar if he's ashamed of the things his son's been accused of. If he was ashamed at the attention Lex brought to their house. Oscar says that there's no shame, hopes that Lex has learned something from the ordeal. Lex reassures him that he has and that there will never be another incident like it again. He's learned the right lessons. He's learned what to do and how to deal with people. There will never be another scandal.

Nerves soothed and breathing calmed, Lex realizes that he's been standing still with his eyes closed for a very long time. He'd almost forgotten that he was in his apartment, waiting for Carmen to return to him with his dropped mojo bag. He waits for a few moments with his eyes still closed, straining to hear her move about the apartment. The world around him is awash in absolute silence. There's not even a random drip of water. No footsteps on hardwoods echo across the vast darkness. He's surrounded by more silence than he's ever experienced. It's unsettling considering all of the things the room has thrown at him over the months he's lived there.

He opens his eyes to persistent darkness. The silence adds to the vast feeling of the space and he snaps his fingers to makes sure his ears still work. The snaps reach his ears immediately and clearly. He waves his hand before his eyes. Still five fingers of shadow with nothing beyond. Heart rate begins to rise, breaths shorten, and there's a tingle dancing across his fingertips. The tips of his ears are twitching and he can't help but to blink.

"Carmen?" he rasps. His voice sounds strange, like he can hear it echoing back to his ears before he hears it from within his head. A faint ringing follows his speech before fading quickly in the silence. The quiet pushes against his throat, forcing him to clear it before speaking again.

"Carmen, are you still in here?"

Lex squeezes the sachet in his fist as he awaits a reply. None comes. He considers taking a step forward, considers searching around the apartment for her. It's unsettling to stand in one place waiting to be rescued by a woman mumbling to herself. He feels detached from his own body, as if everything he is has been reduced to a ball of energy floating just over six feet above the floor.

"Just say something and I'll be quiet again," he tries. His voice has strengthened and is just a couple of breaths above a whisper. He tilts his head forward and focuses all of his efforts to listening for a response. He thinks his eyes are closed, but he can't remember.

He hears something. He waits, trying to resist calling out again. The sound is close. It's just before him, faint and steady. He leans forward a little more but the sound stays the same. Slightly rhythmic, jagged at the edges. It feels familiar. He holds his breath to hear better. It stops.

Silence.

Lex releases a sigh. He closes his mouth as he breathes and hears the faint whisper of his nostrils, air rushing in and out. After realizing that he didn't recognize his own breathing, he laughs, releasing a small bit of tension he's been carrying for what feels like a decade. He feels dumb.

A shadow forms before his eyes, the shape of his companion's head and shoulders. He didn't see her approach. She's simply materialized. The suddenness of her appearance makes Lex jump back.

She doesn't say a thing. The sound she makes is not quite human. The sudden smell of iron fills the air. She sways. He still can't make out her features, but her hair looks disheveled. There's something in the way she's moving. The way she's standing. The sound that comes from somewhere below her shoulders.

Lex feels a hand grip his elbow. He looks down and sees the shadow of an arm barely contrast against the black of the floor. He reaches for her arm, and he feels something sticky. Her hand lands on top of his, adding whatever she's covered in to his wrist and forearm. There's a heat rolling off of her in waves.

He hears a gurgle and a damp smack like someone trying to keep their mouth from watering before a meal. He moves his hand to touch her waist and he feels more warm wet.

His mind seizes. He wants to run, wants to grab Carmen's hands and run. A scream is building between his lungs and his chest heaves in preparation to let it out. He feels tears welling in his eyes. Her sticky, wet palm is still grasping the hand with the sachet and he goes to offer it to her.

Lex hears a faint creaking sound behind her.

He leans closer, trying to look into Carmen's eyes. The faint smell of flowers still floats underneath the smells of death. He can only see shadow, only feel slick traces of wet as her fingers pull away from his. Another damp hand pushes him away from her waist and her silhouette starts to fade. He moves to chase it, moves to keep her from falling back. He extends his hand, but she fades and he's left with darkness. He cannot form words even though air is rushing from his lungs, catching a small click in his throat.

The smell of bile and metal linger in the air. The dark seems to press closer. He hears a faint, wet pop followed by something sliding away. A door slams shut somewhere in front of him and he jumps. He still makes no sound, but hears an odd click as he forces air from his chest. The sachet in his hand teeters on the brink of falling. He's too weak to hold on to it. The darkness feels like it's seeping into his brain. He blinks and it remains, constant. There's a new silence pressing against him. He blinks and the dark remains ever present. He blinks and is blinded by the light that floods the room.

Khaki walls and white trim and pale hardwood floors. White cabinets in the kitchen. White bookcases holding multicolored knick-knacks. His brown-green futon mattress cradled within the blonde wood frame. Ceiling fans overhead turning slowly, their lights bright and steady.

He looks down at the thick streaks of crimson that extends like a paintbrush stroke from his feet to his closet door. They get thicker and darker just before they disappear underneath the door. He looks down at his palms, at the rough-hewn sachet teetering on the tips of his fingers. They're covered in thick globs of glistening, dark red.

eighth

40

Lexington Delaware has never been squeamish over the sight of blood. People thought he'd been a weird kid because of it. Not exactly as weird as the kids he'd ridden bikes with and played on little league teams with, but he'd had quirks. He sometimes remembers the time his buddies were out at the baseball field after a storm. The ground was wet and squishy like a green and brown sponge, water pressing up with each of the boys' steps. Their white shoes had long since turned the color of clay.

They were out searching for places to light their little bombs, pastel- and candy-colored paper things with words like "Big Boom" and "TNT Ultra" stamped in comic book text along the sides. The fuses were thick black threads with loose pigtail curls. He had three of them in his hand, squeezing them to feel their girth. He'd thought they would simply find an old can or a couple of plastic bottles, light the fuses with a borrowed cigarette lighter, then scatter to a safe distance and watch the plastic shrapnel fly.

That was until they came across the fresh carcass of a dead rabbit.

It hadn't been apparent how the coney died, there were no open gashes or twisted limbs. It looked to Lex as if it were simply sleeping in short left field, taking a nap after sprinting from the dugout. One boy grabbed a nearby twig and poked at the rabbit. The trio of them agreed that it was dead. The going theory at the time was that it drowned in a puddle that it couldn't hop from. The boys, after all, were very young.

The idea came wordlessly and suddenly, universally agreed upon and immediately acted on. Lex took the three bombs in his fist and shoved them into the limp, brown body. He'd just been barely able to fit them in, hearing a damp snap as he wedged the third on into place. The boys watched as he twisted the fuses together and ran as he lit them. They had managed to make it to the infield grass before turning to see Lex, standing over the bomb-stuffed rabbit as the sparkling flame of the fuse got closer to the buck-toothed mouth. The boys yelled at the tops of their lungs to get out, to run as fast as he could to the left field fence. Lex stayed where he was. The sparks reached the heads of the bombs, there was a moment where the fizzle seemed to go out, followed by a small blue flash.

The explosion wasn't loud, muffled as it was by the various viscera of the dead bunny. It had sounded like someone standing before him popping an inflated paper bag. The fine red mist that sprayed over him was cold and thick, filled with small chunks of raw and slightly charred rabbit. Some bone lodged itself close to his eye just on the side of his nostril. There wasn't a lot of blood, it hadn't been a very large rabbit. Lex, however, seemed to get most of it on himself, covering his face, his arms, his clothes.

That sensation comes flooding back to him as he stands in the middle of his apartment, staring at the place where the uneven swath of glossy red liquid disappears under the closet door. He drops the sachet that had been precariously perched on his fingertips and it hits the floor with a thick thud. He looks at his hands, at his entire body. His shirt, his pants, shoes, all covered in warm blood. He's shocked at how warm it still is. He's frozen by the idea that the person it belonged to was standing in front of him a few measly moments before. His face twitches and he can feel sticky droplets on his cheek and near his eyes.

When the panic strikes, it takes hold suddenly and completely. He catches sight of himself in the third person. The blood streak on the floor is terrifying in the story it tells. That story is made more macabre by his appearance, bloody hands, bloody shirt, blood spattered across his face. His lungs will not cooperate, his heart pounds against his ribcage to be set free. The ringing in his ears almost drowns out the thoughts racing through his brain. Not quite.

He calls for Carmen, draining his lungs of what little air they'd been willing to hold. His voice echoes off of the walls, adding another high pitch to the ringing he constantly hears. He calls for her again, never moving, never stepping toward the door. All evidence points to her being behind that closet door, stuffed or folded, perhaps hanging in among his polos and work slacks. The next sound to escape his throat is some sort of wild animal groan that morphs into a cry and he can feel tears work their way from his eyes. They sting.

Like a bird, Lex's head darts from one direction to the other and back again. He's become the seeker playing the world's worst game of hide and seek. He doesn't want to move though his mind pleads to flee. His body shakes and his arms stiffen every time he tries to take a breath. He stops his frantic, in-place search for clues while taking a mental inventory of what he sees. The table lamp next to the futon is sitting on its side having been toppled when Carmen hit the side of the frame. The kitchen is pristine, almost sparkling, with the clock above the stove flashing a perpetual midnight.

A small brown sachet lies by the front door like a dead baby rabbit.

At his feet is the other sachet, more red than brown. Still rough hewn, still tied tight at one end. There are deep red dots sprinkled across the crimson handprint covering the bag. An odd artifact of his evening. He wonders if it's more powerful now that it has blood soaking into its weave. Next to the bloody mojo bag is the blood trail, dotted with black bits and pink bits. He hadn't noticed the pale pink and white pieces before and tries to look past them to the thick glob in front of his closet.

This is how he will forever see things whenever he thinks of his small place in the city. A tidy little haven with modern amenities and a horror scene of blood and viscera streaked across the floor. The panic spreads and makes its way, finally, to his legs. He feels sore all over, especially in his legs, from having remained tense for so long. He shuffles his feet, sidestepping the streak, and works his way to the closet. He tries to move quietly lest the unknown hears him and decides to return, plunging his world into darkness and chaos once more. There's an answer, one way or the other, behind that door and he must see it through.

He owes her as much.

He moves along the streak, being careful not to stumble over the futon frame, until he reaches the bright white door. There are no smudges on its surface, no handprints or smears on the handle.

He grasps the doorknob and squeezes it for a moment, thinking about the little red bombs, their fuses dangling between his fingers. He wonders if he will jump out of harms way as he opens the door, if he'll try and run from the inevitable explosion of blood he knows is coming. Or, will curiosity capture his feet, holding them in place while he lets whatever is coming wash over him. He turns the knob and pulls open the door, body tense ready to be overrun. He waits for a torrent of red that never happens. He is, however, not ready for what he sees in the closet.

It's completely empty. Not a stitch of his clothing hang on the hanger rack, not a single pair of shoes rest on the closet floor. The walls and floor are pristine, as if it's never held a stitch of clothing. Lex even checks the ceiling. He checks the wire shelf mounted just above his head. All of it is empty.

Particularly the floor. There's not a drop of blood there. The smear wiping across the floor of the small apartment ends abruptly at the threshold. It's as if someone's taken a sponge and swiped the floor clean right at the closet. He steps in, feeling around the walls and the shelf and the bar in case there's a false panel.

Everything feels solid, frame and drywall and plaster and paint. He places his palm against the back wall of the closet. It's warm to the touch.

He then feels a faint scratching from within the wall and he jumps back, stepping into the bloody streak on the floor and almost tripping.

He struggles to regain his footing, one sole coated in a slick red gel. He steps away from the closet, eyes focused on the back wall until his back touches the corner of the center bookshelf. He's startled for a moment when he hears the creak of the wood and the wobble of the television on its stand. He reaches a hand back to steady everything including himself. He's trying not to panic, but it's a losing battle. He's not felt stable since before they reentered his apartment.

The bookcase is still. The television stops rattling. There's a faint sound of whirring fan blades overhead. The fridge pops as it warms. The heater's fan is off. Lex stands, corner of bookcase pressed against his spine. Ears are ringing, skin itches. Faint whistle as he breathes in through his nostrils. He wants to see what happens next, how the next explosion will look. He waits, but not for very long.

The closet door slams shut and he hears running water coming from the restroom.

Lex tilts his head and glances at the bathroom door then toward the front door.

"I've seen this story already," he says out loud. He's decided not to look for Carmen, abandon her. She's gone somewhere he's not quite ready to follow. He's known that he needs to leave.

He rounds the bookcase and goes straight to the front door. Without looking back, he opens the door and walks out, kicking the little brown sachet out of the way with the side of his foot.

41

"You look like murder," says Merle. He's standing in the hallway, staring toward Lex's apartment. He looks like he's been there for quite a while, hands on hips and head cocked to the side.

The sight of Merle standing in the middle of the hall, taking up space from handrail to hard wall made for a surreal scene. He wonders how a man can seem so large and so small at the same time, wedged in the hallway the way he is. Lex feels oddly self-conscious, pushing down the urge to straighten his clothes. He knows what Merle has just said is true in every sense.

"Not sure what you mean," Lex says, shifting his weight over his heels. He tries to look past Merle, toward the path that will lead him to the stairs and out of that building forever. He understands the cowardice behind the desire to just run away, but he's a man with limits. He's not the heroic type to take up arms for a cause, like finding a badly injured work colleague within the walls of a strange old building.

Merle grins like the Cheshire Cat and leans forward as far as he can without taking a step. He sniffs the air in front of him then rubs the side of his nose with a finger.

"Yes," he says carefully, "I'm quite sure you're not. Listen, honey, I'm not one to judge. I've had my fair share of blood parties in my day, trust me. Let me give you a friendly word of advice."

Merle takes a long pause. Never breaks eye contact with Lex, simply stares at him. Almost through him. Never blinking, alway smiling.

"You had a chance to go and didn't take it," says Merle. "Back when that unfortunate girl lost her footing, you could have just high-tailed it out of here and you would've been fine. Hell, you probably would have come out ahead. But now, your best option is to stay. Turn around, go back to your apartment, and never leave."

"Not sure what you mean, Merle," says Lex through his teeth. The urge to be elsewhere is strengthening. His fists are clinched and he can feel his lips peel away from his teeth in what he hopes is a menacing snarl. He imagines how he probably looks; streaks and spots of blood on his face, bloody hands and clothes, snarling like a rabid dog. It would scare him were he not the one making the face.

"Doesn't change the fact that you should just go back inside, make yourself a cup of coffee, and get very comfortable. There's nothing left for you out there, so you might as well join us here."

It's the joining part that halts Lex's forward momentum. He feels like a bear trap has just snapped around his ankle and he has the choice of either waiting to die or chew his own leg off.

"Are you catching my meaning yet, sweetheart?" Merle continues. "You no longer get to leave by the front door."

"I suppose you're going to stop me. What's the plan, fat man? Sit on me until I give up?"

"Very clever. You're all so cute when you finally figure it out. Lash out like little bratty fucking children. That's okay, I'm not mad at you. I just wanted to let you know that there's nothing but pain waiting for you. Look at yourself, covered in. . .what is that, ketchup? I hope it's red cake icing, otherwise, it'll be hard for you to catch a cab or hop on a bus, don't you think? Tell you what. Why don't you just take yourself back to your apartment and have a nice, hot shower. I'm sure you'll feel so much better about things once you've cleaned yourself off."

"Not going back there."

"Well, you're free to use my shower. I won't peek or nothing, I promise."

Merle's smile has somehow faded a little. It's not as broad, not as toothy. His eyes have gone from menacing to sad, almost mournful. He shrinks a little, seeming to take up less of the hallway that he has.

"You should have left before," he says, almost at a whisper. "It wouldn't have got you if you just left."

"That's what I'm doing now," Lex says with a courage he's not found before. He takes a deep breath and walks toward Merle, toward the steps leading down to the entrance. He moves to push past Merle, but the large man backs away from him at the last moment, seeming to not want to get stained red. Lex doesn't look back as he descends the staircase, two steps at a time.

His thoughts swirl in chaos as he hits the fourth floor landing and turns. The word 'join' keeps echoing through his skull. That the apartment would hold him forever, that he would become part of the building forever. That he would never leave. It all comes back to him and the way the world saw him in the months after Natalie left. He tries to push the thought of Nat aside but it bubbles back up to the surface and he can't shake the idea that it's all happening to him again.

42

HE'D BEEN COMING FROM A VERY BORING CLASS. HE COULDN'T REMEMBER the topic. He couldn't even remember what the subject of the class was anymore. Perhaps some obscure literature in some obscure language translated by an obscure scholar. He was still dazed, trying to push back the feeling of being drugged. He'd always felt a little dopey after leaving that class. He'd dragged himself back to the apartment he shared with Nat and Candice and Stephen and Lucas. He wasn't sure who would be home or what state the apartment would be in when he got there.

He'd reached the door and there were people he didn't know standing around just outside. He thought nothing of it, really. It was a Friday afternoon and people were starting to gather for weekend parties. He'd never understood how people could go without sleep for so long, jumping around and drinking and, if they were capable, fucking all weekend. He liked the quiet little spaces he'd carved out with Nat when things got a little too Bacchanal. He'd shrugged it off and pushed into the living room, expecting to toss his bag down at the nearest empty spot on the floor and beeline to the bathroom.

Candice and Lucas were sitting on the sofa, facing a very serious-looking man in a suit holding a note pad. Candice looked like she'd been crying, her eyes all red and puffy, cheeks drawn. Lucas looked drained, as if he'd just donated every drop of blood he'd had to spare. They'd both looked at Lex the moment he walked in and Candice raised a hand and pointed right at him.

"That's him," she said to the serious man. He turned and Lex could only remember seeing the lines around the man's mouth and the thick black glasses resting across the bridge of his nose. He couldn't even see the man's eyes, just a glint of light off of the glasses as he turned his gaze to Lex.

"What's this all about?" Lex had asked. Lucas snarled, moved to get up and was pulled back onto the sofa by Candice.

"Leave him," she said, eyes darting between the two young men. Her expression was a mixture of pity and anger and confusion. It started to dawn on Lex that he'd just walked into a horrible situation and there would be no escaping it.

"Mr. Delaware," the serious man said. His inflection was monotone as if everything he'd said was scripted and read without rehearsal. "Are you friends with a Miss Natalie Ambrose?"

He'd looked down at his pad before saying her last name. Nat's name said in such flat, clinical tones had made the hair on the back of Lex's neck stand on end. He'd looked around the room, trying to find a clue as to what was happening, why there had been a very out-of-place man standing in their living room asking about Nat. The only thing missing was Rod Serling telling him that he'd entered the Twilight Zone.

That's precisely what it felt like over the following few hours. Candice and Lucas abandoned their spot on the sofa and Lex sat down, face to face with the stranger in glasses, answering questions as they were thrown at him. No he didn't know what was going on. No he hadn't seen Natalie that day. No, there wasn't anything he was hiding from his friends. Yes, he supposed you could call their relationship intimate. They'd been living together for almost four months and they were as close as they'd ever been. Sure, she would disappear for a couple of days here and there, it was never a big deal. No, he didn't think she was having sex with someone else. No, he's never been prone to violent outbursts.

Candice stopped what she'd been doing, endlessly drying dishes that hadn't been washed yet in their small kitchen. She'd stared at Lex for an uncomfortable amount of time and the stranger in glasses noticed. He'd pressed the violence questions a lot more, asking them quickly, sometimes before Lex had even answered the previous one. It left no room for Lex's own questions and he'd been far too polite to interrupt.

No, they'd never gotten into a physical fight. No, things never got rough in the bedroom. Yes, they did have sex in inappropriate places. Sure, he'd worried about getting caught, wasn't that the point? No, she'd never scratched too hard. No, they'd never watched violent porn together. No, he didn't like to watch violent porn alone. He didn't like to watch porn at all. No, he's not gay, what did that have to do with anything?

Lucas shuffled off to the room he shared with Candice and slammed the door. Candice was having a difficult time hiding her tears and finally burst.

"Where is she, Lex?" she'd asked as the stranger in glasses was scribbling something in his notebook. "Just tell us where she is or where you hid her or what you did so that we can just get closure."

He'd felt something turn in his stomach. He'd skipped lunch, hoping that he could pick something up at the apartment before going off to the quiet of the lab. There was nothing there to expel except some coffee and the contents of a water bottle.

He's not sure why he'd never worried about how long Nat had been gone. He'd lost track of it. She'd never wanted him to worry about it and he'd grown accustomed to not pestering her about how long she was going to be gone and where she was going when she left. He looked at Candice, puzzled. He'd felt awkward asking what he was going to need to ask her.

"How long has it been, Candice?" he asked, his voice starting to crack from constantly answering questions. "How long has she been gone this time?"

It was hard to remember exactly what Candice said in response. The bespectacled stranger took a step closer, staring down at Lex as he folded the cover over his little pad and tucked it into his breast pocket along with the pen he'd been writing with. He'd looked like a man on the verge of violence, his patience having been run through. In that moment, Lex had been glad he couldn't see the man's eyes. He might have run screaming. The lines around his mouth, however, deepened into a severe frown that Lex knew meant very bad news for him.

He'd found himself in the back of a dark sedan, hands cuffed behind his back, in what seemed like the blink of an eye. He was leaning against the door, forehead pressed against the glass. He'd tried not to look out of the window. He hadn't wanted to see the spectators looking into the car, snapping pictures with their phones to post to their feeds. His stomach did another backflip when he saw how densely the streets were lined with onlookers. It hadn't simply been fellow students and neighbors and curious passers-by. There were newspaper photographers and television news reporters and bloggers holding up tablets. All were staring at him. All with lenses pointed right at his forehead.

The following few days were a hazy, feverish nightmare. In and out of interrogation rooms, being held in small, windowless concrete bunkers. There was a parade of faces, a barrage of questions from all directions. It had been confusing, the number of places he'd been told to go and the people he'd been told to speak with. Parker had been an enormous help, keeping him pointed in mostly the right direction. He remembers telling Parker that he just knew Nat was going to pop back in at any moment. All they needed to do was wait.

She never did.

The length of her disappearance stretched from days to weeks with all eyes and most fingers directed at Lex. Candice seemed to be leading the charge. He didn't know where she'd gone. No, he doesn't know how he'd lost track of how long she'd been gone. No, they hadn't been fighting. No, he didn't know that he was the last person she'd seen. Yes, he knows how strange it seems. Candice would stand outside his parent's house, leading the vigils to make Lex tell the police where he'd taken her, end the long nightmare.

He didn't know how long his own nightmare lasted. The calendar told him that almost a year passed, but to him it seemed much longer. He was shunned, people whispered whenever he passed. No matter how many times he'd professed his innocence, people stared, thinking that he was guilty of something. Skin like that had to be.

After a while, the police shrugged, not being able to make their timelines match with his alibis. That didn't stop neighbors from their own judgements. That didn't keep the unkind emails away. He changed his phone number, removed himself from social media, barely went outside. Television and newspapers lost interest when the police did. They'd found her car twelve-hundred miles away, so the authorities called off their attack. The car had been abandoned, and the rumor was that they'd found something else with the car, but they'd never said what. Lex wondered if it was a note. His parents wondered if it was her or, worse, some part of her. He'd doubted it. If they'd found something to lead them into the worst conclusion, then it would have made news.

Neighbors and former friends, however, had longer memories. He'd been ostracized by his small group of former friends. None came to visit after he'd been exonerated. None of them even spoke to him, Parker being the lone exception. Neighbors around his parents' place were even worse. He'd stopped going outdoors because parents would pull their children closer whenever he walked nearby. The park at the corner would empty the moment he'd decide to sit on a bench or linger on the corner to watch dogs play. He tried waving to the older people in the community, people who'd predated his folks in the neighborhood, and they would simply frown or scoff. It told him that they'd believed he'd gotten away with something.

That had been the prevailing attitude of most people, that he just had to be guilty of something.

Oscar wasn't having any of it and would berate anyone he caught side-eyeing his son. It was the first time Lex could remember Oscar acting paternal. He'd thought it was out of some softening of his heart, but it turns out that Oscar was more concerned with the last name his son wore. Lex's father wanted him to get back on his feet so that he could work behind him to clean up whatever mess other people thought he'd gotten into.

That isolation destroyed what little confidence he'd earned. His life had been derailed and there seemed to be nothing he could have done about it.

It all started because of the way things seemed. People weren't interested in his fact, only the story they could build around him. This was what was going through his mind as he rounded the landing on the fourth floor on his way out of his apartment building. What story could be told by bloody hands, bloody clothing, brown skin, another missing woman?

43

"YOU'RE NOT GOING TO FIND ANY PEACE OUT THERE," SAYS THE OLD SUPER, standing in the fourth-floor hallway. He's wearing a blue coverall with tools tucked into a utility belt at his waist, their handles protruding at odd angles. The largest flat-head screwdriver Lex has ever seen is sheathed down his thigh like Zorro's rapier. "Probably more of the same. Best you didn't even bother."

His voice is more forceful, speaking at more of a command than rebuke. He still doesn't smile, keeping his birdlike eyes fixed on Lex.

"I'm not finding any peace in here," Lex says, returning the old man's stare.

"You're too busy fighting it to find peace. I knew you were too stupid to get it and not smart enough to get out before you got too involved. You have that optimistic look about you that I can't stand."

"What the hell is this place?"

The old man takes a few steps along the hallway toward Lex. He's smiling just a little, hand resting on the head of a hammer at his hip, the chime of keys pealing from beneath the coveralls. Behind that smile, Lex sees depths of contempt, loathing. He shrinks back a little, temporarily losing his nerve as the old super gets closer. He's hit with the sudden smell of cleaning products and grease and heating oil.

The lurking super looks like a walking grease stain, even more so as he gets closer, as Lex starts to make out the details of his features; the hair flaring out of his ears, the lines radiating from his eyes, the dense bushiness of his eyebrows. The old man looks like he's charging and Lex is directly in his path.

The lights in the hallway flicker and go out for a moment. When they come back on, the old super is no longer charging. The man is no longer in the hallway.

Like a blink, the man is gone. He hears the old man laugh, distant and hollow and he looks to his side. It's coming from the open door to a nearby apartment, a door that had been closed mere seconds before. He looks through the door, then drifts into the apartment within.

Lex looks around the small apartment, similar to his own with a couple of subtle differences. The apartment has an extra door in the far wall which appears to lead to a separate bedroom. The kitchen seems a little larger as does the main living space. There are two very ornate armchairs in the middle of the room facing windows that look out over the street at the front of the building. The darkness has a warmth, streetlights casting the entire scene in amber. The old super is standing at the windows looking down at something in the street. He points at something and addresses Lex without looking up at him.

"You've got trouble and not a little bit," he says. He's almost smiling as he does, the lines in his face deepening, his eyes becoming impossible slits in the folds of his face.

"You haven't answered my question," Lex says. He's shivering.

"Don't have to."

Lex steps to the windows and looks down at what the old man is pointing to. Parked at the curb just outside the building is a black sedan, shining and silent. The two detectives, Newhouse and Flake are nearby, Flake leaning against the driver side door while Newhouse walks laps around the parked car. Flake is speaking with someone just out of view, someone appearing to be standing just outside the door to the building.

"Why are they here?" Lex asks, shoulders suddenly tensing. He feels the familiar defensiveness return, a revival of feelings he'd fought through in the months after he'd been accused of murdering his girlfriend. He stares down at the two cops and sees two other puffs of fog in the air. Unseen people were standing directly below their vantage point, the building blocking his view of them. He didn't need to ask. He knew who it was.

"The pigs were called," says the old super, "by the meddlesome pair that have been following you around. Don't tell me you're too stupid to have even noticed them."

"I don't understand," Lex says. "What did I do to them? And why would they call the cops?"

Lex has a picture of being stalked, of having the couple follow his every step, waiting for him to do something just a little off. He imagines them standing behind him while he shopped for groceries, sitting nearby as he ate his lunch, staring over stall walls as he took a shit. He'd known they were everywhere. He'd stopped seeing them.

"Why the hell do you think I'm going to tell you that, idiot?" the old man pushes himself away from the window and walks around the empty apartment. "I will tell you that we'd thought about putting you in this one. Didn't think you had enough in you for the hungry room upstairs. Management was adamant. They said you had enough to keep the Empty well fed for a very long time. Long enough, at least, for them to find more tenants."

Lex can't take his eyes off of the scene developing down below. Flake is taking out her notebook and starts to write something. There's the flash of a gloved hand and someone is gesturing, pointing at the detective then to the building across the street before disappearing again. Flake nods and writes more in the notebook. Newhouse hasn't stopped moving and occasionally nods when she makes her way around to facing the couple standing sentry at the building.

"You fucking proved me wrong, kid," the old man continues, stopping at the kitchen sink to run his finger along a new bead of silicone. "You got plenty of worries, I give you that. I thought it would get bored with you, run out of juice and just spit you out, but you surprised me. The Empty has quite the nose for the lost. That one bit when you brought that poor girl up to your place and just fucking left her there. Classic! The room just chewed her right up. She had it worse than you."

Lex holds himself still, trying not to react to anything happening around him, anything the old man says. He takes it all in, makes all the connections. His spine stiffens. He doesn't feel sad, doesn't get angry. He just stands and soaks it all in.

"Right now, I can see it in you, all that worry. All that trouble. Just dripping off of you like dirty bath water. This place loves it. Your little room just loves it. That whole thing, just now, with that little girl you brought up. Nguyen Ca Minh. That one is loaded with worries. She's going to last a good, long time in the belly."

Lex can't hide the shock. "Carmen? What did you do to her? You didn't have to kill her."

"Aw, she ain't dead, stud. Not yet. Saving that one for later. For after you've shaken off your entanglements and conceded defeat like the good little boy we know you are. You'll see her again, I'm sure." The old super nods again at the windows before taking a loud, phlegmy sniff.

"This doesn't explain," Lex says carefully, "why the people who have been following me are standing outside with the two cops who questioned me after Felicia's accident."

"Damn, you're slow."

"Who are those people?"

"I know you'll work it out. If not, well, it's not like you're going anywhere any time soon. Plenty of time to puzzle it out."

Lex steps back from the windows and looks around the empty apartment. The walls are painted a dark blue with white trim, the door to the bathroom, and bedroom are open ever so slightly. The shadows behind those doors seem a little deeper. Perhaps it's the shade of blue, lending an austere air to the otherwise small apartment. The air is cooler as well, with the fans whirring at full speed overhead.

Lex's mind races through the possibilities for the identities of his two malefactors. He considers the most extreme ideas, that they're old neighbors still upset about the situation with Nat. They could be related to Natalie somehow, some distant aunt and uncle that demand some sort of revenge, a twisted sense of justice against a man who had nothing to do with why she's missing. This leads him to another conclusion and he looks to the old man as he finally makes the connection.

"There's the fucking light going on behind the eyes," says the old man.

"They're here about Felicia," says Lex. He thinks for a moment before continuing. "They're here about her and they think I had something to do with what happened to her."

"It was your fault after all," says the super, laughing.

"It was an accident. I didn't do anything wrong." Lex is feeling that same tension in his lungs, preventing him from catching a full breath. His blood-caked fingers are flexing, opening and closing fists. "We weren't in the apartment together when whatever spooked her happened."

There's more laughter filling the apartment. It's not coming from the old man, but seems to be drifting into the living room from behind the partially opened doors. The shadows of the apartment are cruelly laughing at him.

"Of course it was you, kid. It's all you, you damned idiot. That girl had worries. That young lady was loaded with them. She was ready to unload them all over the place, leave them here with us. Not as much as you got, but she had a good, fair share. Then, I guess the Empty got a little too greedy, let her get away."

"What the hell is the Empty?" Lex is quivering.

The super holds a palm up and shrugs, "you're standing in it, kid. At least a small part of it. Plenty more in plenty places. Your girl would've run into it sooner or later."

"She didn't have to die."

"Oh, I agree. She just stumbled. You made the girl so scared, she fell over herself trying to get away from you, from your little room. You shouldn't have brought her here if you didn't want her to be sampled, if you know what I mean."

"They're blaming me. For Felicia's fall, they blame me."

"They don't think it was a fall, champ. They think you threw her. Those two sad relics down there are telling the pig all about how their little girl was lured to his home by a serial murderer. They did all their research. They know about how your made that one girl disappear. What was her name?"

"Natalie—"

"Not important."

Lex's teeth are clinched. His entire body feels like it's ready to pounce. He lowers his head and tries to shake it off, looking at the dark whirls of grain in the hardwood floors. The old man continues, seemingly inspecting the walls and millwork near the apartment's door.

"They know who you are. They know what everybody thinks you did and they think you did it to their sweet, innocent little girl. Only, you got caught this time before you could make her disappear. That's what they've been telling the cops, anyway. Trying to get someone to act before you strike again, killer."

Lex feels some truth in what the man is saying. He's never been able to shake the specter of all that exposure, all of that unwanted attention for something he never did. He'd hoped that it was all in the past, that he'd left it behind and was allowed to move on with his life. The job was a first step, the apartment was a second. Independence was within his reach and he'd chosen his homestead poorly.

Images fly through his mind as he inhales deeply and closes his eyes. The puzzling look on Felicia's face as she passed him in the hall, as she'd rushed down the stairs. The way she'd turned and stumbled and fell. The way her body seemed to crumple as it hit the bottom floor. How the hallways and stairs seemed to stretch themselves, like they were sighing after a big meal. He wonders what would have happened had he stayed, had he not gone hunting for booze at such an off hour, leaving his guest to fend for herself. Would she have still fallen to her death? Would the Empty have found another way to claim her?

"Yeah, they've had their eye on you. They saw you try and introduce us to your useless little blonde friend."

"It pushed us away," Lex says, opening his eyes.

"Little bitch was useless. Wouldn't have been worth the trouble. But, then you brought us tonight's little bargain. That pair down there saw you bring her in and they'd seen enough. So, that's why the cops are here. That's why Felicia's parents are trying to get them to break down the doors. They've got pictures. They're probably buzzing you right now, trying to get you to answer. Trying to get you to stop whatever vile thing you're doing to that poor, innocent little lamb you've led to slaughter. They don't know the fucking half of it."

The super has made his way back to the windows and looks out over the street scene. He smiles, or folds his face into what could seem like a smile, could seem like a grimace. One cheek twitches when he blinks. His thin lips stretch impossibly and the shadows around him continue to laugh. Lex hears a drip of water coming from the bathroom.

Lex acts on impulse. He bursts into a full sprint, running for the door. Just before he gets to it, it slams shut before him. He turns and the super is still staring out the window. He grasps the knob and tries to twist, to pull, desperately. It gets warmer and warmer in his hands until it nearly scalds him. He kicks at the door, but it doesn't budge. It stands stolidly, unimpressed by his assault.

The laughter grows more pitched and echoes off of the walls, bounces from the windows. The old super still doesn't move, still admiring the view of the scene below.

Lex looks around the empty apartment for something he can use to pry the door open, He runs to the kitchen and searches all the cabinets and drawers.

"Idiot," says the old man, picking something from his teeth. He shakes his head. "You're about the dumbest one we've had in here."

Lex ignores him and makes a move toward the bedroom. The shadows on the other side of the door are dark, but he scrambles toward it, thinking of perhaps finding the fire escape. The door slams shut, rattling the frame. Just before he reaches it, the doorknob begins to glow red, wisps of smoke rising from it.

The laughter gets louder and Lex hears the faucet in the bathroom open, spilling what sounds like a torrent of water into the sink. He runs to the window and begins pounding on the glass. He tries to unlock it and pull it open, hoping to shout for help, but the lock is stuck. He sees Detective Newhouse stop her orbit around the sedan. Detective Flake is putting away her note pad with one hand and seems to be reaching into her pocket for her keys with the other. The gestures of the gloved hands become more frantic, both hands directing an unseen orchestra.

Lex pounds on the window, hoping to grab their attention. He begins yelling at the top of his lungs. The sound rings in his ears, blending almost in harmony with the laughter that has filled the room. His fists are sore. He's having trouble catching his breath. He steps back to make a run at the window, hoping to force it out with his shoulder.

A hand grasps the nape of his neck and pulls him down to the ground. He looks up at the old man's face just before a fist comes crashing into his nose.

44

"DAMN, THAT FELT GOOD," SAYS THE OLD MAN. "I'VE BEEN WANTING TO do that ever since I met you and I have to say, it was fucking worth the wait."

Lex awakens in the bathtub, face throbbing from his nose outward toward his cheeks. He's having trouble focusing, vision swimming back and forth, side to side, like a new sailor gaining his sea legs. He blinks and reaches a hand toward his forehead, drawing back little at the sight of the caked and cracking dark crimson coating his digits. He feels along the sides of his nose and winces in pain. He's never had a broken nose before.

He can feel the blood drying on his face and wonders what else could happen before he begins to look like a boxer in the middle of a fifteen-rounder. He touches his upper lip and the blood there is still moist. Everything goes gray around the edges and the blinks himself away from passing out. He sits up in the bathtub and looks around.

The light is red, eerie. He'd first thought that everything was tinted red because of all the blood on his face, that he was seeing things. After blinking a few times, trying to focus on the tile, on the towel bars, on the curtain rod over his head, he realizes the room is glowing red. The light fixtures over the sink and mirror are switched off, pale glass ghosts mounted to chromed rods. The red is coming from the tiles, from the tub he's in. He looks over the edge of the tub and the floor is pulsing a deep, unsettling red.

He doesn't hear water running in the sink the way he had before he was knocked out. The tub he's in is dry and he sits up, wincing, to get a better look at his surroundings. He hears a faint breathing behind him and hopes that it's the old man standing just inside the bathroom door, looking down on him in triumphant disdain. He quickly realizes, however, that he's alone in the bathroom, that the breathing is coming from inside the walls, and the door is shut.

"You'll come to like it here," says the old man from behind the door. "You just gotta accept that you're better in than out."

Lex finds his feet and steps from the tub, avoiding looking at himself in the mirror. He presses against the door and puts his hand on the doorknob, gingerly at first. As he wraps his hands around it, he feels a faint throb. It's almost like he's taking the door's pulse, feeling a subtle knock against his palm and fingertips. It feels warm, supple. Not like a doorknob at all. He feels his shoulders relax and some tension release from his chest. Fighting the urge to close his eyes, to lean into the sudden bliss, he twists the knob and pulls open the door.

The rest of the apartment is bathed in a deep violet light, also emanating from the floors and walls and ceilings. The windows look blacked out, throbbing in the frames. His euphoria is growing and Lex has trouble letting go of the doorknob. He's having trouble understanding what's happening, but is starting to not care. He's not felt that good in what seems like years.

"Yeah, let it wash over you," says the old man. Lex looks to his left, toward the source of the voice. The super is standing just by the door to the bedroom, his thumbs hooked into the top of his tool belt with the massive screwdriver dangling down the side of his thigh. Lex smiles. He can't help it. "You're not going to feel anything. The upstairs room did a good job softening you up, but this one's hungry too. Tempted to take you to the other empty ones, let them feed on you too, but I guess it don't matter. All goes to the same place in the end."

The floor starts to ripple below Lex's feet. The ripples work their way up the walls, around the doors. They don't break around his feet, but simply lift him in place, tossing him like a tiny boat on choppy water. He closes his eyes and rides along.

An image floats into focus as he stares at the backs of his eyelids. The sea is dark and vast. Choppy waves interrupt the darkness and he rides along, letting the breeze caress his face. He feels the tug at his clothing, the rise and fall of the sea beneath him. He almost smells the salt in the air. He looks around and the sea stretches onward, infinite in all directions. There's a lightning flash in the distant clouds, throwing the scene into a brief gray contrast. He can see the smaller ripples in the waters, like a torrent bubbling deeply within, struggling to hold itself back. It absorbs all of the fear he may have felt standing on the surface of a roiling sea.

Lex opens his eyes and sees the shadows all around him, human shapes drifting about like dense fog. They dance and float in the still twilight. He can barely see the edges of the room, the deep purple glow throbbing from the walls. He reaches out a hand to a feminine figure seemingly hovering just before him, beckoning him with a shadow and fog. He smiles once more and is lifted from his feet. He feels the floor drop beneath him, feels the gentle peaks of the wavy floor lick the bottoms of his feet, brush against the sides of his toes. He reaches both bloody hands toward the figure. It drifts toward him and he drifts away from her, floating backward. He doesn't mind. His shoulders relax, his ankles release, letting his toes point toward the ground.

The old super saddles to his side as he floats slowly backward toward the bedroom. The old man tilts his head upward, reaches up and pokes Lex in the ribs.

"You're almost there, champ," the old man says, a shade of derision is barely caught by Lex. He doesn't care. "Damn, you're a fucking idiot, you know that? This would all be so much sadder if you just weren't so dumb."

Lex moans his reply. He tries to tell the old man that he won't get away with whatever he's doing in that building. He tries to tell him that there's no such thing as the Empty, that people will come looking for him, that his parents, Parker, detectives who think he's murdered people, all of them will come hunting for him and tear the building apart searching for him.

He then thinks of how easy it had been for Natalie to disappear. How there was a brief search, a once-over of all of her usual spots before the finger pointed squarely at him. The question begins to nag him. How much of her life did they really turn over before Lex became the focus of accusations and recriminations? Did they truly search, unlock the hidden doors of her life before landing on a convenient scapegoat?

He'd been told during the entire process that the authorities felt it was very likely that the disappearance had been all Lex's doing. It was the way they liked to work, go with the simplest solution, pound at the square peg until it fit the round hole. Had they really dedicated themselves to finding the truth, he might not have been dragged through the muck for as long as he had. He tries to think of the person his own disappearance would land on the hardest. Which person out of the handful in his life would become the nail to the investigators' hammers, being pounded down until there was nothing left of their lives?

A sharp pain shoots up Lex's spine and he looks around to find the source. He begins to drop to the floor, the force holding him aloft weakening. He looks at the old super and sees a shadow of concern pass over his eyes. The old man edges closer, putting his face right at Lex's chin.

"Having second thoughts?" asks the old man. His breath smells like motor oil caked in sulphur. "No room for second thoughts, my dumb little lamb."

The pain rises up through the base of his skull and he reaches back to feel if he's been stabbed. Confused, he looks around. There's nothing there. The old man grabs him by the shoulders, his hands like a pair of vices.

Lex thinks again about who would suffer from his absence. Parker would notice first. Lex knows that his best friend would be the first one to sound the alarm, to try and gather a search party. Parker would channel that frantic energy of his into a vicious urban search that would leave no alley unchecked. He knows that authorities would question Parker and all of his answers would turn their doubts back on them. Nothing would stick to his friend. They could try and pin Lex's vanishing on him and he would use a psychological jujitsu and force them to keep searching.

"No one will miss you, loser," croaks the old man. "You're not wanted, you've hardly been noticed. What makes you think that anyone would notice after you've finally found some kind of use for your life."

The face of his father flashes before him. He's not sure if Oscar would let it show, but he knows the man would take it very poorly. He would take it out on strangers, take it out on well-wishers. He would then retreat to the private place he shares with Lorraine and grieve deeply. Lex isn't sure how he knows this, but he is certain that the grief would touch his father in whatever light places he has left, turning them a bitter dark.

The old man's hands grip Lex's shoulders tighter as he realizes that Lex is no longer drifting backward, that the floor is no longer rippling and moving. All of the shadowy, smoky figures about the room have stopped their waltz. The figure that once gestured toward him stands still, frozen in her reach. The old man's eyes are the picture of strain, his lips pulled back to reveal a partially-toothed grimace.

"You are unwanted, freak," the old man growls. He leans ever closer, his forehead almost in Lex's jaw. Wisps of wiry hair pass between his lips.

Lex pictures his mother's face, wondering what she will do when he no longer exists. Will she sit vigil, waiting by the door for him to return home? Pretend to take it in stride that he hadn't returned yet, go about her everyday life the best she could. She would take the support she'd get from her neighbors gratefully. She would smile faintly, put on a brave face, say all the right things to the well-wishers.

What torrent of sorrow would rage behind the composure she maintains? Lex can see her in private moments, when she comforts Oscar. She's holding his head against her shoulder, hand pressed against his damp cheek. Her tears mixing with his, their sobs in sync. Ragged breathing muffled by the pillows in their room, the dark drapes hiding their loss.

Lex's pain ricochets inside his skull and lands behind his eyes. His fingertips go numb. He struggles to flush the image from his mind, the image of his parents weeping in silence, their sadness unseen. Firm hands on his shoulders try and push him back, try to guide him toward the bedroom. The old man has his head down as he focuses all of his strength in the effort of steering Lex the final few feet into oblivion. The shadow figures in the room seem to solidify, details forming where they'd been mere suggestions before. Eyes and noses and ears and fingernails at the ends of pointing fingers.

Lex feels his resolve strengthen, knows he must stand his ground. He begins to lean back into the old man, providing more resistance. The old man tries for an advantage, tries to gain leverage. He uses his low center of gravity to throw the larger, younger man off of his feet. Lex grapples with the man, resists with all of his strength, but can feel himself slipping. Feels himself begin to fall backward. He grasps at the old man's tool belt, trying to find something to use. The man shifts his hips while stepping to try and throw Lex.

Lex feels his ankles leave the floor. He tries to grab the old man, but he's too strong. Muscles flexing like rows of rubber bands, tensing with little effort. The old man's grip becomes pincer-like, adding to the pain in Lex's spine.

Lex feels around the tool belt in search of one final advantage. He grasps the handle of the old man's screwdriver and pulls it free from the tool belt. The old super doesn't notice, focused as he is on throwing Lex, on pushing him through the bedroom door and into the heart of the building. Lex is frantic. In one final, desperate flail, Lex jabs the long flathead screwdriver upward through the old man's cheek.

A soft crunch as the flat tip erupts from the top of the man's head over his eye.

45

EVERYTHING GOES STILL IN AN INSTANT. THE OLD MAN STOPS STRUGGLING even though he's moments away from throwing his quarry. Lex relaxes as blood pours over the handle of the screwdriver, over his hand and down his arm. There's a new faint, warm spray across his face. He smells bile and onions and rot. The old man pulls away and Lex looks into his eyes. They're frozen in a state of shock and fear. Blood has begun to pool around the irises. Red tears start to leak from the corner of his eye and down his cheek. He's not shaking, he doesn't make a sound. He simply stands, weakened.

The shadows in the room become faint once more. Wisps of smoke roll off of them and they begin to scatter. Their edges disappear as the figures become formless lumps. Then they're just clouds floating above the floor. Some hold in place for longer. The female figure that beckoned Lex remains a few more moments. Suddenly, they're all gone.

The room brightens, light from the street below spilling into the apartment through the windows. The scene begins to take gruesome shape as the old man in Dickies coveralls starts to whither. The liquid pouring from his wounds is a deep, ancient red and flows like warm maple syrup. Lex is frozen, still holding the long screwdriver in its place just under the wilting old man's chin, who gets smaller as the liquid oozes from the body. Eyes bulge from their sockets and, in one final rattling gasp, the old man falls away, sliding from the tool.

Lex stands for a moment in the artificial twilight, the apartment silent and empty. He's covered in red ooze, smiling, holding his weapon like a dagger. He looks at the ceiling and notices a small spray of red dots tracing an arc directly overhead. He looks down at the growing pool of dark crimson at his feet. The liquid gets darker the more it spills from the old man's corpse.

He takes a deep breath, releasing the screwdriver from his grip, and begins to laugh. In that laugh, he releases all of the tension, all of the guilt. He lets go of the burden of loneliness, the pain of solitude. He takes in a newfound freedom and spreads his arms at his sides like wings. He closes his eyes and lets a new ease wash over him. He feels free and light. There is one final thing that he knows he must do.

Slowly, Lex walks to the door of the apartment, ignoring the burgundy trail he's leaving from just outside the bedroom. He opens the door, staining the doorknob as he grasps and turns it. Just outside the door, standing in the hallway is Merle Ogden, face frozen in an expression of terror.

"Is it over?" he asks. He tries to look past Lex, tries to see what's happening inside the fourth-floor apartment. Lex steps aside to allow Merle passage, but the man seems too frightened to move. "Just tell me, is it all done?"

"No," says Lex, smiling. He passes Merle and pats him on the shoulder, leaving a dark crimson handprint on the large man's bathrobe. "I'm not going to be here when it starts up again, though. I'd suggest you not be here, either."

Merle gasps, suppressing a gag as he stares at the handprint on his shoulder. He then whimpers his way back to the fifth floor, shuffling his feet the whole way.

Lex leaves a diminishing red trail down the remaining flights of stairs to the first floor, making sure to run his fingers along the walls where he can. The syrupy liquid on his hands has begun to dry as he traces his fingers along pale gray textured wallpaper.

He stops at the mailboxes, staring forward toward the metal-framed glass door. He's not sure how much time has passed from the time he saw Flake and Newhouse speaking to the old couple stalking his every move. As he rounded the landing at the top of the first flight of stairs, he wondered if he'd be too late. He wondered if the small crowd gathering at the entrance to the building would still be there, waiting to confirm recriminations.

Staring at the front door, he sees that he's just in time. Standing just outside the doors, their backs to him, are the couple. He can hear that they are yelling though he can't quite make out exactly what they are saying. He sees, just beyond the couple, the two detectives. The women seem to be on the verge of some very violent action. Flake's patience has disintegrated and Newhouse stands with her hand resting on the handle of her service pistol. Lex would guess that the strap securing the handgun in the holster has been unsnapped and Newhouse's fingers are gently caressing the safety.

Before he takes another step, Lex glances at his reflection in the darkened glass. His face is streaked red with dots of darker red and chunks of something unknown scattered among his features. His nose is a little swollen and not quite sitting as straight as it had that morning. His clothes are blotted with crimson, thicker at the shoulders and across his chest. His sleeves are completely dyed as are the fronts of his trousers. His hands are coated and caked in varying shades of deep, dark maroon from finger tips to wrists. He smiles at the reflection, hoping that his image makes a lasting impression on the participants of the scene outside.

He glides to the door unnoticed.

Lex stands, hands resting on the push bar just inside the building. He waits.

ACKNOWLEDGEMENTS

As with many firsts, this book would not have been possible without the cabal of supporters, direct and otherwise, who helped me bring this novel to life. Thanks as always to Janice and Fred Dudley for encouraging the explorations of my imagination. These characters and this story came about from the practiced probing of an admittedly verdant imagination (yes, I know I just used that word, gimme a break!) and following where it led.

Thank you to my wife, Crissy, who patiently attended while I spent days and nights, week in and week out, pounding away at the keyboard of this old MacBook Pro, trying to find the words for the pictures in my head.

Thank you to Bashirah Muttalib for the care she took in the editing of this novel. How lucky am I to have someone so kind, generous and experienced help me through this process. This book is where it is because of you.

Thank you to Whitney Patel and to my fellow experiential creatives at 160over90. It continues to be an honor to work among such a gifted slate of designers and artists.

Finally, thanks to my Covid family and my D*C family. Your encouragement has meant more than I have the capability to say.

Now to you, gentle reader. Sleep tight.

www.ingramcontent.com/pod-product-compliance
Lightning Source LLC
Chambersburg PA
CBHW030545310726
48979CB00010B/2034/J

* 9 7 8 1 7 3 6 6 1 6 0 0 0 *